DOLCI DI LOVE

SARAH-KATE LYNCH lives for much of the year on the wild west coast of New Zealand but escapes whenever she can to such far-flung corners of the world as the vineyards of Champagne, the streets of New York, and the hilltop towns of Tuscany. Sometimes she allows her husband, film art director Mark Robins, to come with her. You can read more about her, or just look at the pictures, at www.sarah-katelynch.com.

Dolci di Love

or

The Sweetheart *Cantucci*

A NOVEL

Sarah-Kate Lynch

A PLUME BOOK

PLUME
Published by the Penguin Group
Penguin Group (USA) Inc., 375 Hudson Street, New York, New York 10014, U.S.A.
Penguin Group (Canada), 90 Eglinton Avenue East, Suite 700, Toronto, Ontario,
Canada M4P 2Y3 (a division of Pearson Penguin Canada Inc.) • Penguin Books
Ltd., 80 Strand, London WC2R 0RL, England • Penguin Ireland, 25 St. Stephen's
Green, Dublin 2, Ireland (a division of Penguin Books Ltd.) • Penguin Group
(Australia), 250 Camberwell Road, Camberwell, Victoria 3124, Australia (a division
of Pearson Australia Group Pty. Ltd.) • Penguin Books India Pvt. Ltd., 11 Community
Centre, Panchsheel Park, New Delhi – 110 017, India • Penguin Group (NZ), 67 Apollo
Drive, Rosedale, North Shore 0632, New Zealand (a division of Pearson New Zealand
Ltd.) • Penguin Books (South Africa) (Pty.) Ltd., 24 Sturdee Avenue, Rosebank,
Johannesburg 2196, South Africa

Penguin Books Ltd., Registered Offices: 80 Strand, London WC2R 0RL, England

First published by Plume, a member of Penguin Group (USA) Inc.

First Printing, April 2011
10 9 8 7 6 5 4 3

Ⓟ REGISTERED TRADEMARK—MARCA REGISTRADA

LIBRARY OF CONGRESS CATALOGING-IN-PUBLICATION DATA
Lynch, Sarah-Kate.
   Dolci di love : a novel / Sarah-Kate Lynch.
      p. cm.
   ISBN 978-0-452-29675-6 (pbk. : alk. paper) 1. Businesswomen—Fiction. 2. Mar-
ried people—Fiction. 3. Americans—Italy—Fiction. 4. Bakeries—Fiction. 5. Domestic
fiction.   I. Title.
   PR9639.4.L96D65 2011
   823'.92—dc22   2010043216

Printed in the United States of America
Set in Janson Text • Designed by Eve L. Kirch

For my mother, Margaret Lynch,

and all the world's helpful widows

Dolci di Love

Chapter 1

Daniel's other woman and two bright-eyed beautiful children were sitting under the insole of his left golf shoe when Lily first found them. They were laminated.

Despite the shock of finding the photo and the immediate awful certainty deep in her bones that these children were indeed her husband's, this most practical of details struck her. They were laminated, which made a point all by itself.

The layers of Lily's life-as-she-knew-it might be flying off into the ether, helplessly transparent, never to be seen together again, but the layers of this other life she knew nothing about were fixed sturdily right there in her hand, bonded for eternity.

Lamination was forever, after all. That was what it was for. You didn't laminate things that didn't matter or that you weren't sure about; things like your Fairway shopping list or the Italian heels clipped out of the latest *Vogue*.

You only laminated absolute necessities, sureties; things that you needed to last longer than they were meant to when they were printed on paper that could be spattered by ketchup or yellowed by the sun.

The surprise woman and two children were accordingly announced to Lily as a trio in need of top-level maintenance. So important were they to Daniel, her husband, that he wanted to protect them forever against all the foot rot, shoe sweat, and whatever other peril the Manhattan Woods Golf Club held for them. So important were they that he wanted to keep them close to him for time immemorial, or however long plastic lasted, which Lily happened to know was about five hundred years. Long after Daniel was dead and buried, after she was, after everyone in the photo was, after the golf shoe—save, perhaps, the two brown aglets from the tips of the laces—had decomposed, this snapshot of a happy "family" would remain.

Daniel's foot fungus of the year before, Lily thought, as she put the shoe back in its place. Was this picture-perfect threesome responsible for that? Could they have created extra moisture under his sole? Produced a perfect breeding ground for rogue spores after eighteen holes in the Hudson Valley? He'd spent a fortune at the podiatrist; she knew, because she paid the bills.

She straightened both the golf shoes on their shelf, although she didn't know why. Surely there was something else she should be doing. Her life had just been turned upside down. She should have thought to laminate that, to preserve that forever just the way she liked it.

The annoying thing was, if she'd known she had to, she would have. Lily was by nature a laminator. She was famous for dotting *i*'s and crossing *t*'s, but a person had to know that an *i* needed dotting or a *t* crossing in the first place. If they were sitting there looking to all intents and purposes already dotted and crossed then there were usually a million other things to be getting on with in the meantime.

She wondered why Daniel had chosen his golf shoe.

Was it so he could take the little family out of his sports bag when he drove to the club with Jordie and Dave, gazing at those beautiful childish faces in the back of Jordie's SUV while up front they talked about real estate and the Knicks?

That didn't seem private enough, somehow. Unless Jordie and

Dave knew about it, which she doubted because Jordie actually only talked about real estate and the Knicks and Dave didn't talk at all. She couldn't see the three of them analyzing the perils of a bent tee, let alone infidelity.

No, she was pretty certain that the laminated photo was not related to the golf itself.

She looked around her husband's closet. The rest of his shoes were neatly laid side by side across three shelves: all black and nearly identical. Why, he had the most boring taste in shoes of any man alive. How could she never have noticed that before?

Obviously, he couldn't hide anything in any of these lookalike shoes because he would waste too much time trying to find it. He had a pair of gray running shoes, but she supposed they would be too sweaty to house the little plastic family (the resulting foot fungus would likely kill him), and his one pair of loafers—she picked them up and had a close look—had a glued-on insole.

The brown and white golf shoes with their flirty leather fringe were really the obvious choice, she reasoned. He could slip into his closet and easily snatch a few private moments to gaze at his secret photo. Also, Lily did not play golf. She'd tried it years before but considered it a waste of time. She could burn calories more efficiently a dozen other ways so had left Daniel to his golfing years before. He knew she would never have anything to do with those shoes.

In fact, normally she wouldn't have anything to do with his closet. She had one of her own on the other side of the wall from where his suits hung three inches apart from each other. Her closet was the same size, but there was no space between her clothes, and her shoes were all completely different plus, as far as she knew, held no secrets, apart from the cost of one particular pair about which she lied for no reason other than it seemed ridiculous to pay that much.

It was Pearl, her assistant at Heigelmann's, who was to blame for her being in there. It was Daniel's birthday Saturday and Lily had been going to get him a polo shirt, a good one, but had been surprised at the response from Pearl when asked to organize this.

"Whatever you say," Pearl had said, with attitude. "Just not blue and not green, right?"

They'd worked together seven years; Lily knew to pay attention to attitude.

"Oh, really? And why is that?" she asked, curious because Daniel suited both those colors. Green brought out his eyes and blue the shots of silver that were further claiming his thick blond hair. He was a handsome man and only improving with age but seemed not to notice this himself. She loved that about him. That and his kindness. His smile. His no-fuss way of handling things. No fuss? She had that right.

"Because you gave him a blue shirt for his last birthday and a green one at Christmas," Pearl informed her, with one of her special disapproving head waggles. She was really a very good assistant but at times like this Lily wanted to pull on one of her shiny black ringlets. Lily could remember how many product units were transported in any given week from Virginia to Vermont and how much it cost, down to the penny, so why couldn't she remember what gifts she'd given her husband?

"You could always get him a tie," Pearl suggested.

"Oh, well, Daniel doesn't really wear ties," Lily said although of course he did and what's more Pearl had probably seen him in one at least a dozen times. "Not that much," she added limply. "Anymore, that is." Pearl pursed her lips and raised her eyebrows so high it was a miracle they didn't shoot right off of her head.

"Actually, you know what?" Lily pressed a finger to her lips, feigning a sudden inspiration. "I've just had another idea. Thanks, Pearl, but I think I'll take care of this myself."

She racked her brains for the rest of the day trying to come up with an alternative gift, finally remembering that Daniel had complained in recent weeks, in as much as he ever really complained, that the sprigs on his golf shoes were loose, or old, or tired, or something.

She hadn't paid much attention when he mentioned it but in light of the shirt situation, she decided she would break the tradition she'd unwittingly embraced and would replace his golf shoes instead. She just couldn't remember what size he took.

Should she have known? she wondered, again looking around his closet. Would a wife who remembered previous gifts and knew her husband's shoe size be less likely to find a laminated photo of a beautiful woman and two children hidden under his insole?

It was searching for his size that had brought her into his closet. She'd picked up the shoe, turned it upside down, and dislodged his secret spotless-forever family. If she'd known his shoe size, or even reached for the other shoe, the spotless-forever family would have remained a secret.

Looking down at the laminated picture she was still clutching, Lily felt the need to sit. Were she prone to explosive displays of emotion she would be indulging in one right now, she knew that, but she was not. Her emotions—a neat, controlled collection as a rule—seemed bewildered, with her body not far behind. Her legs were trembling, she realized. That was why she needed to sit. This was a normal reflex. This was good.

She sat, light as a feather, on the edge of her bed. The little girl in the photo was about five, she thought, and the boy was not much more than a baby.

A baby.

A crumpled gargle-like whimper, an almost cute puppyish noise, escaped without her permission.

She stared at the woman in the picture, running her thumb along the sharp edge of the hard plastic. She wasn't exactly pretty, the woman, not in the all-American way that Lily was, but she had that wild, defiant sort of beauty that "other" women often seemed to possess; not dangerous exactly, but close. Her lips were thin, her cheekbones sharp, her dark unruly hair was being blown across her face in the wind, and she was smiling, sort of, at the photographer, who was no doubt Daniel, Lily's husband, to whom Lily had been married for sixteen years and who formed one half of the perfect couple everyone said they were.

Another choked gargle escaped her as she ran her fingers over the little girl. She had her mother's hair, long and dark, and that same defiant wildness, but she had Daniel's eyes, his dimpled chin. She stood slightly in front of her mother, not touching her, and looked boldly at the camera as if challenging Daniel to even take the photo.

The baby was the happiest of them all, his face turned toward his mamma as he laughed at what the wind was doing to her hair. He was wearing a T-shirt and something stripy on his bottom half, which didn't really match. Lily had drawers full of clothes that this baby would look better in. One sausage arm was raised in the air as his fat round hand with its tiny plump fingers snatched at a glossy black tendril the wind was whisking just out of his reach. He looked exactly like Daniel did in all his baby photos. Exactly.

She should be crying, she knew that. Howling even. But crying seemed too insignificant a response, howling an insult. Tears and moans were for everyday heartbreak. This was something else. Again, she felt it, in the quiver in her arm, in the light bead of sweat on her forehead: bewilderment.

Lily had built a career on not being bewildered. Indeed, she was famous for her certainty. It had got her as far as being VP of a Fortune 500 company—one of the country's biggest—this unwavering natural instinct. It had brought her wealth and success. It had become her most prized possession and she trusted it.

Yet right now as she confronted what was undoubtedly the biggest crisis of her personal life, her ability to know what to do lay huddled in a distant cave, licking its wounds, shunning the light, leaving her all on her own.

The thing was that Lily considered her marriage to Daniel, indeed Daniel himself now she came to think about it, as the pin in the grenade of her life: not the most exciting feature, perhaps, but pull it out and everything would explode. The bits would fly as far as the sun and she would never reclaim them.

So what if she focused more on her job these days than on her husband—what woman in her situation wouldn't? She could hardly take a few years off to stare at an empty crib. Married women without children had no choice but to concentrate on their careers and it happened almost naturally that they climbed the ladder more quickly. It was no problem for Lily to stay later in the office, after all, because she had no blond-haired boy to pick up from nursery school, no green-eyed girl's ballet performance to dash off to.

And at forty-four there was never going to be a blond-haired boy or a green-eyed girl for Lily. She knew that, she had been through all that; she had accepted it years ago.

Absentmindedly, she turned the picture over and to her further shock there was half a photo of Daniel and the woman and baby on the other side. Well, there was a whole photo but only half of Daniel was in it. The little girl must have taken the picture and it was on a crazy angle, with just the bottom parts of the two adults and one fat striped leg of the baby.

Daniel was wearing the Prada belt Lily had given him for an earlier birthday. (Always polo shirts indeed!) His thirty-fifth, maybe? She'd bought it herself, at Bergdorf Goodman, after a particularly promising OB-GYN appointment. She remembered wafting through the store feeling as if she were floating on a river of champagne. *This time*, she'd almost sung to herself, *this time*. The belt had cost her nearly $300, but she wouldn't have cared if it was $3,000. And in the end, there was no *this time*.

Daniel's arms were not in the picture so she couldn't tell if they were around the woman, but their hips were touching, hers slightly in front. Take away the fact that the children looked so much like Daniel, could these be the hips of two mere acquaintances? Lily looked closer, the whole photo was only the size of a playing card and the hips were all in one triangular half. Still, the woman appeared to be pressing into her husband's groin. She was quite curvy, or hippy, really, if you were going to be critical. She would have trouble finding jeans to fit properly, which was maybe why she went for the wraparound dress—a paisley pattern the green of Daniel's eyes—that showed off her impressive cleavage and small waist, but made less of her bottom half.

In the triangular part of the photo that didn't contain her husband and the woman and baby, a soft light was setting on distant golden hills dotted with pencil-like pine trees. Straight rows of cascading greenery, grapes no doubt, ran in stripes toward the plump weathered dome of a honey-colored church with a bell tower tucked in behind it.

She sucked back another whimper.

She thought she knew where the photo had been taken. And knowing that made her even more certain that there was no mistake, that her life as she knew it was over.

There certainly weren't churches like that in New York or anywhere near it. The church looked like it was in Italy.

Daniel was mad about Italy, always had been. When they'd

first met, he'd told her about the elderly Italian neighbors who had adopted him as an honorary grandson when he was just a little boy and added him to their rough-and-tumble extended family. An only child whose own home life was far from a barrel of laughs, these neighbors—oh, why could she not think of their names?—had provided him with some sort of happy refuge when he most needed it.

Daniel had wanted to go to Italy for their honeymoon, even, but Lily felt it was too far and too hard after the exhausting exercise of organizing a wedding.

They'd gone instead to a tiny romantic cottage in Maine where the weather had been abysmal but they hadn't cared.

When Lily had woken the first morning there, her new husband's warm body pressed against her, snoring politely, the stress of the nuptials over and done with, she had experienced her first ever wave of complete and utter happiness.

Even sitting there, staring at the photo of Daniel's love children all these years later, she could recall it as though it were yesterday. The sensation had overwhelmed her, brought gooseflesh to her skin, tears to her eyes, a contentment to her heart that she had not even dreamed was possible.

She remembered lying there, naked, as the rain danced on the roof above her, watching Daniel sleep and reveling in the promise of their wonderful future together.

They'd been so in love then, so happy. She had thought they still were. Compared with many of their divorced or miserably still-married friends, Lily and Daniel were paragons of good old-fashioned stability despite the unspoken heartbreak that blossomed between them. Daniel never treated her with anything other than respect and devotion. He was kind, considerate, loving. And she was too. Or so she thought. Their commitment to each other was often remarked upon and, so she had been told, envied. She was proud of their marriage, of him, of herself.

She stood up, still clutching the photo, and walked to their bedroom window, gazing out at the view. If she leaned against the right hand pane, she could see down West Seventy-second Street to Central Park. The trees this morning were shimmering in the gentle summer breeze. Normally she loved those trees. She loved the park. She loved her apartment, her life.

She wondered how long it had been since she had actually considered whether she was truly still in love with Daniel. After sixteen years of marriage it just wasn't something she thought about that often. There were so many other things to think about. She had a full schedule and an all-consuming job. Who had time to sit around and ponder the state of their marriage, especially when it showed all the vital signs of being perfectly secure?

She looked at the church in the photo again.

She had tolerated, if not entirely shared, Daniel's passion for Italy, especially the food and wine, and supported him whole-heartedly when he worked out a way to manipulate his amateur enthusiasm into something resembling a career, chiseling out a niche for himself as a buyer of Italian wines, importing ballsy brunellos and rich vino nobiles for sommeliers to dispense at Manhattan's favorite eating and drinking haunts.

And she was busy at Heigelmann's so it had never worried her that he spent one week out of every four in Tuscany. He had done it for the past ten years. He was there right now, quite possibly in the company of this exotic looking creature and her children.

She felt a physical ache in her chest that she assumed was her heart in the process of breaking, but the surprising thing was the ache didn't feel entirely new. In fact, it felt all too familiar. Perhaps a person could only take so much hurt and disappointment. Perhaps a person reached a point where anything else, anything worse, would just ricochet off without leaving a dent.

What Lily mostly felt—give or take a quiver or two—was empty. How fitting. Tragic, but fitting. Empty!

All these years she had tortured her body, her mind, and that poor aching heart—not to mention her bank account—trying for a baby. And failing. She wasn't used to failure, she struggled to deal with it, but what had kept her going through the dark days had been her obvious success at work and her quiet assumption at home that Daniel loved her no matter what, that it was she who mattered most to him, not these wisps of the future that she couldn't manage to conjure into being.

But there he was, all this time, turning her wisps into flesh-and-blood reality on the other side of the world with someone else.

Lily looked at her watch. It was eleven o'clock on a Sunday morning.

She slipped the photo into the pocket of her silk robe, walked down the hallway into the kitchen, and opened the refrigerator door. A bottle of crisp white pinot grigio stood there boldly, unopened. She'd been trying to cut down; wine played havoc with her waistline now her thirties had marched into history, and in the past few years she'd gotten in the habit of drinking alone in the weeks when Daniel was away.

She had never smoked, didn't care for recreational drugs, and had long resisted the lure of chocolate. The odd glass of wine, she supposed, had become her chosen vice. And somewhere along the line one glass in the evening after work had perhaps turned into two, then three until some nights she had been getting through a bottle.

She loved the warm, floaty cushion of well-being that each

mouthful brought with it, but did not appreciate the puffy eyes and dull head the next morning. And the calories!

Daniel had been gone three days and she'd not touched a drop.

She pulled out the cork and poured a generous helping into a tall crystal glass.

Chapter 2

Violetta awoke feeling her sister's big toe prodding her armpit. She lifted her head up off the pillow and there at the opposite end of the rickety old bed was Luciana, her wizened snout twitching, her eyes twinkling, her wrinkled smile stretching across ancient lips to reveal a haphazard collection of jauntily crooked teeth.

"It aches!" Luciana crowed, pushing her toe into Violetta's armpit again. "I'm sure of it, sister. Yes, all praise to Santa Ana di Chisa. It definitely aches!"

Violetta rubbed at her own wizened snout.

"And that tingles, doesn't it?" cried Luciana. "I know it does. It tingles! And I can smell it! Can you smell it? I can smell it!"

They both lifted their faces, mole-like, into the air and sniffed.

"Orange blossom!" trilled Luciana. "As clear as the age spots on your cheek, Violetta. Orange blossom!"

Violetta nodded. For decades the heady aroma of out-of-season orange blossom had been the sisters' one shared clue that the day was going to be one of their special ones. The separate clues were that Violetta would wake with an itchy nose and Luciana with an aching toe. Then the orange blossom would hit them, there'd be a flurry of excitement, and before they knew it, they'd be calling a meeting and hatching a plan.

"Oh, I'm just in the mood too," Luciana said. "Or I will be

when I can get this tired old body up and running. Could you give that toe a rub? It gets worse every time. How's the tingling?"

"Do you need to be quite so cheerful?" Violetta asked. Her own ancient body felt like a lump of unmolded clay left abandoned in the summer heat; dry and misshapen, nothing now could ever give it back the promise of the past. "If you start the day in the best of moods it leaves you nowhere else to go."

Nonetheless she reached back under the bed covers with one hand to find her sister's foot, using the other hand to draw back the flimsy curtain that was only just keeping out the first meek rays of the early morning sun.

Outside, a gentle Tuscan mist clung juicily to the low-slung hills of the Val D'Orcia. Behind them, dark clouds lurked moodily across the horizon. No wonder the sun was meek this morning. It was going to rain.

Violetta twitched her nose again. Usually she quite liked the tingling—it was exciting; like an infinitely more useful version of a sneeze. But today, not so much. Today something was different.

She let go of Luciana's toe, extricated herself creakily from the pile of quilts and blankets, and shuffled over to the lopsided dresser in the corner of the small, dark room.

From the middle shelf she lifted a tarnished frame bearing a photo of a handsome young man in army uniform. She brought the picture up to her lips and planted a kiss on it, then let out a startled cry.

"What in the devil's name is *he* doing here?" she asked, glaring at the photo.

Luciana looked up and before the blunder could blossom into anything bigger, told her sister to bring the picture to her. "Don't go making a fuss," she said, a warning tone in her voice. "It doesn't mean a thing except your eyes are getting worse."

Shaking her head in disbelief at the prospect of something else about her person getting worse, Violetta delivered the photo as she was bid then shuffled back to another tarnished frame farther along the shelf with what appeared to be the same photo. This one she held at arm's length first—her eyes, indeed, were heading downhill fast—and after establishing it was definitely the right one, plonked another kiss on it.

"Good morning, Salvatore," she said. "I hope you slept well." A pain shot through her chest, almost winding her. She'd felt it before, she thought. Or was it a new ache to add to the list of complications confounding her?

"And good morning to you, Silvio," Luciana said to her photo. "And you just watch where you put yourself or it'll be back in the napkin drawer."

"I'll put on the coffee," Violetta said, ignoring her. "It's time to get up. We have a lot to do today even if most of it is only thinking."

Thinking did not require doing the splits or sprinting around the *piazza grande*, was Luciana's opinion, so could actually be done while lying down. But Violetta was the boss. She was ten months older and in charge of all major decision-making, plus she had the all-important sixth sense when it came to matters of the heart, so Luciana, as always, was happy to follow orders.

"I agree," she said. "And I've already started my thinking, have you?"

"I'm thinking we are owed a happy ending or two right about now, so we'd better get off our behinds and do something about it."

"There is really no need to be so cranky," Luciana chided. "We got our happy ending with Enrico and the mechanic's daughter," she reminded her sister. "Although it did take her finding him underneath his motorcycle covered in cherry brandy. The look on her face when she realized it wasn't blood! That was 'the moment' as I recall."

"Yes," said Violetta, softening a smidgeon. "That was 'the moment.'" Even with worry nipping at her soul like a kitten at a ball of wool, she could still appreciate the moment.

"I just love the moment," Luciana sighed. "Although it's surprising how often a great big mess is involved."

"Well, love is a great big messy business," Violetta pointed out. "Now hop to it."

And so Luciana hopped. But as Violetta busied herself in the kitchen she felt a shiver wriggle up her curving spine and jump through her chest to join the ache that sat there like a watchful pigeon, looking for trouble—and finding it.

It was her nose, her wrinkled nose: It hadn't tingled at all. Not once. Not even for a second. Nor had it picked up, no matter how hard she sniffed, so much as the faintest suggestion of the sweet seductive scent of orange blossom.

Chapter 3

In the days when Lily and her sister Rose still spoke to each other, they'd had a term for having one too many margaritas and booking outlandish things on the Internet. They called it Tipsy Tourism.

Tipsy Tourism was behind their going to Madison Square Garden to see Madonna perform live solely on the grounds that Rose had heard someone say her underarm skin sagged just like a normal woman's.

"She doesn't even like Madonna," Rose's husband Al told Lily when he heard their plan. "Neither of you do."

He was even more aggrieved closer to the time when it transpired that he would have to stay at home and look after Jack, their six-month-old baby, and played the guilt card so expertly that Rose tried to cancel.

"I thought you wanted to see the woman wobble," Lily reminded her. "I mean really wobble."

They went, they took binoculars, they danced, they sang, they had a blast.

A year later, they celebrated Lily's new promotion with so much champagne that they went back to her apartment, lurched straight on to the Internet, and Tipsy Tourism got the better of them again. This time they booked a spa weekend in New Hampshire.

The trip, when it rolled around, was exactly what they both

needed. Lily was working fourteen-hour days and Rose was exhausted from the trials of mothering a precocious toddler.

But by the afternoon of the first day it was clear to Lily that Rose was not her usual self.

"Are you going to tell me what's wrong?" Lily asked, as they soaked in side-by-side mud baths, bodies slick with goo, sliced kiwi cooling their closed eyes.

"I'm pregnant," Rose said.

"That's fantastic news, you must be thrilled!" Lily enthused as authentically as she could manage, but tears slid down the side of her face leaving sad, pale streaks in the mud.

Worse, when Harry was born, it simply felt to Lily that he should have been hers. And he did seem to fit perfectly in her arms. It just wasn't plausible she had to hand him back to someone else.

Worse still, despite the fact she could talk to Rose for hours about a button falling off a shirt or a dust ball returning to the same place under the coffee table, she could not talk to her about this.

In fact, she found herself unable to talk to Rose about anything, the unbearable beauty of Harry sticking in her throat so awkwardly that it was easier to avoid her all together.

She used work as an excuse for not making the journey up to Connecticut for weekends and stopped asking her sister into the city for special occasions. Rose, guilty about her fertile body, plus hormonal and tired, obliged by increasingly taking offense.

At one stage, four months passed without Lily laying eyes on her sister and nephews, and the next time they met it started badly and ended worse.

"I'm pregnant again," Rose said as they surveyed the stilettos in Barneys. "Twins. I'm so sorry, Lily. Really, I don't know what else to say. Just, after everything you've been through, I'm sorry."

Lily smiled in a way that, she did not then know, she was already famous for at Heigelmann's. "Nonsense. Congratulations!" she said. "I'm delighted for you." Then she bustled Rose to the lingerie department and tried to make her accept a gift of a lacy bra and matching panties.

Rose stood miserably in the changing room mirror, her post–baby fat glistening in the harsh fluorescent lighting.

"I feel like a circus elephant stuffed into a tiny tutu," she said. "And I'm going to look like two circus elephants stuffed into a tiny tutu in a month's time. If not three. Thank you but no, Lily. I feel gross. You're very generous but I don't want them. You get them."

"It's a maternity bra," Lily said. "What am I going to do with one of those?"

They parted on awful terms, Rose crying and Lily remaining aloof and unflinching. She could not help herself. It was that or collapse on the floor and never get up again. That Rose had been afraid to tell her about the new babies only made it worse. It made Lily's desperation real. It turned the possibility she would never be a mother herself into such a bleak and definite prospect that she didn't know what to do with it.

The twins, Emily and Charlotte, duly arrived and Lily did go to see them, but only once, at their christening.

"Thank you so much for coming," Rose said, eyes shining, a baby in each arm as she met her sister on the steps of the church.

"Thank you for inviting me," Lily answered stiffly, feeling Daniel's hand on the small of her back as though he was scared she might fall backward.

The sight of her sister and those four beautiful children gathered around the baptismal font with the Virgin Mary beaming beatifically down on them had almost done it.

She managed to stay a polite hour at the lunch afterward but didn't even have to ask Daniel to take her home. He knew. Toddler Harry, full of sugary party drinks, broke free of his older brother Jack and clutched dramatically at her leg, howling, as she tried to leave.

"We hate babies," he roared. "We hate them."

Those babies were now at school. Lily sent cards and gifts (which Pearl shopped for) on birthdays and at Christmas, but that was all.

Which was why she got such a shock the morning after finding Daniel's secret family to be woken by the doorman calling to say her sister was in the lobby.

"My sister?" she croaked, looking at her watch. It was past seven. She should have been up an hour ago.

"Yes, Mrs. Turner. Your sister," she heard him ask whomever he had down there for a name. "Rose. Rose Rickman. Shall I send her up?"

"Send her up? I guess so. Yes."

She couldn't imagine what had happened to bring Rose to the city after all this time. She must have left home before five.

Pulling on her robe she looked automatically in the bathroom mirror and was appalled by the face staring back at her. She was a complete mess. Yesterday's makeup had traveled to bits of her face that really didn't suit it and her thick blond hair, which she paid a fortune to have straightened twice a week and which normally sat in a neat twist at the nape of her neck, looked like a joke someone would play using an upturned mop.

She threw some water on her face and gave it a quick wipe with a washcloth, only partially repairing the damage before Rose rang the buzzer and she went, heart hammering, to let her in.

"Well, thank God, you're all right!" Rose blew in, her usual boisterous self, no trace of the years of stony silence between them.

She had put on more weight, Lily noticed, reeling from the shock of looking at her, listening to her, having her there in the hallway. But the weight suited her. She looked like exactly what she was: a slightly harassed but otherwise happy suburban mother, all flushed naked cheeks, glossy lips, and haphazard clothing. Her hair was loosely fixed in a cascading up-do and she wore boyfriend jeans with flat shoes, a crumpled shirt, and an old pashmina that had seen better days.

"All right?" Lily was stiff with embarrassment. Was there something she didn't know? What on earth had happened? "Of course I'm all right. Why wouldn't I be?"

Rose gave something between a snort and a laugh. "Are you kidding me?" she asked. "You called me last night to tell me about Daniel's little situation in Italy and I couldn't sleep for worrying about you. Don't you remember?"

Lily clutched her robe tighter to her chest. "I *called* you?"

"Yes, about the floozy."

"The *floozy*?"

Rose shook her head in exasperation. "Oh for Pete's sake, Lily, let's just cut the crap," she said, as she snatched off the pashmina that was slipping from her shoulder and stuffed it in her enormous tote bag. "And can we get out of the hallway? Come on, I've been up half the night, I feel like a horse's ass and I need coffee."

"Cut what crap?" Lily asked, attempting to disguise her mortification as she followed her sister to the kitchen. "You know, you can't just barge your way into my apartment and—"

But Rose was having none of that. "You know, I left Al at home with a bunch of screaming kids," she said, rounding on her sister, "two who have the raging chicken pox and one who is refusing to leave the house owing to 'girl germs,' because I was scared to death my sister who hasn't spoken to me in however long was going to do something stupid like kill herself."

"Kill myself?"

"Yes!" Rose seethed, banging the coffee pot into the holder. "You think just because you disappear from my life I don't still think about you? I don't still worry about you? I worry like crazy, and believe me, I have enough problems of my own to be getting on with. And I can only imagine what you've been going through, Lily, and if we could swap places I probably would, truly I would, today of all days, I fricking would, but I can't. This is it. This is what we've got and we have to get on with it, but just look at you, Lily—you're a mess. And you were drunk on the phone. Drunk! You sounded just like Mom."

Shame ripped the scab from Lily's open wound and for a split second she considered flying into Rose's arms and howling with the grief she'd long used her expert composure to conceal.

She knew her sister would sweep her up without a moment's hesitation—she'd always been the more forgiving one, the more loving, lovable one—but Lily had taken refuge behind her cool, distant exterior for so long, she didn't know how to step away from it. She just stood there, tightening her robe at her throat until she was saved by Rose's cell phone ringing again.

"What is it now?" Rose barked. "Well, I don't know. Tell her you'll give her a ton of candy if she doesn't scratch them. Be inventive!" She rolled her eyes. "Then tell him that there are probably more girl germs at our house than in the whole of the neighborhood, including the toilet doors, and he'll die if he stays inside all day because chicken pox germs are the worst of all and they're unisex."

Resting the phone on her shoulder, she poured two cups of coffee. "Jesus, Al, I'm here trying to sort out this mess with Lily and you—No, she's fine. Same as always." She turned to look at Lily, still frozen in the same spot. "Al says hi," she said briskly but then her face softened. "Hey, buddy," she said. "How ya doing?

I know they itch but that'll stop if you just let them be. Maybe Daddy will read you some Harry Potter if you ask him nicely. Wanna try that? OK, yes, or watch *Transformers*, sure, whatever. I'll be home soon." She laughed. "Yes, I'll tell her. Bye-bye."

She slid the phone back into her bag. "Harry says he misses you."

Lily said nothing. She was afraid of what would happen if she opened her mouth.

"Although, actually, to be more precise, he 'mitheth' you owing to an unfortunate incident involving a baseball bat and a front tooth," Rose plonked herself down at the table. "Come on, Lily, sit down would you? You're making the place look untidy."

Lily cleared her throat and slowly sat, trying to block out any thoughts of Rose's messy, noisy house full of itchy lovable children.

"Al's not at work?" she asked. Al was a builder, specializing in renovating old colonials, of which there were many where they lived in Connecticut.

"Work? What's that?" Rose answered dryly. "Half the poor schmucks up our way have lost their life savings in some Ponzi scheme, whatever that is, so houses are staying pretty much un-renovated. There is no work."

"Al's unemployed? I thought he was the best in the business."

"Well, there still has to be business to be the best in, I suppose. And at the moment there isn't. I'm back teaching fifth grade and Al's being a househusband, although frankly he sucks at it and what's worse, there's no money to work on our own house so it remains a dump. A leaky dump that smells of rotten carpet. You don't know how lucky you are, Lily, I tell you."

As soon as she'd said it, she looked fit to suck the words right back. "Oh, crap, I don't mean it like that," she sighed. "You know I don't. It's just about the money."

"If you need money, Rose," Lily said coldly, "I'm sure we can sort something out."

"I don't need money, or at least I don't want any of yours, that's not what I mean either." Rose's cell phone started ringing again. "Oh for Pete's sake! What does he want now?"

She answered and listened, fuming. "Did you check the linen press? Or the drier? Or the fricking drawers in their fricking room? Well, I don't know, Al—keep trying. What do you expect me to do from here?"

She flipped her phone closed and threw it back in her bag.

"It looks to me as though you're needed more at the rotten-smelling dump than you are here," Lily said, rising from the table and taking her still-full coffee cup to the kitchen sink. "As you can see, I am perfectly fine and I'm just sorry you wasted your time coming to check on me."

"OK, Miss High-and-Mighty, so this is how you're going to play it?" Rose's cheeks were starting to redden, a sure sign she was building to blow her top. Lily had seen it a hundred times before. As a child, Rose's tantrums had been legendary, although it had not usually been Lily who caused them; rather she had been the one to soothe her sister and bring her back to good humor.

"Treat me like some piece of dog dirt on the bottom of your fancy-pants shoe, why don't you. See if I care! And while we're at it, let me tell you something. I am *not* needed more at the rotten-smelling dump than I am here, but I'm going home anyway. And let me tell you something else: You're wrong about you being fine, Lily. You are not fine. And you know what? I can't feel sorry for you any longer. I just can't. I've felt so sorry for you for so long, but I'm done with that. Where has it got us? We used to be best friends! So close! And now? Now you're obviously drink-ing your way into an early grave just like Mom did, and I'm not going to turn myself inside out trying to stop you the way we tried to stop her. The two of us. Together. Remember?"

Rose and Lily did not talk about their mother. The painful experience of being Carmel Watson's daughters was something they shared at DNA level but rarely out loud, and never since she had died, slowly and with very little dignity, when the sisters were in their early twenties.

For Rose to exhume her now, and to compare Lily to her—a bitter, angry woman who died of cirrhosis after a miserable life spent shriveled in rage and resentment—was unforgivable.

"You really should go now," Lily said. "And as you think so little of me, I think it's best that you never come back."

"Don't you worry, I'm going," Rose answered, snatching up her bag. "And don't you worry a second time because I'm not coming back—not until you call me stone-cold sober and beg me to."

"Thanks for the feedback, I'll take that on board," Lily said, knowing how much Rose hated business jargon and ushering her stiffly up the hall like an unwanted client.

Furious, Rose pulled open the door but paused and blew out a lungful of air before she walked through it. "You're my sister and I love you," she said, turning to Lily, the color in her cheeks softening. "I don't think so little of you. I think so much of you. That's the trouble. You have looked out for me my whole life and I probably wouldn't even be here if it wasn't for you, but don't stay this cold, lonely person you've turned into, Lily. It's not the real you. I know it isn't. Please, go find Daniel. For God's sake, work it out with him. Sure, it's Tipsy Tourism, but it's not a bad idea. Just please, please, I beg you, don't sweep this one under the carpet, Lil."

"Good-bye, Rose," Lily said and shut the door in her face. Tipsy Tourism? What the hell was she talking about?

Chapter 4

Violetta and Luciana shuffled sideways out of their cramped living quarters and through the swinging door into the adjoining bakeshop like a pair of crippled crabs.

Their family, the Ferrettis, had been making and selling their famous *cantucci* since well before the sisters were born nearly a hundred years earlier, and very little had changed in all that time.

Their *cantucci*—a mouthwateringly delicious Italian cookie that could be dipped in sweet wine, dunked in coffee, or eaten for no particular reason at any time of the day or night—was made strictly to the traditional family recipe. They used only the finest flour, the best sugar, the freshest eggs, the plumpest hazelnuts, and their secret ingredient: Ferretti fingers to hand shape the morsels into the perfect bite-size mouthfuls. The Ferretti *cantucci* may have been a little plain to look at, but all the love and history that went into each tiny crumb made it taste like a beacon of artisan integrity, and after all these years it still enjoyed the best reputation in Tuscany.

This was something to which the sisters clung fiercely, not just because it was their birthright but because the Borsolini brothers down the hill were now selling *cantucci* too.

They didn't make it themselves, they brought it in from Milano, and it tasted like *cacca* according to Violetta. But the vast Borsolini, which now extended much further than the original brothers, did a roaring trade in their store selling truckloads of this commercial confection in a variety of different flavors and colors. Green cherry and white chocolate? Crystallized ginger and pistachio? Black forest? The Borsolini *cantucci* might have looked dazzling, but it had all the artisan integrity of an iPod. Worse, one of the younger sons had quite a flair for window dressing and displayed the family's multi-colored wares with significant drama, changing it at least once a week.

The Ferretti sisters did their best to ignore this, continuing to make their authentic Tuscan morning, afternoon, or evening treat by hand, themselves, although in small, and getting smaller, amounts.

Their store's single marble counter bore a sparse collection of large fluted glass bowls inside of which were heaped piles of their homemade cookies. They had no confirmed-bachelor offspring to throw together any eye-catching displays: Their window had an empty table and a single chair in it.

On this particular morning, the morning of the ache but not the itch, Violetta pushed one of the fluted bowls aside as she leaned on the counter to catch her breath. The sisters were running late but getting anywhere seemed to take twice as long these days. Even bending over to pick up a tea towel could take half an hour if the shoulders, hips, and knees refused to line up and cooperate. Sometimes, a tea towel just had to stay on the ground until someone with better-oiled parts visited and could more easily return it to its rightful position.

"When did we get so old?" Violetta asked her sister.

"I think it was the eighties," Luciana replied. "But who can remember?"

They laughed, a noise which, at their age, generally sounded a lot like two desert animals fighting over a squeaky toy, but today Violetta's chortle hit a feeble note.

She felt her age and she was scared, yes, there it was, scared, of what lay around the corner. Ageing was not for the fainthearted. It hurt and it took a lot of time and in the end what did you get? A hole in the ground and a headstone if you were lucky. And there was still so much to be done!

The sisters' slow progress around the counter was interrupted by a rattle on the *pasticceria* door.

"Here we go," Violetta grumbled as two Danish backpackers clattered into the store and headed for the *cantucci* bowls.

The two sisters immediately started hissing like busted steam pipes as Luciana flapped her apron at the surprised tourists while Violetta shook her head and, muttering angrily into her chest, hobbled over to the giant Danes and gave them a shove back in the direction of the door they had just come through.

They pretty quickly got the idea and stumbled back out onto the street where they stood for a moment, stunned, while Violetta continued to shoo them away through the glass door as though sick to death of large, good-looking, blond people trying to buy *cantucci*, of all things, in a *cantucci* shop, of all places, in their lovely hilltop town of Montevedova. *Ridicolo!*

"I guess we could always put the CLOSED sign up," suggested Luciana.

"I don't think so! We don't want our *cantucci* to be as easy to come by as that Borsolini *cacca*. As long as people want to buy it and we don't let them, we have the upper hand."

She checked that the sign still said OPEN, turned the lock so no one else could get in, then the two of them shuffled over to a set of dusty shelves at the back of the store.

With quite some effort, they pushed and pulled at one of the shoulder-height ledges until finally the whole thing slid away, revealing a hidden stairwell behind the wall.

"Are you ready?" Violetta asked. Luciana nodded and they

started their descent, resting on each of three separate landings, then working their way along a narrow passage until they found themselves outside a large wooden door upon which Violetta performed a complicated knock before pushing it open.

The two old ladies stepped into the warm, welcoming lamp-lit comfort of a large cozy room. Medieval tapestries hung from the dark oak walls, half-restored frescoes lurking beneath them, while at the far end of the room three lava lamps glooped and burped inside the enormous open fireplace. A table beneath one of the frescoes, remarkable only in that everyone in it—even the lambs and donkeys—had red hair, bore a carafe of sweet *vin santo* and a dozen small crystal glasses.

This was the headquarters of *La Lega Segreta de Rammendatrici Vedove*—the Secret League of Widowed Darners.

The sisters had initially started the League to fill the void left by the deaths of their twin husbands, Salvatore and Silvio, killed far from home in East Africa during World War II.

As they mourned the men they had adored, they filled hole after hole in the toes and heels of various socks, and within a few months had attracted dozens of other widowed members.

At that stage, the surviving men of Montevedova tried to muscle in on the action, turning up to meetings to get pie-eyed on grappa and telling long-winded stories about things they probably had not done on the battlefields.

This made the widows sad that the men they had lost had been such good sorts while the men that were left behind were such a pain in the rear. They disbanded the open league, annexed the basement beneath the cathedral while the parish was briefly between priests, and re-formed the secret league.

They also decided that darning hose was perhaps a tiny bit boring and not worth having a league for, but that the pursuit of true love—the likes of which they had all been lucky enough to have and still treasured—was far more philanthropic. In other words, they decided to mend hearts instead of socks.

When Violetta's nose tingled, Luciana's toe throbbed, and orange blossom perfume filled the air, it meant a new *calzino rotto*—secret code for a broken heart—was about to come their way. The trick was to identify the *calzino rotto* as soon as possible and get mending.

The widows believed in love with all their hearts, and no one more than Violetta, but in recent years it seemed that happy endings were harder to come by and added to this, League numbers—thanks to natural attrition—had dwindled to an even dozen.

Modern technology helped plug the gaps to a certain extent. As soon as the tingling and throbbing and perfuming took place, Luciana would wave a scarf out their bedroom window, catching the attention of the widow Ciacci who lived across the lane and had a cell phone. She was then in charge of informing the other widows who still had appropriate use of eyes and fingers that a special meeting was to take place right away. This saved ageing bodies from scuttling up and down the steep streets of Montevedova knocking on doors and hissing at windows, which had once been the way it was done. With the League's average age hovering somewhere perilously close to ninety-two, this was no longer feasible.

On this occasion, most of the widows were already gathered by the time the sisters arrived, having entered through the other secret door behind the baptismal font in the church behind the *pasticceria*. Eight were sitting up in straight-backed wooden chairs in their favored semicircle, while the ninth—the widow Rossellini—slept peacefully, drooling slightly from the half smile she had been wearing when she had nodded off.

"*Buongiorno!*" the ones who were awake called when the sisters shuffled in.

"Where's the widow Del Grasso?" Violetta asked. Experience had taught her that complications arose when instructions were issued while a League member was absent. Only half the ears in the League worked at the best of times, two-thirds of the eyes were faulty, and it could not be said that remembering things was anybody's strongest point. They achieved their best results when they were all together and could ask the widow next to them what had just been said and what they should do about it.

"I definitely texted her," the widow Ciacci said.

"Widow Mazzetti, can you be in charge of bringing her up to speed later on?" Violetta asked. The widow Mazzetti nodded vigorously. She was something of a Goody Two–shoes and loved a chore.

"As for the rest of you, today is the day, so those of you who can see, keep your eyes open, those of you who can hear, keep your ears open, and those of you who are asleep, stay as you are."

They all looked at the snoozing widow Rossellini, who obliged.

"Any activity leading to the identification of a likely *calzino* candidate should be reported to either Widow Ciacci up here or—Widow Ercolani, are you on duty at the tourist office downtown?" asked Violetta. "Good. Or to Widow Ercolani down there. Widow Pacini will be stationed in the doorway of her *alimentare* between the two. Everyone else, everywhere else, please maintain your usual spots in your own doorways and let's pray to Santa Ana di Chisa that the day goes smoothly."

At this, there was a furtive knocking at the door and someone sprang up, not as speedy a process as it sounds, and pulled it open.

It was the twelfth widow, the widow Del Grasso. And she was not alone.

Chapter 5

Fear fluttering in her chest, Lily flew to the home office she and Daniel shared in the room that they had once called the Nursery but which they now referred to as the Library.

The computer was turned on. An empty wine bottle and a glass sat next to it along with a yellow legal pad covered in scrawled times and destinations. The empty wine bottle was a worry because there was another one in the kitchen.

Oh, no, Lily pleaded silently. Oh, please, please, no.

She sat down and clicked on the first unread message in her e-mail in-box.

It was an itinerary that had her flying out of JFK at 5:15 P.M. that evening for Rome. Business Class. Nonrefundable.

Worse, the second unread message was from a rental car company, confirming her rental of a car—a stick shift!—from Fiumicino airport.

The third unread message was from the Hotel Prato confirming her stay for a week in Montevedova.

Montevedova? Is that where she thought Daniel was? But why? Surely he could be anywhere in Tuscany. She didn't know where he stayed when he was away. She assumed he traveled around visiting vineyards, meeting winemakers, tasting wine.

She noticed then that her Web browser window was still open, and not without trepidation, she clicked on the history bar. Down dropped a lengthy menu of Internet sites she had trolled the previous night, many of them featuring searches for Tuscan red wines and, subsequently, churches.

Using her sober morning powers of deduction, she checked the last Web site before she had obviously moved on to making her airline booking and was barely surprised to find the church in the golf shoe.

"The church of the Madonna di San Biagio is found on the slopes of the hill of Montevedova," the Web site revealed, "at the bottom of a picturesque avenue flanked by towering cypresses."

It was one of the most famous churches—a shepherdess having witnessed a miracle there, of course—in a part of Tuscany renowned for its wine, which was why, even under the influence of two bottles of the stuff, she'd appeared to have had no trouble finding it.

But finding it was one thing, deciding to go there quite another. It was beyond impulsive and Lily had little time for impulse.

Mind you, she'd bought an exercise bike on the Internet once, late at night, and forgotten she'd done so. She'd similarly put herself (for all of twelve hours) on Facebook. There was a hidden supply of makeup advertised by Cindy Crawford currently stashed in their basement that arrived one morning to her great surprise. She'd thought that an excellent idea at midnight after a few glasses of wine. But wanting to look like Cindy Crawford made a lot more sense than this. Daniel was coming back in a couple of days anyway, and by then she would have worked out a plan to deal with the situation. She didn't understand why, pinot grigio aside, she'd wanted to speed up the whole process before she was properly equipped to handle it.

Then she clicked back on her e-mail program and noticed the message below the Alitalia flight confirmation. She hadn't spotted it before because it wasn't in bold; it had already been opened and she must have read it. It was from Daniel.

This in itself was odd. He rarely contacted her in the weeks he was away. He was only gone for seven or eight days and nothing urgent ever cropped up. She had a number for him somewhere, or Pearl did, because he used a different cell phone in Italy to save money on expensive roaming fees, but she'd never had to use it.

Had Daniel been lying particularly low when he was out of the country? This had never occurred to her before, but there was no reason why it should. She had nothing to be suspicious about. Until yesterday she'd been under the impression he was the perfect husband.

It was such a strange new world, this realm of the cheated-on wife. It was like turning a different colored light on an old familiar scene: All the same things were still in all the same places, yet it now seemed unrecognizable.

This was Daniel she was talking about. Daniel.

She clicked on his e-mail.

"Lily darling," he wrote. *"So sorry to drop this on you but something's come up over here and I need to deal with it right away or face possible financial ruin and you know how much I'd like that. Turns out there's another American distributor trying to lure my suppliers away from me and I need to do some serious fast-talking to avert disaster. I know you had plans for my birthday Saturday but I'm sorry I don't think I'll be home till next week. I'll make it up to you when I get back, I promise. And could you be a darling and let Jordie know I won't make it to golf on Sunday? I don't have his details with me. Amore, Daniel."*

Well, that certainly helped put together the events of the previous night. She must have gone to check her e-mail for some reason, perhaps after the first bottle, found this from Daniel, opened a second bottle, surfed the Net, weighed up her options, and . . .

And come up with the perfectly rational plan of going straight

over to God-knew-where to confront her husband and his laminated love-family.

She may as well have ordered a boatload of Viagra and a penis
extension.

It was utterly absurd. But it was probably what any deranged
drunk person fiddling on the Internet would do under the
circumstances.

Still, Lily was not deranged or drunk now. She was a little
queasy, her potassium levels perilously low thanks to the pinot
grigio. And she was ashamed that she couldn't remember
doing what she had done. She wanted to put it behind her. Or
underneath.

Rose didn't know what she was talking about—there was
nothing wrong with sweeping things under the carpet. That's
what carpets were for. Without them, the world would be full of
plain old floorboards, covered in dust and riddled with termites.
No one wanted to see that.

Life was about solutions. That's what everyone wanted and that
was what Lily was known for delivering. If sweeping something
under the carpet was the most effective way to deal with a problem,
Lily would sweep. She never swept more than she had to, never
less. She was simply as good with a broom as any other corporate
executive with a commensurate CV. It was just one course of action
she could take in a given set of circumstances. An option.

And in this current set of circumstances, a good one. On balance, her preference.

Women like Lily just did not go dashing off to Italy to chase
their cheating husbands, she thought, casting her eye once more
over her wine-soused alter ego's itinerary. She had other com-
mitments. Her job, for instance. The one she should have been
at an hour ago.

She snatched up the evidence of her drinking spree and was

carrying it into the kitchen when the phone rang, giving her such a fright she dropped the bottle, which glanced painfully off the side of her foot and rolled under the table.

The home phone rang so rarely, it occurred to her, as she hopped over to answer it. Was that just when Daniel was away? Or was it all the time?

It was Pearl on the line, wondering where she was. Lily felt a spasm of irritation at this because Pearl started work at 8:30 and it was currently 8:31. Her assistant had given her all of one minute before sending out the search party.

"Well, seven years and I've never walked into an empty office before," Pearl pointed out. "I thought you might have been kidnapped or beat up or hit by a bus or something."

It was true, Lily was a stickler for punctuality. Pearl would be expecting a pretty good excuse. But seeing the dropped wine bottle under the table, Lily couldn't quite come up with one.

"Has the data on the Eastern Seaboard retrenchments come in yet?" she asked instead.

"What retrenchments?" Pearl asked. "I don't know anything about any retrenchments."

"Oh, perhaps the ball is still in Bob Hayward's court," Lily said, knowing that Bob's assistant Meredith was Pearl's sworn enemy and it would drive her crazy to think Meredith was in on something she wasn't. "We might just have to hang fire on that. Can you remind me what we have on this morning?"

She crouched to reach for the bottle and was conjuring up the explicit details for a fictional bout of food poisoning when she saw Rose's shawl poured like spilt milk on the floor beneath a chair. She reached for it, bunched it up, and held it against her face as Pearl itemized the day's heaving schedule.

The pashmina was soft and pink, like Rose herself, and smelled vaguely of Paris, a fragrance Lily had picked out for her years before and which suited her so much, Lily couldn't imagine her ever smelling of anything else.

Lily used to know her sister so well. She used to know Daniel too. And now look at her. Look at all of them. The empty pinot grigio bottle rocked slightly on the bare floor.

"So, you have Todd and his offsider from R and D coming in at ten," Pearl was saying, "but I could shift them to this afternoon because we have a window at 2:15. And Finance wants you to present your quarterly projections at eleven today, not tomorrow. I saw the spreadsheet on your computer, and it looks like you have it nailed already, so are you OK with that?"

I don't know what I am OK with, Lily thought. *Am I OK with flying to Italy to stalk my straying husband? Is that what I am doing? Who in their right mind does that?*

But then again, the ghost of Paris-smelling Rose seemed to whisper from her pashmina, who *ignores* it?

Against the steady staccato of Pearl's further suggestions, Lily once more pressed her sister's shawl into her face and breathed in. She didn't want to be a cold, lonely person like their mother. She didn't want to be anything like their mother.

She wanted to be the woman she started out as, or turned into before disappointment got her all tangled up and frozen. She wanted Daniel. She wanted his warm body pressed against hers while the rain danced on the roof above them. She wanted to be in love. Maybe then she could get back some of what was missing, recapture some of the lost whatever-it-was these last difficult years had stolen from her.

Out of nowhere she remembered a picnic in Central Park with her husband and Rose and Al—before they had kids. Al had mocked her for bringing organic apples—it was pre–Whole Foods days when organic still meant ugly—and no one would eat the fruit after Al said his looked like Richard Nixon.

So Lily snatched the apples up and juggled with them.

She'd taken juggling classes at college, she told them, mainly because she had a thing for the teacher who left halfway through the semester to join, not that surprisingly, the circus.

She wasn't making it up. It wasn't a dream. A long time ago, she used to juggle. She used to be fun.

Still crouched beside the kitchen table, Lily realized that she couldn't summon up her usual concern for the quarterly projections.

This was a first. Usually she cared about them so much she had no room left to care about anything else. But not today.

"I'm so sorry," she interrupted Pearl, who was still talking about them, and Meredith's chances of delivering Bob's on time, which in Pearl's opinion were next to nil, what with all the time she wasted yakking around the water cooler and flirting with Desmond in Accounts Payable who was married with three small children and also apparently cheating with Alyssa, the scrawny redhead in Payroll.

Lily stood up straight and borrowed directly from Daniel's e-mail. "It's just that something's come up and I need to deal with it right away. I'm so sorry, Pearl, but I won't be coming in and I can only apologize for not letting you know sooner. Do you think you can cope without me?" She could feel the shock of responsibility and opportunity straighten Pearl's ringlets through the phone line. Pearl would have a fine time coping without her, she knew that for a fact.

"Well, sure, I can, if that's what you want," Pearl said. "You don't need me to come by and help with whatever's come up?"

Pearl, despite her best attempts, had never gotten farther than the lobby of Lily's apartment building, which was just the way Lily liked it.

"Thanks, Pearl, but I'll take care of it myself."

"Well, see you tomorrow then, I guess," her assistant said, miffed.

"Actually, I may be away for a little longer," Lily told her and despite never having taken a sick day in more than a decade of being VP, Logistics, Eastern Distribution, for Heigelmann's; despite knowing her husband had betrayed her and was possibly continuing to do so even as she spoke; and despite the hangover that lurched from one temple to the other inside her aching head, Lily felt a tremor of determination in her belly.

She put down the phone, wrapped Rose's pashmina around her shoulders, and went in search of her suitcase.

Chapter 6

"This is Fiorella Fiorucci," the widow Del Grasso announced to the League. "She was sitting outside on my doorstep this morning when I went to water my geraniums."

The other widows all looked to Violetta. Membership was at an all-time low, but that didn't mean just anyone could join. It was secret, after all. New widows were generally already known to the group before their loved one was lost and usually there was a gentle approach made from someone who had a particular connection once the difficult yearlong mourning period was over.

No one could recall seeing Fiorella Fiorucci ever before and what's more, she was wearing a bright orange shift with big pink flowers on it when the rest of them were in head-to-toe black.

"My no-good son-of-a-so-and-so husband has finally gone and bought the big one," Fiorella Fiorucci told the group. "So I want in."

The widows, still speechless, all looked to Violetta again.

"You want in?" Violetta repeated.

"Are you deaf? Yes, I want in. I'm a widow now. I qualify."

"We know each other, apparently, from meeting at the library, but to be honest . . ." the widow Del Grasso started, clearly embarrassed. Her memory had been a little unreliable of late so she supposed it was quite possible she did know Fiorella but had forgotten. This was thoroughly vexing but, she supposed, nowhere near as vexing as forgetting to take the rollers out of her hair before going to Mass or forgetting to put her shoes on to go to the market. In fact, in comparison, it was hardly vexing at all. "To be honest," she continued more brightly, "I didn't know she was even married."

"Why would you?" Fiorella shrugged. "Why would anyone? My husband ran off with my sister in 1977 and has been living in Naples ever since, may God spit on his soul once he's finished dragging it out through the sorry wretch's intestines." She pushed her thick spectacles back up on to her nose and wrinkled it.

If toads wore thick spectacles and gaudy shifts, she could almost have been mistaken for one.

"Erm, we're sorry for your loss," Violetta said, somewhat unconvincingly to break the ensuing awkward silence. "But I'm not quite sure that you're what we're looking for." The true love of a good man certainly did not seem to be a feature of this interloper's recent past, and the true love of a good man was the number one requirement for entry into the League. "And anyway, there isn't an opening."

"Oh, and you can afford to be so fussy? I can darn four socks so well in a single hour that you'd never even know they once had holes in them," Fiorella said. "My cousin Enzo sells them at the market in San Quirico as new. Gets two euro a pair."

The widows coughed shiftily and scuffed their slippers on the floor.

"The thing is," Violetta said carefully, "that darning socks is not entirely what the League is about."

"Oh, I know that," answered Fiorella. "I've seen the sad sacks that start out all mopey and blue, then get all miraculously jazzed up by you lot though they don't even know it and next thing they're all lovey-dovey, having the time of their lives. I'm on to you."

It was a secret league. Despite more than two hundred and

fifty happy endings being produced over the years, no one was supposed to be on to them.

"What's more," continued Fiorella, pushing those enormous spectacles back up her nose again, "I'm a part-time shelf stacker at the pharmacy on the way out of town. Not the one right in the middle where everyone goes for the boring stuff. Trust me, we get it all where I am. There's not a condom or a pregnancy test or a happy pill that passes out of that place without me seeing who it's headed for. I have my finger on the pulse, let me tell you. More than the pharmacist, that's for sure. He's hopped up on goofballs half the time. Doesn't know his own name unless he checks his driver's license."

The stunned widows didn't know where to look now. Information the likes of which came out of the pharmacy on the way out of town, they could definitely use, but it was clear that Fiorella Fiorucci was a handful.

The widow Mazzetti, who had memorized the League's rule book and knew every clause and addendum going back as far as 1947, looked fit to burst a blood vessel. She was as much a stickler for the rules as Violetta, who narrowed her eyes, cleared her throat, and exhorted Fiorella to tell the group more about her late husband.

"What's to tell?" said Fiorella. "Sixty-four years ago he came back from the war and told me that my childhood sweetheart, Eduardo, had died in his arms on the battlefield. A little while later, we got married. A little while after that Eduardo came home, minus a leg but otherwise still the man I loved with all my heart and soul, the man I thought I would spend the rest of my life with."

The atmosphere in the room changed from being stunned to being sympathetic, which under the circumstances was quite a shift.

"That must have been terrible," Luciana said, moving slightly in front of her sister.

"Yes, well, in those days a girl did not leave her husband just because he was a lying, cheating bully who had tricked her out of eternal happiness."

"No, I suppose they didn't," agreed several of the widows.

"And what happened to Eduardo?" Luciana wanted to know.

"Oh, we met again, just the once, and he gave me a locket with a picture of the two of us in it. I have it still." She fished it out from beneath her gaudy shift and opened it, showing the room a faded sepia photo of her young self—same glasses—and an adoring boy soldier. "He said I should forgive myself because anyone would have fallen for Lorenzo's trickery, he was known for it, and that I should try to be happy with him anyway. Then he went home and died. I think it was a broken heart, although others said septicemia."

"A good man," one of the widows uttered to a chorus of "*sí, sí.*"

"I've felt like a widow my entire married life, to be honest," said Fiorella. "Even though that overgrown *gnocchi* lived with me for thirty years and managed another thirty with my whining gasbag of a sister before doing the decent thing and falling under a truck."

There was another awkward silence.

"You seem a little crotchety," ventured Luciana.

"We're supposed to be, aren't we?" Fiorella said. "You all are."

"Yes, but we're only pretending," pointed out Violetta.

"Well, maybe so am I."

"If she is, she's very good at it," the widow Benedicti muttered to no one in particular.

"Look, I know what it's like to be old and invisible," Fiorella said, fingering her locket as she looked around the room. "We can sit quietly in our darkened doorways feeling like we're not worth the contents of your average chamber pot, not doing anything for anybody—Italy is full of women just like us. Every hilltop town in Tuscany has at least two dozen. It's the curse of old age! But I've seen how you lot use your powers as scratchy old dames for good, not evil, and what can I say—I like it. So shoot me! My own happiness may have been snatched away from me by the giant sweaty hands of a complete and utter deadbeat, but if I can help someone else find happiness, I will. It's what Eduardo would want."

At this, the widow Rossellini woke herself up with a rumbling snore. "I don't feel so well," she said.

"Your color's not good," agreed the widow sitting next to her.

"She's not been feeling so great the last few weeks," chimed in another.

"Her daughter's been trying for months to get her to go to, you know, the *microwave*," whispered another.

"The microwave?" repeated Fiorella.

The widows fell silent. The microwave was their euphemism for the glistening hospital block that had been built just a few years before, a couple of miles south of the town. Rising out of the pristine landscape very much like a shiny modern kitchen appliance, once women their age went into it, they were likely to shrivel and, if not disappear altogether, emerge a shadow of their former selves—if they were lucky. The unlucky ones emerged a shadow of their former selves minus an arm, it was rumored, a bosom, or an internal organ. Those even less fortunate never emerged at all.

Women their age would do anything to avoid going into the microwave.

"She just needs a week or two in bed to get her color back," said the widow sitting next to her. "I'll take her home and sit with her a while."

"I'll help," said someone else, as the widow Rossellini was indeed very unsteady on her feet.

"Me too," piped up another.

"Well, looks like there could be an opening after all," Fiorella said cheerfully as the room started to empty, and before Violetta could give her an old-fashioned tune-up for her rudeness and insensitivity, Luciana jumped in with uncustomary presumption.

"Yes, at least temporarily, it seems there is," she said. "Fiorella Fiorucci, would you care to join our league?"

"You bet," came the answer. "But do you have anything to eat other than this *cantucci*? I swiped some from over by the ginger supper and it's horrible. What do you put in it? Cement? All the *vin santo* in Christendom isn't going to help that, let me tell you."

She moved off to help herself to the small amount of *vin santo* that was still available anyway, at which Violetta turned angrily to her sister.

"What on earth were you thinking?" she asked.

"I was thinking she has a certain something," Luciana answered.

"That she does," Violetta answered. "But it is the wrong sort of something."

Chapter 7

The last-minute complications of deserting her life on such short notice required a lot more work than Lily had anticipated, her tightly packed schedule being almost as time-consuming to cancel as it was to keep.

Luckily Tipsy Tourism stretched to business class and she slept fitfully on the flight, with the help of more than her fair share of champagne, but arrived in rainy Rome feeling tired and aghast that one important aspect of coming to Italy she had overlooked was that everyone spoke Italian.

Not only could she not understand a word, she couldn't even follow the gesticulations, which she was sure could be blamed for how she ended up in the world's smallest rental car. It was a Fiat 500 but 500 of what? she asked. She had never seen a car so small. It was the size of a sneaker. Her baggage only just fit in the tiny trunk, and she had to put the seat back as far as it would go to accommodate her long legs.

She spent the first half hour driving around the airport parking lot trying to find the exit and then pressed the wrong button on her rented GPS so that it would only operate with a voice proclaiming to be Dermott in what she thought was an Irish accent.

She could make little sense of anything other than *left* and *right*, but in fact these two words turned out to be enough to direct her north on the A1 toward Firenze, which she worked out was Florence, which she was pretty sure was in Tuscany, so it was taking her in the right direction.

It was pouring and the Italians seemed to drive with a ferocity that suggested they were racing either away from raging flames licking at their rear fenders or toward loved ones taking their last gasps before the machines were turned off. At first Lily's leg trembled on the accelerator as she carefully switched lanes in the poor visibility and did her best to avoid vehicles moving faster than hers, which was all of them.

Soon, however, she caught the rhythm of the *autostrada* and relaxed enough to consider her surroundings. The view from the A1 was not one likely to show up on postcards or romantic book covers.

To her left, she could see distant smokestacks and strange isolated collections of industrial buildings piled like children's blocks on the gloomy skyline. If not for the roadside billboards in a foreign language, she could have been on a big highway almost anywhere. But to her right the impression was, she guessed, a little more Italian. Fields of something tall and slender stretched as far as she could see, swaying in the wind and rain, then fading away to a faraway spine of misty mountains.

Faraway spines of misty mountains did not usually crop up in Lily's world on a Tuesday morning. What a normal Tuesday morning brought was a strenuous session with her personal trainer at the gym, followed by a shower, a chive and egg white omelet, a green tea, a fine-tooth combing of countless spreadsheets, and then the weekly statistics meeting with other Heigelmann's HODs.

At the thought of her usual omelet, she felt a pang of hunger but could not quite stomach the thought of stopping at the giant roadside gas stations, which seemed to be the only option. Starving seemed imminently preferable to doing further battle with a foreign language over the presence of pesticides or preservatives in whatever fare was on offer, which she doubted would suit her particular palate anyway.

Eventually, Dermott directed her off the freeway toward the spine of misty mountains, where it became clear why most other people were also driving very small cars: They were on very small roads.

In some places they were not even wide enough for two sneakers to pass each other. On one corner, Lily found herself swerving off the road, jamming on the brakes and shutting her eyes as an ancient farmer in a three-wheeled contraption came hurtling toward her.

He missed, but only by the skin of his teeth.

She remembered then a similarly antique farmer blocking the road with his tractor and a motley herd of cows when she and Daniel were in Maine on their honeymoon.

The old man was puttering down the road without a care in the world, completely oblivious to the fact that Daniel and Lily were stuck behind him.

"I should have boned up on my country horn-honking etiquette before we came away," Daniel had said. "I don't suppose you did?"

When they did honk the horn, only one ornery cow took any notice. It stopped and glared at them in such an intimidating fashion that Daniel lost his nerve and said he thought the side of the road actually looked quite comfortable and perhaps they should stay there instead of going back to their cottage. Lily laughed so much she nearly peed her pants.

It seemed like a long time since she'd laughed like that. Now she and Daniel were both so seriously grown up and busy, what they mostly did was a lot of quiet, unemotional getting-on-with-it.

Maybe that's what went on in all sixteen-year marriages.

Maybe no one nearly peed their pants outside the first flush of love.

"Continue straight ahead," Dermott said in his cheerful Irish accent, which confused her into taking her foot off the clutch and stalling the little car.

She turned the key in the ignition but found herself unable to pull back out onto the road, staying instead on the same tilted angle in the grass, the passenger window pressed up against a shimmering wet hedge of shiny green leaves and tiny purple flowers.

Unemotional getting-on-with-it certainly wasn't what she thought the future held when she and Daniel were in bed drinking wine and eating cheese out of the wrapper without even getting up for a knife on their honeymoon. She'd wanted love, happiness, laughter, fun. All the things anyone wanted when they got married.

She'd wanted children, a family.

It had all seemed so perfectly within reach in the beginning. They had no money and a fifth-floor walk-up that smelled horribly of mold and mothballs, but they had all those wonderful dreams. That was their wealth in those days: their limitless hope, their electrifying potential.

It was the babies' fault. Those smiling, pink-cheeked, plump, sweet-smelling babies with whom she had never been blessed. Their absence had just sapped the pant-peeing happiness right out of her. That's where the laughter had gone.

The rain fell in glassy curtains across her windshield, the wipers sweeping them open and closed. Out the window a thick mist was rolling across the fields toward her. She realized she hadn't even brought an umbrella. She could have been in Washington.

Tuscany? It was hard to know what all the fuss was about. And what did she think she was going to achieve in Montevedova anyway? If she found Daniel at this point she wasn't quite sure what she would do with him. She could not begin to think how the conversation would start, let alone end. It was all so uncivilized.

She was out of her mind coming here without a plan.

Lily didn't usually open an eyelid without a plan. Ever since she was a little girl, she'd liked to know what was around the corner. It had driven Rose mad for as long as she could remember. "Let's just see what happens," Rose had said to her older sister more than once, more than a dozen times, possibly more than a hundred. "Try going with the flow, Lily."

But Lily didn't trust the flow. The flow took frightening turns and threatening twists. She assumed it was their mother's fault. Something about never knowing from one day to the next what "mood" Carmel would be in had unsettled Lily from an early age. As soon as she worked out that if she could control a situation, the results were more predictable, she started controlling the situation.

Nothing in Lily's adult life had just casually cropped up. She'd orchestrated it all: Ivy League scholarship, Yale business degree, good job, handsome husband, great salary. Even the view from their apartment on Seventy-second Street was pretty much the one she'd always had in mind and just needed to find and acquire within her predestined time frame.

The only dream she hadn't been able to make come true were her three beautiful children: Edward, after Daniel's father; Rose, after Rose; and then either Amelia or Angus, depending.

She'd persevered with this plan every bit as hard as she had for anything else, if not harder: She'd tried IVF treatments, egg donation, surrogate motherhood, and—finally—adoption. She bit her lip and shook away that memory. It didn't matter because in the end it had all come to nothing.

The sharp *rat-a-tat-tat* of someone knocking at her window

brought her smartly back to the present. Flustered, she scrambled to press the right button to open the window, first accidentally locking all the doors, then opening the passenger window before finally her own.

"Continue straight ahead," chirruped Dermott, who had been maintaining a haughty silence until then. "Continue straight ahead."

Rattled, Lily looked up to see an Italian man of about her own age bending in beneath a huge white umbrella to look at her. His hair was curly and shoulder length, his eyes brown and big and his eyelashes so thick and long they would not have looked out of place on a supermodel, but his face was otherwise craggy, slightly unshaven. He was good-looking but carried a little extra weight and he had an intense sort of seriousness about him.

"I saw you stopped here," he said in heavily accented but perfectly understandable English. "Is anything the matter?"

He was wearing a white linen shirt that was getting splattered by the rain bouncing off his umbrella, creating little splodges that clung to his skin.

"I'm so sorry," Lily said, finding, to her embarrassment, that her voice was shaky. Those babies. Those wretched lost babies. "I've just driven from Rome and I'm not sure about these tiny little roads. I pulled over to . . . Well, there was a . . . Am I blocking you?"

She looked in her rearview mirror and saw his car—a black Range Rover—parked behind her, its hazard lights blinking. It wasn't her fault he was driving such a vast machine that he couldn't get past. But anyway, he was right, she needed to get going. She couldn't stay there forever.

"I'll get going right away," she said, turning the car over again even though it was already idling, which made a horrible noise and confused her as much as the windows.

"Continue straight ahead," Dermott repeated.

"Oh, I'm so sorry," Lily said to the man. "Will you shut up!" she snapped at Dermott. "I was going straight ahead anyway."

The man laughed, and perhaps because she had just been lamenting the lack of laughter in her recent life, this grated.

"Yes, very funny, but if you'll excuse me I'll be on my way," she said, taking her foot off the clutch and stalling the car again.

Dermott had the good sense to stay silent, but the long-haired Italian was not as attuned to Lily as her GPS was.

"I think you are a damsel in distress and I must help you," he said.

"Actually, there's no such thing as damsels in distress where I come from," Lily said, smiling sweetly up at him. "Really, I'm fine, there's nothing wrong. I'm not lost, I'm just resting, and anyway I have this Irish fellow here helping me. If this is the road to Montevedova, which I believe it is, I can't really go wrong and all I have to do is drive right up to my hotel when I get there and I'm all set."

The Italian man nodded, but in a way that did not particularly look as though he was agreeing with her.

"Alessandro D'Agnello at your service," he said with a polite little bow, as though she had not just explained how much she didn't need his service. "I think perhaps you have not been to Montevedova before."

"Oh, you do, do you? And why is that?"

"Perhaps you can tell me the name of your hotel."

He was getting quite wet now, nearly soaked through. The splodges had joined up. She could see how brown his smooth skin was beneath the linen.

"Well, even if I could remember the name, which I can't, I wouldn't tell you," Lily said. "Look, I appreciate your concern, but, honestly, I really don't need your service, so if you would just step back, I'll be on my way."

Alessandro smiled gently and stood back as asked. "Of course. I apologize. But just be aware that you cannot drive in Montevedova. Cars are not permitted."

Lily took her foot off the accelerator again.

"They're not?"

"They are not."

"Not even a car as small as this one?"

"Not even."

"So how do I get to my hotel?"

"This is why I ask you where it is. There are parking lots surrounding the town and depending where your hotel is, I can tell you which is closest."

The information about her hotel was in her suitcase in the trunk and Lily did not feel like getting out to retrieve it.

"Or perhaps you would like to follow me," Alessandro offered. "I can take you to the main parking lot near the tourist office and help you work it out from there."

"Continue straight ahead," Dermott interjected again, and Lily was sure he sounded more forceful, as though incensed that someone other than himself was offering navigational guidance.

"No, really, thank you." She managed another smile at Alessandro. "You're very kind but truly, I'm fine. Thanks for the tip about the tourist office though. I'll head straight there."

"Well, OK, if you are sure," Alessandro said, with a polite shrug. "*Buongiorno, signora*, and I hope you enjoy your stay."

He stood back and watched as she pulled cautiously out into the narrow lane and drove away. It was not every day he happened upon a beautiful blonde woman parked up on the road near his house. In fact, he couldn't recall it ever happening before, although there was no shortage of beautiful blonde women in Montevedova and its surrounds if you were looking for them, not that he was interested, not in general.

This beautiful blonde though? She was different. An American, obviously, older than most of the backpackers who traipsed through the town in droves over the summer. What was she doing driving there alone—no husband, no children, no friend to keep her company?

Alessandro climbed into his Range Rover and turned up the unpaved *strada bianca* toward his villa. She hadn't liked it when he called her a damsel in distress, but that didn't mean she wasn't one. And regardless of her flustered state, she retained a sort of elegance he found very attractive. She had a long neck, he'd noticed, her collar bones ending in delicate points at the base of her throat, leaving the perfect space for a single diamond to sit on a tiny gold chain.

Her blue-and-white striped top did not show any extra flesh the way so many women chose to, just that tantalizing bit of throat and her slim wrists, smooth hands, and long fingers.

She'd not been wearing a wedding ring, he had of course noticed that. But he had also noticed the trouble brewing behind her wide blue eyes. She was a damsel in distress, if ever there was one, even if she didn't know it herself.

Alessandro didn't normally go down that particular track. It was too soon for that. It was too soon to even be thinking too soon. It made him feel guilty, a little, but mostly, as usual, just downhearted.

Still, the mysterious blonde stayed with him as he threw open the doors of his villa, turned up his favorite Bellini aria, and put the coffeepot on for his late-morning espresso.

"I'm not lost, just resting," he said to himself, then to the cat, then to his housekeeper, the widow Benedicti, who bustled in the door not long after him and whose chipmunk cheeks looked even pinker and shinier than usual.

Chapter 8

Daniel sat outside a pleasantly crowded café just off the piazza around the corner from his hotel, emptying a carafe of wine as he smoked his fourth cigarette in a row.

In Italy, Daniel smoked.

In Italy, Daniel was a different person.

In Italy he didn't go jogging in the mornings or play golf at the weekends. He didn't wave away the sommelier at lunch, he didn't scrimp on the olive oil, he didn't pass on dessert. In Italy he didn't do any of the things he usually did. It was like being on vacation but not from his job because it was his job that brought him here. It was like being on vacation from his usual self.

He exhaled slowly and watched through the smoke as a tall blonde woman slid her way between two tables nearby. She sat down, pushed her sunglasses up on her head, and flicked him a smile as she met his gaze.

She looked like Lily. Not as slim or as beautiful but she had that same sort of casual chic that Lily had. It was one of the first things he'd noticed about her, the woman who would become his wife: the way she moved with an almost accidental grace, like satin sliding off a marble tabletop.

He'd known from the first glimpse of her that he wanted to marry her, yet he hadn't even believed that things like that really happened until then. He'd thought it was just something foolish that lovestruck couples said after the fact to make each other feel like it was meant to be.

But the truth was, the second he saw Lily across the restaurant Jordie dragged him to after some sweaty squash game all those years ago, he knew. He just knew. Well, he didn't know that he was going to marry her. But he knew that he wanted to. Just like that. *Kapow.*

Turned out Lily was a friend of Jordie's date—they never did find out if it was a set up or not, but if either of them suspected it at the time, they hadn't shown it. Afterward, they never cared how they met, only that they did.

Daniel just watched her, mostly, that first night; the way she ate so delicately, spoke freely, laughed easily, and had no idea how many eyes in the room lingered on her delectable neck, her tiny ear lobes, her perfect mouth.

He'd been smitten. So smitten, in fact, that he realized all the other love or lust affairs he'd had before then had been ridiculous, hardly more than schoolboy flirtations in comparison.

Loving Lily had been an ache from the very beginning, an ache so deep he couldn't tell where it started and where it finished, what shape it was, an ache that consumed him till he won her heart and consumed him still.

He'd never feel like that about anyone else, ever, even if he lived to be a hundred, which he hoped he wouldn't because living to be forty-five he'd made so many mistakes he didn't know how to even begin fixing them.

Sometimes, when he was shaving, Daniel met his own eyes in the mirror and was astonished to see the same person he once was looking back at him. How could that be? He still appeared so clean cut on the outside. So dependable, so ordinary, so the same as ever. But those tidy good looks, that impassive exterior belied the secrets and private shames that scurried around inside him, searching for places to hide.

It got so that he started shaving in the shower, no mirror, never mind the odd nick.

The blonde woman sitting alone at the table was chatting on her cell phone now. Actually, she had big earlobes, a shorter neck. She wasn't so much like Lily after all, Daniel thought, lighting another cigarette. She had her own style and she looked happy, this blonde woman. Uncomplicated. And happy.

If it had been Lily sitting at that table and someone else's husband smoking cigarettes and looking at her, he doubted *happy* would have been the word that sprang to mind. He'd admire the beauty, this other husband, he may even find himself briefly enamored. But he'd quickly sense the darkness lurking behind that exquisite face and would find his eyes roving to a less thorny rose, someone not as good to look at, perhaps, but with a twinkle in her eye.

Lily's sadness had stolen her twinkle. The blonde sitting two tables away from him still had hers.

Daniel poured himself another glass of wine. The thought of Lily's sadness was something he did not want to further contemplate. He'd contemplated it enough already, knew that there was little if anything he could do to alleviate it. In New York he was the useless husband of an unhappy wife, but here he didn't have to be, or at least he didn't have to see the unhappiness. This too was a sort of vacation. Not that he begrudged his wife her grief, her sorrow. It was his too, after all. To begin with, they shared it, the same way they shared all the good things in life, the greatness, the laughter.

But Lily's sadness had gradually overtaken everything else about her. He wondered, often, when the tipping point had been. He knew when it had started, and when it had gotten worse, but he couldn't pinpoint the exact moment when it consumed her completely.

He was disappointed about the first miscarriage, of course,

but not overwhelmingly so, fatherhood being an island he knew he wanted to visit, but wasn't sure he wanted to stay on.

Every failed attempt after that hurt him more and more, but that was nothing compared to what it did to Lily. Each tragedy seemed to chip away at her until she was like a statue remodeled over the centuries: the same piece of stone that had always stood there but an entirely different image. Smaller. Sharper. It wasn't as though she cried all the time, or became suicidal, or resorted to hysterics, although he thought he might have preferred that, ill-equipped as he was to deal with that sort of behavior. Instead, she just retreated, the lights went off, and it took him too long to realize he was sitting in the dark. Alone.

By then, he had screwed up too badly to do anything much about it.

His own cell phone rang then and when he looked at who was calling, his heart sank. Still, he picked it up and waited for the voice on the other end to start where she had left off half an hour ago.

"I told you, it's just a few days," he said, tiredly, when he finally got a word in. "I know, and I'm sorry, but I'll figure something out. I promise. I just need a bit of time."

He listened for a while longer, then gently took the phone from his ear, laid it on his thigh, and turned it off.

A waiter approached, a man who looked old enough to be Daniel's father and who wore a similar look of something bordering on contempt but not quite.

He ordered another liter of wine and slid his old self into his back pocket along with his phone. Then the blonde woman asked if she could join him.

She wasn't Lily, but she was close.

Chapter 9

The widow Benedicti was usually so particular about her cleaning that spiders quivered in their webs merely at the sound of her rusty Renault rattling up Alessandro's drive.

On this particular occasion, however, the spiders were safe to stay where they were, eating flies and looking creepy, because cleaning was the last thing on her mind.

She whizzed around the villa halfheartedly dislodging dirt from one spot to another and monitoring her employer's whereabouts should she get the chance to use his phone.

The widow Benedicti loved Alessandro. All the widows did. All the women of Montevedova did, as it happened. He was kind, handsome, and rich.

More important than that, even, he was also a man known to lift an elderly woman over a puddle or a child out of a high chair, or to stop and help attach a problematic exhaust pipe to a worn-down clunker of a car.

He was a good and decent man, in other words. Plus, his heart had been broken.

Various members of the League had put him forward as a likely candidate for their attention several times over the past couple of years, but for one reason or another the right woman had never turned up to be helped into his arms.

Until now. The widow Benedicti had just seen Alessandro with her very own eyes stopped on the side of the road talking to a glamorous blonde who looked just like Grace Kelly in *Rear Window*.

The widow Benedicti loved Grace Kelly in *Rear Window*.

Unfortunately, she had been playing Patience on her cell phone during the night so when she went to report this all-important sighting of a romantic possibility for one of their favorite possibilities to Widow Ciacci, its battery was as flat as a frittata. As soon as she was able, she got on Alessandro's landline and alerted the widow Ciacci to the fact that it seemed like Alessandro's time had finally come.

She gave a quick description of the glamorous blonde but was then startled by Alessandro coming into the kitchen and asking why his pillowcases had been turned inside out, not laundered, so she had to hang up.

"You young things expect everything to be just so," she grumbled as she hid her embarrassment at being caught doing such a sloppy job. "In my day we didn't even have pillowcases. We didn't even have pillows. We didn't have a bed. Just straw."

"I'm sorry for your hardship," Alessandro said with real sympathy. "And if that's still the situation, I would very happily buy you a new bed and all the linen you require, but in the meantime, I do indeed like my pillowcases to be just so."

Chapter 10

"This hotel you ask for is closed down for renovations," a wrinkled old woman in a voluminous black smock told Lily when she asked at the tourist office for directions.

"But I only booked it yesterday," Lily disputed.

"Yes, it close suddenly for very urgent repair," the old woman said.

"Hotel Prato is closed?" the pretty young girl also working in the office interrupted. "I thought—"

"I take care of this!" the old woman snapped. "Shoo!" She turned to Lily. "Is no problem. You have booking now at only other hotel in Montevedova. Hotel Adesso. Very nice."

"Is it also four star?" Lily wanted to know.

"Is no star. But Hotel Prato also is no star, just say so on Internet. Hotel Adesso very nice."

Lily considered arguing, but this woman did not look the type to meddle with. "Well, is it far?" she asked instead.

"Yes," the old woman said. "And road is steep." She peered over the counter at Lily's kitten heels and out through the doors of the office to the pouring rain. "And is very wet."

Indeed, by the time Lily got to the medieval arched gate at the entrance of the old town, about fifty yards behind the tourist office, she was already saturated.

She stopped briefly, sheltered by the town's ancient portal. Montevedova as far as she could see consisted of a single stupidly steep curving cobbled lane, the Via del Corso. Crooked rows of two- or three-story buildings loomed in from either side, their shuttered windows like inquisitive eyes peering down at those who scuttled below.

On a nice day, it might have had some charm, but not today. Today it was, just as the old woman said, steep and wet.

Lily stepped back out into the rain, her wheeled suitcase skittering over the slippery cobbles and quickly developing something of a noisy limp, drawing extra attention.

Two young men sitting in the open window of a busy café stopped talking and stared as she passed; a group of workmen huddled behind the plastic sheeting covering a scaffolded church front laughed as one of them blew smoke rings in her direction; an old woman eyed her carefully from the doorway of a tiny grocery store as she fiddled with a cell phone in her apron pocket.

Still it poured. Still Lily climbed. Finally, the lane flattened out a little and forked—albeit even more steeply—in opposite directions. At the T of this junction, on the flat bit, was an open foyer beneath a grander building. Gratefully, Lily again sought respite from the rain.

She heaved her bag up on to the raised parapet and with frozen fingers pulled off Rose's pashmina, which she had wrapped around her head, then unscrunched her soggy map. It looked as though she had just as far to go again to make it to her hotel and the moment she realized this, the rain started to fall even harder. Water flowed from either side of the Corso into the middle and gushed down the hill like a river.

A gangly black dog joined her on her dry parapet, shaking itself and spraying her from head to foot before shooting her a coy look and mooching off. That women her age should dream of coming to places like this for long lunches, golden vistas, and the thrill of hot sex with young, well-built men seemed preposterous.

Suddenly though, above the solid *plink-plink* of the rain, she realized that someone nearby was playing the violin. It was a gentle piece not at all in keeping with the torrid weather and she strained to hear more. The noisy downpour was actually providing a sort of rhythmic timpani, the overall effect being quite orchestral. The violin swelled up and Lily closed her eyes. The long lunches and golden vistas suddenly seemed a little more likely. But this brief flirtation with the romance of Tuscany was crushed almost immediately by the sound of a howling baby.

Lily had heard somewhere that mothers had a special radar allowing them to pick out their own baby's cries from a sea of similar cries, hormones jumping for joy as they did. Obviously, she had no experience of this, but what she knew to be absolutely true was that women who would never be mothers were sensitive to babies crying too, the difference being that women who would never be mothers picked up the sound of every child. And their hormones didn't jump for joy, they ran around like chickens with their heads cut off.

In the same way a certain Eagles song could take Lily back to drinking beer on Fire Island with Rose one sultry August when they were teenagers, down to feeling the sunburn on her neck and the sand beneath her toes, the sound of a baby crying could plummet her into the depths of her childlessness.

She seemed to feel it right down in her empty womb, where some useless attachment tightened and pulled at her insides. She felt it then as she stood listening to the violin music dancing the light fantastic to the drumbeat of the fat raindrops hitting the Via del Corso.

This particular crying infant was beneath an enormous red umbrella moving up the middle of the steep lane toward the parapet. Water sprayed out beneath the wheels of an ancient pram and as it got closer she saw the umbrella was attached to its handle so that the even more ancient man pushing it could use both hands to do so. And he needed both. Montevedova and baby carriages were not an ideal combination in any weather.

Lily willed the old man to keep pushing the crying baby up one of the steep lanes to either side of her, but he didn't, instead approaching her sanctuary and battling unsuccessfully to get the pram over the lip of the parapet and out of the rain. She knew she should go and help as he pushed and pulled, releasing what sounded to her, in any language, like a string of curses as he struggled, but she was frozen to her spot.

The crying got louder and the old man stopped his swearing and instead leaned in toward the baby and made soothing noises.

Lily turned away, dry eyes prickling, but turned back when she heard the sound of a nearby door slamming. A young man, no more than twenty or so, appeared in the entrance of a shop diagonally across from them. He shot Lily a quick, appreciative look, scrunched his face up into the rain, then hunched his shoulders and dashed across the lane.

He babbled a greeting to the older man and together they hoisted the pram into the dry recess. The old man shook himself off while the younger man reached in and fetched out the child.

It occurred to Lily at that point that the baby he was pulling out into the cool wet air could possibly be Daniel's but the infant who emerged was a girl: a fact heralded by the pink ribbon tied around her otherwise unisex fat bald head. Upon being picked up, the baby girl roared in fury, her chubby thighs kicking angrily beneath a frilly white dress. She threw her head furiously from side to side, face crumpled like a big red raisin, and howled. But the young man had only to jiggle her in the air a handful of times, make a few cooing noises, and the wailing stopped, the plump fists that had been banging the air suddenly stretched happily out to her sides. Within moments she was gurgling and laughing as he lifted her up and down and spoke to her in a sing-song voice.

Lily couldn't look away. If she did, she thought, she would crumble into a mountain of wet pebbles and be swept down the drain with the water from the torrential downpour. Why had she been denied one of these precious creatures? What had she done wrong? Where was the justice?

The two men shared a joke and the younger planted a kiss on the baby's forehead, which made her squeal—this time with delight.

He had turned her despair into joy so effortlessly. She wondered if he knew what a gift that was.

Daniel, on the other hand, had always been awkward with other people's children. He held them at funny angles and didn't know what to do or say. It was strange, really, because he'd always insisted he wanted children as much as she did and she'd assumed he'd be different with their own, but in the six days and seventeen hours they'd had Baby Grace—she allowed herself to just think that precious name—he'd still seemed not reluctant, exactly, not even uncertain. Overawed, perhaps. She wondered what her husband was like with his Italian children, if he'd ever got the hang of it, if it now came naturally to him, this thing she herself had been given less than a week to display a flair for.

She closed her mind to the subject, the thoughts she didn't want to have stiffening her already-brittle bones.

Across the parapet, the baby was being put back in her pram, the umbrella was reattached, and after the young man helped lift the carriage back onto the lane, her perilous journey continued farther up the hill in the opposite direction to which Lily's hotel was marked on her map.

The younger man looked after them for a while, peeking out from underneath the shelter, then moved his gaze to Lily.

"*Buongiorno, signora!*" he called, nodding in the direction of the rain. "*Piove a catinelle,* no?"

"I'm sorry," she said. "I don't speak Italian."

"Ah, sorry. *Turista?*"

"No," said Lily. "I mean, yes. *Sí. Turista.*" The violin music was gone. She was cold, desperate for a shower and dry clothes. The rain wasn't going away. She would have to brave it to get to her hotel. She started collecting her things.

"Alberto," the young man said, walking toward her, holding out his hand for her to shake. "You would like to come for some wine at my shop, perhaps?"

He had short, spiky, dark hair, Alberto, and a sort of boyish charm that had its appeal, as did the glass of wine, but the tugging at her insides that had arrived with the baby's cries tautened further within her. She wanted to be alone, somewhere dark and quiet.

"Maybe some other time." She smiled politely.

"Are you sure? This rain look like to stay for some time . . . I am just sitting down to my lunch. I have bread and prosciutto and tomatoes from my grandmother's garden—she bring them to me just now and said I should share them with the first pretty blonde woman I see, then I look out the window and here you are. Seems like fate, no?"

"Not to me, it doesn't," Lily said more forcefully than she meant to. "I'm sorry, but I'm tired and would just like to get to my hotel."

Alberto held up his hands.

"OK, OK," he said, but his smile was still warm. "I understand. No problem. Welcome to Montevedova anyway, no?"

"*Sí.*" She smiled. "Thank you."

"*Ciao, ciao,*" he said, and, collar up, he took off.

By the time Lily reached the torn and tattered canopy of the

Hotel Adesso she had pulled a calf muscle, wrenched her shoulder, and decided that whatever small, dry luxuries no-star accommodation could offer, she would gratefully accept.

She stopped under the canopy, dripping, and rubbed her palm where the handle of her bag had cut off the circulation just as a foul stench hit her square in the face.

Every door in the hotel opened and a rumble of mutual disgust and anger billowed through the three-story building, ending with a shriek as a uniformed housemaid came running down the hallway, hand over her nose.

"What's going on?" Lily asked, as the maid gulped for fresh air and rubbed her stomach, grimacing.

"The drains," she said. "There is big problem."

"With all of them?"

"They are flowing over. In the bathroom."

"But I'm supposed to stay here!"

"I think not today," the housemaid said. "Try Hotel Prato. Is four stars."

The lobby at the end of the hallway was filling with angry guests demanding information from the lone, harried receptionist, and Lily's dream of no-star refuge drained away.

"I can't believe this," she said. "Hotel Prato is closed for renovations. I don't suppose you know of anywhere else?"

"Hotel Prato closed? Are you—" But the rest of the housemaid's response was swallowed by an almighty holler coming from a diminutive gray-haired woman who appeared in the lobby and continued to make an enthusiastically vocal fuss. "*Scusi*," the housemaid said, then covered her face with a handkerchief and dashed back down the hall.

The raindrops bounced furiously off the cobbles in front of her as Lily contemplated the Corso once again. But the stench was not getting any sweeter, the lobby any emptier. She lurched back out into the lane, body pitched against the weather, and headed uphill, but she had gone barely a dozen steps when she came to a tiny ivy-covered building on the opposite side with a FOR RENT sign written in wobbly letters in its darkened window.

Without stopping to think further, Lily pitched in the door, her bag listing sideways as she hauled it in behind her, her purse slipping from her grasp and sliding across the floor, a large unseemly looking puddle forming beneath her.

The space was cozily dark, but she didn't need to see much to figure out it was no ordinary house. It was some sort of shop, she thought, as her eyes adjusted. A bakeshop. It was tiny, barely larger than her beloved closet at home, but infinitely better-smelling. Facing her was an *L*-shaped marble counter set out galley-style from the walls. On this counter sat a dozen or so enormous fluted glass bowls, some on raised plinths so they sat at different heights, in a palette of dark reds and blues and greens. The way the scant light reflected through the dusty air— bouncing off a chandelier, of all things, then striking the bowls and shimmering around the outside of the room—gave Lily the impression of being in the middle of a stained-glass window.

A scent she couldn't quite place seemed to leach out of the walls. At first she thought it was cinnamon, then vanilla, then something more floral, like lavender. It was oddly comforting, like being wrapped in a satin-lined coat. Indeed, she could no longer hear the rain beating down, and with the heat in the room and the spiciness in the air, her bones loosened, her blood warmed, her color started to return.

In the window bearing the FOR RENT sign, a lonely wrought-iron chair sat neatly waiting beside a tiny round table. The tiled floor beneath her kitten heels was a slightly crazed mosaic in faded burnt orange, dull turquoise, and gray.

She stepped forward and saw that the bowls were full of what looked like biscotti; the Italian cookies she never ate when they came with coffee or the check at Babbo or 'Cesca.

Her mouth watered. It had been a long time since she had eaten anything.

Behind the counter, against the back wall, stood a set of shelves, on which sat a dusty collection of spice jars and faded cookie boxes. They looked old-fashioned to Lily, as though they had been sitting there for many, many years.

In fact, it looked like the whole store had been sitting there for many, many years. If it was a store. It certainly wasn't the sort of place with which Heigelmann's would trifle. There was no room for more than five customers, tops, and there didn't seem to be a cash register. Or anyone working there.

The biscotti, upon further inspection, differed from the similar cookies Lily turned down at Babbo or 'Cesca, which were oval shaped and smooth. These ones were slightly unconventional: their shapes uneven and the surfaces a little craggy.

Also, unless she was mistaken—and there was that enchanting light shimmering about the room giving everything a slightly ethereal glow, so her eyes could have been playing tricks on her—there was a fine layer of dust over the cookies.

Maybe it wasn't a shop but a museum of some sort. Either way, this room was obviously not for rent, but that didn't mean there wasn't another one that was, and she hardly had any other options.

She stepped out of the puddle she had made on the floor. "Hello!" she called out. "Anyone here?"

Chapter 11

The widow Ercolani waited until Lily had left the tourist office and slowly dialed the widow Ciacci's number.

"She was booked into Prato," she duly reported, "so I've flushed her up to Adesso to get her closer to you, but I really can't see what all the fuss is about."

The widow Ercolani did not like Grace Kelly in *Rear Window*. She was more of a Sophia Loren fan.

"Never mind what all the fuss is about," the widow Ciacci said briskly. It was common knowledge that the widow Ercolani had her granddaughter Adriana earmarked for Alessandro, but a good man was wasted on that hussy. "What else can you tell us about her?"

"She's tall and American."

"American? Oh! And what else?"

"Hm?"

"I said what else? She's tall and American and . . . ?"

"And that's not enough? I thought we'd be giving her a miss in the circumstances. Besides, she was too thin for someone that height and not dressed for the weather or the climb." The widow Ercolani did not have to pretend to be crotchety. It came to her quite naturally.

"Well, it's Alessandro's heart we're mending, isn't it?" the widow Ciacci reminded her. "And it's not up to us how that gets done or who does it. It's up to Violetta."

The widow Ercolani harrumphed. Her crotchetiness extended as far as Violetta. And beyond.

"Well, it's not like we're getting the results we used to, these days," she sniffed. "The last three cases we've worked on have been nothing short of disastrous."

It was true. There had been a bad run. First they'd tried to fix the baker's son up with a woman who had a rare allergy to flour; then they'd tried to reunite the draper with her high school sweetheart, unaware of his newly formed gambling problem; and most recently they pushed the curvaceous mayor's secretary into the arms of a man who turned out to have a boyfriend in Cortona. These disasters had been a long time in the planning and execution and the dreadful results had hit the widows hard.

Times were tough and getting tougher, that much was obvious, but the widow Ciacci didn't want to get into that right now. She had a sore tooth and didn't feel like squeezing details out of the widow Ercolani like pips out of a lemon.

"The problem is that we're falling down on our intelligence gathering," she said rather pointedly. "Which, might I remind you, it is your job to help provide."

"That is not the problem," the widow Ercolani argued. "The problem is that Violetta's getting too old and crumbly to work her magic." The widow Ercolani was feeling pretty old and crumbly herself. Her ears rang, her hips ached, and she had spent her pension on chocolate so could not afford any painkillers.

"I'll look forward to hearing you discussing that directly with Violetta at the meeting later today, shall I?" the widow Ciacci suggested.

"I'm sorry. What was that?"

"Oh, never mind. I need to get on to the plumbing at the Hotel Adesso."

"Whatever you say," grumbled the widow Ercolani. "I've done my bit."

Up the hill, Violetta got such a fright when she heard Lily call from the *pasticceria* that she spat out a mouthful of coffee clear across the table, only missing her sister by the merest of smidgeons.

"She's here already," Luciana said, unfazed. "That was quick."

"That stupid doorbell!" spluttered Violetta.

Where had the time gone? It seemed like she'd only just issued her instructions and gone to the WC—an almost full-time occupation at her stage—and now this Lily woman was on the other side of the door calling out for them.

On top of not having an itchy nose or smelling orange blossom and being bulldozed by her usually placid younger sister into accepting the irritating and unsuitable Fiorella Fiorucci into the League, she felt wrong-footed, to say the least.

She took another sip of her coffee. She could barely taste it. Never mind a sixth sense, she was now back down to five, if not four. This, on top of everything, catapulted her into the filthiest of moods.

"What are you looking at me like that for?" she snapped at her sister. "I'm allowed to sit down for five minutes and enjoy my coffee without you mooning at me across the table like an old heifer, aren't I?"

"If I'm an old heifer, you're an even older one," pointed out Luciana. "And anyway, what's got your giblets in a pickle?"

"My giblets are not in a pickle," Violetta said. "I'm just devising the rest of the plan."

"I thought we already had the plan," Luciana said, her chair scraping against the floor as she slowly stood up. "You take Grace Kelly upstairs and pump her for information while Ciacci and I meet with Benedicti and the others to start devising our strategy for Alessandro, then we—"

"Yes, yes, I do know how it works, Luciana. I am the director of this league, you might recall."

"And this is you *not* in a pickle?" Luciana lifted her sagging eyelids to have a really good look at her sister. She was right, she was old. She'd been old for a long time and she looked especially old today. Luciana felt a tiny tremor of something down near her still-throbbing toe that had nothing to do with a broken heart other than, possibly, her own.

"Are you all right, Violetta?" she asked quietly.

This was met with what she thought was a snort, although it could have come from any part of her aged sibling. "I'm always all right," Violetta said as she stiffly rose from the table. "As usual, I'll do the talking. Now step to it."

Chapter 12

Lily heard muffled grumblings, the scraping of chairs, and the soft scuff of shuffling feet before the door in the rear corner of the bakeshop creaked open and out hobbled two almost identical old women, both dressed in black, both with thin gray hair scraped into wispy buns, both so wrinkled their faces looked like dried autumn leaves.

They stood hip to hip behind the counter, and after a moment or two of looking her up and down, one of them started a breathless monologue of which Lily understood not a syllable, while the other looked on, nodding shakily in agreement.

"I'm sorry, please—I'm not following, I don't speak Italian," Lily said, attempting to staunch the flow. "I'm here about the place to rent."

The chattering old woman just kept chattering and the nodding one nodding.

"The place to rent?" Lily said, louder. "Is it a room? An apartment?" She moved over to the window and tapped at the sign. *"Apartamento? Rento?"*

The nodding woman then said something to the chattering one. They both stopped and looked her up and down again, then the nodding one left the shop.

This took quite a long time. She moved very slowly.

"So about this room," Lily said when the nodding old lady had made her way out the door. "If there's anything you can tell me . . . It's just that I'm slightly desperate."

The remaining old woman clasped both hands beneath her chin and squinted so hard that her wrinkles surfed over each other to the edges of her face like ripples in a pond. Her small dark eyes gleamed beneath layers of drooping lid. Finally, she hobbled around the counter and over to Lily, grasping one of her hands. Her fingers were swollen and bent, but they were surprisingly soft and warm.

She stood about as tall as Lily's chest. Lily could see the hair thinning around her center part, could pick out the worn patches on the collar of her black cotton dress. She smelled of daphne. It was not what Lily had expected from the look of her. In Lily's experience, which was admittedly limited, people this old did not generally smell this good.

She felt a lump rise in her throat, an inexplicable surge of misplaced affection. She was tired, jet-lagged, out of her comfort zone.

"No speako Italiano," she told the old woman, feeling hopelessly unsophisticated. Years before, Daniel had suggested they take lessons, but she hadn't seen the point.

The old woman squeezed her hand tighter, then, with a robust tug, started to pull her around the tiny store, leaning on her slightly as she knocked at the glass bowls, tapped at the floor, pointed to the sign in the window, all the while continuing to chatter happily away in Italian.

Lily smiled and nodded because she was still dripping wet, bone-shatteringly tired, and didn't know what else to do. Taking this as a sign of acquiescence, the old woman let go of her hand and rather spryly grabbed at the handle of her suitcase. For someone so crippled, she managed to pull it remarkably swiftly behind the counter and through the door she and her sister had come out of.

Lily waited a moment until she realized the woman wasn't coming back, and followed. The back room had the same dim lighting and a similar intoxicating smell but was even warmer than the shop and was dominated by a large refectory-style table, used so often its top was no longer level but dipped and rose in a smooth landscape of curves and hollows. Two chairs sat at each end, and there was a single bed piled high with quilts pushed against the far wall. Behind the table was a kitchen of sorts with curtained shelves and a tiny television on top of a freestanding box on legs that Lily assumed was in lieu of a refrigerator.

"This is the apartment?" she asked. She needed to lie down and it was toasty warm and, despite its simplicity, strangely inviting. But the bed in the corner didn't even look long enough for her.

"I'm sorry, but you know, I don't think it's quite what I'm looking for," she told the old woman, who merely blew her a sort of raspberry and pointed to the ceiling. It was painted pale yellow, or nicotine color, and bore another unlikely chandelier.

"Yes, it's lovely, but still," Lily said and reached for her bag. But the little old lady clung to it, shaking her head, a steely glint in those small black eyes as she opened another door that Lily had assumed was a cupboard and disappeared into it.

"Oh, for Pete's sake," she grumbled but again followed. It wasn't a cupboard at all, but a narrow stairwell that led up to another room, infinitely bigger and brighter, with a double bed, a bigger chandelier, an enormous television, and that same strangely spicy sweet scent.

The bed looked so inviting that Lily wanted nothing more than to just lie down on the spongy covers and drift away into glorious nothingness.

The ceiling in this room had been painted, fresco style, between the weathered beams in a pale blue-and-yellow delicate floral pattern with curlicues of mauve and green at each end. It reminded Lily of something; she didn't quite know what, but it was something good.

The old Italian woman stood in the middle of the room mumbling incoherently, but as Lily looked around and weighed up the prospect of staying put, it occurred to her that it wasn't mumbling at all but a repetition of the same sequence of words.

"*Mi chiamo* Violetta," the old woman was saying. "*Mi chiamo Violetta.*" She tapped at the hollow chest where her bosoms had once been (they now sagged jauntily below, one significantly higher than the other). "Violetta," she said again. "*Capita?* Violetta. Violetta."

"Oh, of course!" Lily answered, as it seeped in that the woman was introducing herself. She acknowledged this by giving a silly little bow of her upper body that probably wasn't the custom in everyday Italy unless you were meeting the Pope. "Violetta," she repeated. "Pleased to meet you. I'm Lily. *Mi chiamo* Lily? Is that how you say it?"

Violetta raised the sparse hedges of her eyebrows. "Lee-lee," she tried the word out, shrugging her shoulders. "Lee-lee. OK." Then she hobbled to the faded floral curtains behind her, throwing them open to reveal a large picture window facing out to the valley that rolled down the hill from the town.

Lily took a step forward.

In the time she had been inside, the rain had stopped, and although the mist still clung to pockets of undulating land and wafted greedily around huddled clumps of trees, enough of the foreign landscape was emerging in front of her eyes to take her breath away.

"Oh my goodness!" she said moving closer, a throbbing blister, hunger, and her anxiety retreating.

The view was astonishing. Suddenly she definitely could see the long lunches and the youthful sexual athletics.

What's more, as she watched, the dreary mist continued to rise, revealing a rolling carpet of different vibrant greens stretching away from Montevedova toward the horizon. Trails of pencil pines meandered down distant ridges, neat stands of olives crisscrossed emerald fields, rows of grapes marched up and down gentle hillsides. Tiny orange-hued villas appeared before her eyes, tucked in between little explosions of foliage.

A pigeon—such ugly creatures at home—flapped gracefully over the terra-cotta tiled roof just below her, drawing her eye as it departed to another little hilltop town floating above a recalcitrant band of mist like a beheaded cardinal's hat in the distance.

"It's beautiful," she breathed. "Just beautiful."

"*Sì, molto bello*," Violetta agreed, without much emotion. "*Molto bello.*"

"*Molto bello*," Lily repeated, opening the window and leaning out. How could this astonishing vista, this extraordinary landscape, have been hiding behind all that rain and dreary mire as she drove here?

Down below her, to the left, something large and round was trying to emerge but kept being snatched away by a rogue cloud of fog. When it finally reappeared for good, it brought its whole coppered dome and bell tower with it, revealing itself to be Madonna di San Biagio—the church in the photo in Daniel's shoe.

With that, the mist seemed to disappear altogether and Lily saw everything very clearly. She was in this place for a reason and it did not leave room for awe.

Stony-faced, she turned away and let Violetta show her the tiny bathroom, with its minute shower stall, a child-size lavatory, and not so much as a single cabinet for storage.

The room wasn't what Lily would have chosen, but it was spotlessly clean and dry and she was wet and exhausted.

"You know what? I think I'll take it," she told Violetta. "For a few nights at least. Is that OK?"

"*Sí, sí*, OK, OK," the old woman said, patting the cover on the bed.

Lily's body ached to lie down on it. If she could just catch a few hours sleep, a few minutes even, she would be able to think more clearly.

She took 500 euro out of her wallet and was surprised when Violetta grabbed it all but was too worn out to attempt further conversation. Instead, she held a finger to her lips in what she hoped was the international language of "let's keep this whole thing our little secret" and waited until the old woman reciprocated, which she did, following this up with another long string of something undecipherable and a dismissive wave good-bye.

As soon as she was gone, Lily slipped off her kitten heels, peeled off her sodden clothes, lay back on the bed, and almost immediately drifted off into blissful oblivion.

Chapter 13

The widows were not a happy bunch when Violetta hobbled down to meet them in the basement.

"You are wrong," one group was shouting at another.

"No, you are wrong," the other group was shouting back.

"You're both wrong," a third splinter was joining in the fray.

Thinking they were arguing about Lily and Alessandro, Violetta bit her lip and scuttled over to her sister, who was standing beneath the ginger supper knocking back a glass of *vin santo*.

"What's going on?" Violetta whispered.

"Fiorella brought a *torta della nonna*," explained Luciana, pointing to the table where there was nothing but a few crumbs left on a crumpled paper plate.

"She did what?"

"She brought a *torta della nonna* and it was extremely delicious, but it's started something of a debate," Luciana said.

"You use whole eggs in the pastry," an angry voice cried.

"No, you just use the yolks!"

"You use orange zest."

"No, vanilla."

"No, a tablespoon of olive oil."

"It's not the pastry that makes a good *torta della nonna* anyway, it's the filling!"

"Ricotta," went up one chorus.

"*No* ricotta," went up another.

Violetta walked into the middle of this heated battle and silenced the lot of them with just one look, which ended on Fiorella sitting happily on a chair with pastry crumbs cascading down her cleavage.

"We do not have *torta della nonna* at meetings of the Secret League of Widowed Darners," Violetta said coldly. "We have *cantucci*."

"Oh, really," Fiorella scoffed. "Says who?"

"Says me," Violetta answered.

The widow Mazzetti held the rule book up and shook it, although it had nearly killed her not to have a slice or two of such a good-looking *torta*.

"Says the rules," Violetta confirmed.

Fiorella was not a woman used to female company, or company of any kind for that matter, and was getting the distinct impression that she wasn't very good at it. "Right. Fine. Whatever you say." She shrugged. "It's only *dolci*. I just thought some of us could do with a bit of sweetening up."

"Never mind that, are we really going to help out that stuck-up American ice princess?" the widow Ercolani asked, cutting to the chase. She was suffering from indigestion so hadn't had any *torta*, although perhaps she could have done with some sweetening. "We're asking for trouble involving an 'outsider,' if you ask me," she added. "And who's to say she won't whisk Alessandro away once we've done our bit."

The widow Benedicti hadn't thought of this and turned, panicked, to Violetta for assurance.

The League was officially a democracy, so decisions were meant to be made based on a majority rule, but really, Violetta was the leader and always had been; it was a divine situation, a bit like the Dalai Lama, only in black.

And the truth was that Violetta had always felt she possessed a sixth sense when it came to matters of the heart, and was helped in this regard by Luciana, who possessed five-and-a-half.

Usually, she knew exactly what to do and who to do it to, but today no bells were ringing, no signs were flashing, her mind was as clear as minestrone. Was Alessandro really their *calzino rotto*? And could Lily truly be the woman to soothe his broken heart?

Where before she felt nothing but certainty, today she felt like the *cornetto* she'd had for breakfast was lodged in her chest and would never move. That was all.

"What about Roberto, the bus driver, from Cremona," Luciana suggested, stepping helpfully into the breach. "Remember we set him up with Angelica from the language school? Bit of a bumpy start as I recall but they've got children now, and grandchildren."

"Cremona isn't a foreign country," the widow Ercolani pointed out.

"Put your hand up if you have ever been to Cremona," Violetta commanded, retrieving her wits and seizing the opportunity.

Not a single hand rose.

"And put your hand up if you have ever been to America."

Again, not a single hand rose.

"Therefore I think we can safely say that America is no more foreign than Cremona."

This seemed to satisfy the group at large but Fiorella felt moved to voice her own skepticism. "So, let me get this straight, this blonde *turista* is seen talking to old droopy drawers out in the valley and on those grounds you decide this is the love match?"

"This blonde *turista* is seen talking to old droopy drawers on one of Violetta's special days," the widow Benedicti stressed. "That's the key. And by the way, he does not have droopy drawers." That Alessandro fitted his drawers quite well had already been discussed on a number of occasions.

"Right. Good system," drawled Fiorella, rolling her eyes, something she did with practiced skill.

On any other occasion Violetta might have shut her up with a vicious stare or got the widow Mazzetti to refer again to the rule book for statutes regarding ethnicity, but the events of the day had unsettled her too badly and still there was that sharp pain in her chest, poking at her from the inside like an evil finger.

In the past she had found that a sticky issue could sometimes be resolved by pulling a bit of darning-related wisdom out of her pocket, and given the circumstances, she decided to try this again.

"Might I remind you," she told the assembled widows, "that our job is not to judge the sock by its color or even the quality of its wool, but to simply fix the hole, be it in the toe or the heel."

Her pronouncement was met with silence at first, then a couple of heads nodded, and a couple more, and eventually the whole room was full of nodding heads.

And just one pair of rolling eyes.

Chapter 14

The early morning light threw a friendly shaft across Lily's face and for a few sleepy moments she thought she was at home in the Seventy-second Street apartment.

She opened her eyes, stretched out her arms, and took a few bleary beats to remember she was not lying next to Daniel on the Hästens mattress she'd bought herself, even though it cost the same as a car, for her fortieth birthday. Daniel was missing, the sheets were a shade of apricot she would never let into her building, let alone her home, and the electricity in her arm hair told her they were also polyester.

She rolled onto her side, looking at the vast expanse of empty bed beside her.

She rolled onto her back again. Blew out a sigh. Let the despair of her miserable situation fully descend.

Once it had settled near rock bottom, she realized she'd been there before. Mornings, if she was honest with herself, had been miserable for a long time.

This was why at home she organized herself a jam-packed schedule, which started the moment her eyes flew open and which she faced, undaunted, with determined enthusiasm. She liked it that way. She organized it that way. The devil finds work for idle hands, the nuns had always said, and Lily found it to also be true of the mind. The devil finds work for an idle mind.

She sat up in her synthetic bed, the static electricity snatching at her silk pajamas. She needed to get out and work up a sweat, but as she stood to seek out her running shoes she caught a glimpse of the view waiting quietly out the picture-postcard window.

Tuscany, a place she had never been the slightest bit anxious to see despite the many opportunities, a place she'd not even thought to imagine and which on first impression had sadly underwhelmed her. Yet here it was and here she was and again it took her breath away.

She moved closer to the window and gazed out at the rolling patchwork sea of greens; so many different shades and each one deeper or brighter or more dazzling than the one right next to it. She realized that if she had imagined Tuscany, she would have seen it as burnt orange and golden; vibrant colors but harsh and arid compared to the moist and thriving sprawl of grasses, grapes, olives, forests, and fields that stretched below her.

It was so beautiful it was impossible to concentrate on what had brought her there.

Instead, she leaned against the window frame and watched daylight crawl across the landscape, the offensive shade of apricot on the electric sheets and her wretched heart forgotten as she just let the world's natural shades unfurl in front of her.

She kept thinking she should go, do something, get on with it—whatever it was—but watching the sun creep higher in the sky, spreading its fingers slowly across the rolling hills and valleys, was completely mesmerizing.

It wasn't till she heard the sound of something being dropped with a clatter below her that she registered how ravenous she was. She couldn't think what time it would be in New York or how many meals she must have missed. She'd had nothing since the flight the day before. She was starving.

She crossed the room and looked out the other window up

and down the Corso. The Hotel Adesso looked remarkably unscathed by its plumbing disaster of the day before; it looked to be sleeping, just like the rest of the street, shuttered and silent. The sun was yet to wake the town with its golden touch the way it had woken Lily and the valley.

She wondered if Daniel was asleep somewhere nearby, his face relaxed, his blond hair sticking up on one side like it did before he washed it in the morning, the dark dangerous woman tossing restlessly beside him.

Another pang knocked at her insides, and it wasn't hunger. It was Daniel. She turned away from the beautiful view.

She should be angry, she thought as she washed her hair in the tiny shower. She should not be marveling at the ridiculous view or calmly wondering about her cheating husband's hair, she should be enraged. But she wasn't. She knew rage only too well, thanks to her mother. Rage involved spankings and slaps; shouting and screaming; sharp objects thrown at small heads; terrifying threats; foul language; utter, uncontrollable, high-decibel fury.

Lily felt something, and it was big—she was there in Montevedova after all—but it wasn't loud and explosive in her mother's vein. It was more complicated than that, like the sort of itch that could drive a person mad, or an ache so deep its source was unfathomable.

She searched her face in the mirror for any outward signs of crisis but found no fury there either, a little tightness around the eyes, perhaps, a slightly haunted expression.

Once upon a time she'd seen herself as maybe not beautiful—who admitted to that—but as agreeable. She still conceded to the positive overall package: the blonde hair, the good cheekbones, the clear skin for someone of her vintage, the slender body that she worked so hard to maintain.

She stopped drying herself and looked at that body: the gap between the top of her firm thighs, her sharp hips, her ribs, her small but manageably pert breasts, her collarbone, square shoulders.

It was slender, her body. She had made it slender. She kept it slender. The size of her body Lily could control and did, with a dedication matched only by professional athletes and actresses.

This had become more and more important to her as time went by because with every babyless year that passed, Lily was reminded that this wretched collection of flesh and bone had a mind of its own when it came to the thing she, the heart and soul of Lily, most wanted.

No specialist could tell her exactly why she could not carry a baby to full term.

She'd been to all the conventional experts, obviously, even a psychiatrist in case there was some secret emotional issue sabotaging her plans for motherhood, but no, in the circumstances, she'd passed that test with flying colors. She'd been to naturopaths, homeopaths, acupuncturists, herbal gurus, reflexologists, reiki practitioners, iridologists; she'd even had her hair tested—by a strange-smelling man with a beard down to his navel—to see if it perhaps held some hideous secret. It didn't.

She'd done everything she possibly could to prepare her body for the treasured role of motherhood. She gave up alcohol, coffee, soda, seafood, and cheese. She upped her fatty acids, her omega-3s, her dietary fiber, and took folic acid, selenium, and zinc supplements. But her body had let her down, so now, to pay it back, she punished it by keeping it at a size two. All that dedication and she'd ended up a clothes hanger.

Still, she had good clothes, she had to admit, as she pulled on white Capri pants and a soft pink boatneck top, then made her way downstairs, contemplating the foolishness of renting an apartment that required her to walk through someone else's to get outside. There would no doubt be many an awkward encounter with Violetta and her funny little doppelganger.

Indeed, she heard the two sisters chirruping to each other as she came down the stairs, although they hushed up upon seeing her in the kitchen—but only briefly.

"*Mia sorella*, Luciana," Violetta said, thrusting her sister out toward their guest. "Luciana. Luciana. Luciana."

"Luciana? Oh, good morning," Lily said. "And good morning to you, Violetta."

The refectory table and much of the kitchen floor was covered in flour. In fact, if Lily hadn't known what a beautiful day it was outside she might have thought it had been snowing. Inside. Violetta had so much flour on her face she looked like a wizened old geisha and Luciana's black smock was now almost completely white.

At first, Lily tried to sidestep them both and scoot out of their way, but it soon became obvious that they had other plans. Before she knew what was happening, she had been herded to one end of the floury refectory table and pushed into a chair while one old woman thrust some sort of a croissant into one hand and the other old woman forced a strong cup of coffee into the other.

"Actually, I thought I would go out for breakfast," Lily said, starting to get up, but Violetta—or was it Luciana, she had trouble telling one from the other—forced her back down into her seat.

"I couldn't," Lily protested, looking at the croissant, pushing it away. "Honestly, pastry doesn't . . . I don't . . . I thought they were French . . . I'm more of a . . ."

The two sisters stared at her, blinking uncomprehendingly. They were really quite intimidating for little old ladies.

"Well, just a little bite perhaps," Lily said, to be polite, and took a nibble. It tasted pretty good, actually, although she could feel the buttery fat settle on the roof of her mouth. It was not a feeling she was used to. She gulped the coffee and, by way of diverting attention from the pastry, pointed out the old ladies' side window that looked out on to a bland building opposite.

"A lovely day, I see," she said, nonetheless. "I thought I would try a little sightseeing or a walk in the countryside."

One of the sisters then shuffled over to the curtained shelves and emerged with a large enamel container of flour, while the other reached in for a similar container of sugar.

To Lily's great surprise, Violetta (she thought) emptied most of the flour on to the table in front of her with a clumsy flourish. It billowed up like an atom-bomb cloud, explaining the snowy sensation in the room.

"Oh, I'm sorry," Lily said, pushing her chair back, assuming it was a mistake.

But Luciana then moved in and proceeded to dump a pile of sugar on top of the flour.

The two old women looked at her and made twin twiddling gestures in front of their faces. Their hands were like the knotted branch ends of twisted old trees.

With matching smiles, they plunged those gnarled digits into the pile of flour and sugar on the table and started to mix it.

It flew everywhere, up in the air, on to the floor, all over them. The dry ingredients danced like a well-stoked fire.

"You know, I'm pretty sure there has been an amazing invention that might help you with this," Lily said. "It's called a bowl. Maybe I could get you one?"

The sisters chirruped between each other again, then one of them pushed the half-eaten pastry closer to Lily. She picked it up and took another nibble.

They watched her curiously for a moment, then Violetta

shuffled to the refrigerator and came back with a dozen eggs, some of which she proceeded to break into the mixture right there on the table while Luciana, with her arthritic fingers, attempted to mix this now-much-wetter combination.

"And spoons," Lily said, unable to drag her eyes away from the strange sight. "You should try using mixing spoons. I'm sure it would make all the difference."

Luciana winced and stood back from the table. Violetta moved in and took over.

"I should help you, I can see that," Lily said, "but it's just that I'm not really a kitchen person."

Luciana then brought a small saucepan of melted butter to the table and poured it onto the mixture, which had turned into a lumpy yellow dough. Violetta stepped away and straightened her back as much as she could, which wasn't much, and Luciana took over.

It was clear to Lily now why their cookies were crooked. These little old ladies were past their use-by date when it came to making them and it was painful to watch them try. But it was also slightly wonderful: like modern ballet. They were doing it anyway, no matter how pleasing the results.

And the smell, now that the warm butter had hit the sugar, was making her dizzy. It was just so . . . well, she didn't know what it was but it brought an unexpected lump to her throat.

"There are also machines for this these days, you know," she said, a catch in her voice. "There are mixers and food processors and wands and all sorts of things."

Violetta and Luciana kept swapping places, lifting buttery, floury, curled, clawlike hands in the air as they stepped back and forth, perfectly in tune with each other.

Lily felt an inexplicable tear roll down her cheek as one of them hobbled away to get a bowl of hazelnuts, which were then worked clumsily into the dough before Violetta clawed it into two large chunks. Luciana halved the chunks again and rolled them into four uneven logs on a baking pan, which Violetta put in the oven.

"I keep cashmere sweaters in my oven," Lily told the sisters, wiping her eyes as they dumped more flour and sugar on the messy table and started all over again. How on earth did those misshapen logs ever turn into biscotti?

"Although I have a sister too—Rose," she continued. "And she cooked a Thanksgiving turkey in it once. In my oven, that is."

Out came the eggs, *splat*, into the mixture.

"It was after the second miscarriage, I think," Lily continued. "I didn't think I had a thing in the world to give thanks for, but Rose would not be put off coming. She just arrived with her baby and a bottle of champagne. And Al, of course, carrying a hamper heaving with a huge turkey, his mother's secret stuffing recipe and pecan pie, which, by the way, I can't bear."

Violetta added more melted butter to the second *cantucci* mixture.

Lily could remember emptying more than one bottle of champagne that Thanksgiving.

Actually, she thought it might have been after the third miscarriage. And she'd thought there was nothing to give thanks for then! Little had she known that five precious incomplete angels in all would be snatched away from her before she ever got to know them.

"And then there was Grace," she said, so dreamily it was almost a whisper. "Baby Grace."

Also snatched away, but not before Lily got to know her.

"She, I actually got to hold in my arms for six whole days. I swear, I must have kissed that little head a thousand times." If she closed her eyes she could still feel the silky touch of Grace's downy golden hair on her lips, her cheek: a sensation like no other.

"Sometimes I catch a whiff of talcum powder on someone else's baby and it's like I'm back in Tennessee with her in my arms and everything I ever wanted in the whole wide world nestled right there in one tiny bundle."

Then, poof, just as quickly, that would be gone and she'd be swallowed up again by what she didn't have.

"Grace," Lily repeated softly. "It's so long since I've said it out loud."

At that, a plume of smoke erupted rudely out of the ancient oven and the elderly sisters both flew at it with flapping aprons, great clouds of flour mushrooming in front of them. Lily shook herself as if waking from a trance and the image of all those little pink all-in-ones that would never be worn flew off into the corners of the smoky room. She could not imagine why she had been burbling on like that. Just as well the old women couldn't understand a word of it.

"Unless you need me to call the fire brigade," she said, "I think I'll be on my way." And while Luciana and Violetta were sidetracked trying to rescue their burning cookie logs, she slipped out of the room.

Chapter 15

"What was she saying?" Luciana asked, waving smoke away from her face after Lily left the room.

"There's trouble with *bambino*," Violetta told her. "Not having them, that is. I don't know what happened but it's not ideal."

"So, she's been married before. Big deal. So has Alessandro. Better that way I always think. And speaking of thinking, it didn't occur to you to mention to Lily that you are perfectly fluent in her own language?"

"Perfectly fluent? I don't think so." Violetta had learned to speak a number of foreign languages in the early forties, but as no one expected her to, she often didn't let on that she could, and the sisters gathered some of their best information this way.

But in this instance, Luciana was possibly right. Violetta should have told Lily she understood what she was saying, but there hadn't been the opportunity to stop her. Or if there was, Violetta had missed it. Just another awkward misstep to put her off her stride! And Lily spilling her beans had made her even more confused than she already was.

"Something is not right here," she said, poking one of the burnt cookie trumpets with a finger. "Something is seriously not right."

Luciana gave a little cough.

"Something has seriously not been right for a while," she agreed, poking at a second one. "And I'm glad you brought it up because I know you find it difficult, but we most certainly can't keep up this pretence. We can't ignore it any longer, Violetta. Fiorella is right about our teeth."

There was an awkward silence.

"Fiorella? Teeth? What on earth are you talking about?" Violetta asked.

"I'm talking about the *cantucci*," Luciana said. "Violetta, I think it's time. We can't keep pretending we're managing it."

"Ferrettis have been making *cantucci* in Montevedova since 1898," Violetta insisted, shaking her head. "It's the best in Tuscany, everybody says so. Even the Pope. Three popes."

"Yes, everybody says it's the best but everybody buys the Borsolinis'. We need money, Violetta. We need to go to the doctor. You're getting grayer in the face with every passing day, my hips are killing me, and everyone we know needs dentures."

"There's nothing wrong with me," Violetta said, that tightness in her chest turning something inexplicable inside her again. "And I'm not talking about the *cantucci*. I don't want to talk about that. I'm talking about the match, our *calzino*. There's something not right with this match. Alessandro is too much of a lost soul to end up with another lost soul and I think that's what this woman, this Lily, is. It's a worry to me."

"Never mind that."

"How can you say that, Luciana? We must mind it! The world needs love and lovers now more than it ever has. We're trying to do Santa Ana di Chisa's work with dwindling resources and—"

"Violetta, you need to think of yourself, and of me. I'm talking about us. We need pills for our arthritis. My hands hurt all the time. We have no money."

"We have five hundred euros for the room."

"I know the League is your vocation but the *cantucci* provides us with a living, and we have to face the fact that it's getting too hard for us to turn it out. All we have left is our reputation and if we're not careful we're going to lose that too."

At that moment, the widow Ciacci put her head in the side window—something she could only do by standing on her own kitchen chair out in the alleyway that led off the Corso.

"I think it's time you got a smoke alarm," she said, coughing. "Or an apprentice. Really, you'll burn to a crisp and then where will we be?"

"In the safe hands of Fiorella Fiorucci no doubt," Violetta said. "I'm surprised she isn't in here taking over our kitchen already. Too aggressive by far, if you ask me."

"Oh, but did you taste her *torta della nonna*?" the widow Ciacci enthused. "She mixes ricotta with the custard, I believe. And perhaps there's a bit of booze in there somewhere as well. And she can still bend enough to play *baci*! There's no one else left in the League who can do that."

This was the last thing Violetta wanted to hear. "The reason for this unscheduled stopover?" she inquired.

"Two things: one, the widow Benedicti has faxed through Alessandro's schedule for the week so we can orchestrate some connections and the other, there's a kid in your *pasticceria* talking to Grace Kelly. It's that strange little girl from the other side of the piazza who's always getting in fights and breaking things."

Chapter 16

After her escape from the kitchen, Lily took a moment in the bakeshop to collect herself, leaning on the marble counter and considering the contents of the closest *cantucci* bowl.

Those poor old women. What were they thinking? That the two of them had ever produced enough cookies to operate a business was astounding. That they were still trying to do so was something else.

She picked a piece of *cantucci* out of the bowl, blew off the dust and held it up to the golden light filtering through from the Corso. The cookie was still hard, no matter what its age, and would look tantalizing enough, she thought, to a person of a sweet-toothed persuasion. The hazelnuts seemed robust and there was even a slight gloss to them. She sniffed the cookie and was surprised by a fresh scent, a bit like the seashore but with a lingering spiciness. She turned it again in the light. For a confection that was well past its best, it was holding up remarkably well.

Outside, the sleepy morning quiet was rudely interrupted by a disturbance that grew louder as its vortex neared the store. Through the dirty window Lily saw a blur of bright colors whiz by, a whirling collection of arms, legs, shrieks, and mirth. The door flew open, the bell clanged, the cacophony filled the tiny room, the door closed, the shrill young voices dissolved, and through the backlit dust that spun in a frenzy before falling like a glittering gold show curtain to the floor, emerged a small dark angel.

The dust settled. The *cantucci* fell from Lily's fingers back into the bowl with a solid *clack*.

The small dark angel was the little girl from the photo in Daniel's golf shoe.

She was a year or two older, perhaps, and wearing a set of costume party wings on her back, but otherwise she looked exactly the same.

Lily had known the moment she saw the photo that the children were Daniel's, but to see this child in the flesh? She even had his legs, long and slim but splaying out slightly from the hips. Her chin was his, her open face. Daniel had been a good-looking kid and this girl, his *daughter*, had inherited his looks, although she was dark where he was fair. Her eyes were green though, just like Daniel's, exactly like them. She wasn't cute, not in the childish adorable sense, but she was truly arresting in a way that would last forever, unlike cute, which came and went.

The wings were made of pale yellow gauze fitted around wire frames and strapped to her shoulders like a backpack. She was puffing as if she had been running.

She did not turn back to see if the cyclone of arms and legs was coming into the store with her. She stood her ground, looking at Lily.

"Who are you?" she asked, in very good English. Her beautiful face was alive and inquisitive. She had confidence in herself. Confidence and beauty: the perfect combination.

Oh, I want one, Lily's biological clock chimed ineptly. I want one, I want one, I want one.

She opened her mouth to speak, but her longing choked her as it occurred that the child might be aware of her, might know that her father had a wife called Lily—some ugly evil creature ruining his life on the other side of the world.

Something not unlike the flickering embers of someone else's anger licked at her then. Would the Daniel she knew and loved paint her this way? Was it possible he actually saw her like that?

"I'm Lillian Watson," she said, pulling the name she was born with out of her pocket like a crumpled sunhat, surprised that her voice sounded so solid when the rest of her felt like it could disappear into a whorl of golden dust. "And who might you be?"

"I'm Francesca," the girl answered with a heartbreaking smile, sidling sideways up to the counter. "What's wrong with you?"

Lily was taken aback. She brushed at her cheeks to make sure no tears had escaped, pushed back her hair, forced a smile.

"What's wrong with me? Well, nothing that I can think of. Why do you ask?"

"Usually when people come to stay with the Ferretti sisters they have something wrong with them." Francesca said. "But they don't usually work in the store. Or help with the *cantucci*. Are you going to help with the *cantucci*? I think it would be good if you did."

"Oh, well, I'm not really staying here," Lily said. "Not for long anyway and I'm certainly not likely to be helping with the *cantucci*. That's this biscotti, right?"

"Biscotti is all cookies, *cantucci* is what we make here in Tuscany and the Ferrettis make the best."

"But does anyone buy it?"

Francesca shrugged. "I don't think they're allowed. The Ferrettis don't usually let people in the store. They are too mean. Except if there's something wrong with you. I only came in because I saw it was you."

"Me?" A flush of panic.

"You, not them. They can be scary and they have hands like, like, *allora*, like Captain Hook." She lifted up fingers just like Daniel's, long with knobby knuckles, and curled them into claws. "You know, in *Peter Pan*."

Oh, how that further flamed Lily's bravely burning embers. Of course Daniel had read his daughter *Peter Pan*. It had been his favorite book as a child, hers too. They'd bought countless copies for the children of friends and more for their own imaginary children.

Francesca wasn't an angel at all.

"You're Tinker Bell," Lily said.

Francesca looked pleased. "They're not real wings," she said. "I can't fly."

"I love that book," Lily told her. "I used to read it to my sister when I was about your age and we'd listen to it as well, I guess on the record player. You couldn't turn the page of the book until Tinker Bell rang her little bell."

Lily wondered where those books were, the one she had bought for her own children, if they'd been relegated to the charity store like so much of the other baby paraphernalia she had collected over the years or if they were stashed somewhere in the apartment. Or maybe Daniel had brought them here. Would he do that?

Francesca came right up to the counter, her nose at fluted *cantucci* bowl level. She peered in to the bowl then up at Lily.

"I don't know what is a record player. Have you seen it at the movies?" she asked. "*Peter Pan*?"

Those eyes. Daniel's eyes.

"I don't think it was on at the movies when I was little."

"What about now?" Francesca asked.

"Now I'm grown up, I don't really go to the movies," she said. Francesca looked disappointed.

Please don't ask me if I have children, Lily begged. She couldn't bear that question from anyone, let alone . . .

"But you are American?" Francesca asked.

"Yes, I am," Lily answered then, keen to move on: "What about you? Are you from here? From Montevedova?"

"Yes, but I'm going to America one day," Francesca said, swiveling her slender little hips. "And I'm going on my own. I'm going to go to the movies and do hip-hop, and I'm not taking Ernesto with me."

"Ernesto?" Lily asked. She couldn't help herself.

"My little brother," Francesca said with a sigh. "He is a pain in my ass."

"You speak wonderful English for a little girl, Francesca," Lily told her, "but I'm not sure *ass* is a word you should be using."

"My papa makes me have lessons and I am nearly seven," Francesca informed her. "So that's not little. Ernesto is little."

Nearly seven. Lily turned away and fumbled for an imaginary something in her purse. She did not want Francesca to see her face. Nearly *seven*. That made her just a year younger than Grace. Grace would be nearly eight now.

That year after they lost her, that year when her world collapsed yet again, leaving her in pieces she could never put back together, all she'd had to cling to was work. Work and Daniel. Because one stopped her from thinking and the other knew what she thought. And yet, in that year, that same horrendous, hideous year, Daniel had not been thinking what she was thinking at all, not suffering what she was suffering. He had been coming here and creating himself this perfect parallel universe.

Everything she ever wanted, but without her.

The flames of her missing anger lunged up inside her, licking at her, burning her. They required immediate dousing.

"I'm sorry, sweetie," she said to Francesca. "I have to get going now. Do you have somewhere to be? School, maybe?"

"It's summer," Francesca said, her pretty smile gone. "There is no school."

She reluctantly followed Lily to the door and waited until Lily waved her through it, but as she passed in front that blur of color—a group of girls about the same age as she, it turned out— came clattering back up the lane.

As soon as she saw them, Francesca stepped back into the shop, pressing herself, her fairy wings, hard into Lily's empty body.

Lily saw the look that rippled through the gang of girls, felt Francesca shrink away from them. One girl snickered, and the others followed suit—that same shrill fracas—then they broke into a run and scattered, calling out what, Lily did not know, but Francesca stayed pressed into her.

The wings, up close, had a series of little holes in them, as if the fairy wearing them had long ago been gunned down. Her dress, Lily realized, was not as clean as it could have been. A thin crescent of dirt fringed each fingernail. Her hair had not recently been brushed. Who was looking after her?

When the slap of the girls' sandals had completely faded, Francesca relaxed and stepped out into the street as if nothing had happened.

She turned around and in the split second that Lily saw her pull her expression together, Lily realized she had been too quick to identify confidence in the child.

She showed it all right, but it wasn't quite the natural resource Lily had originally assumed. In front of those other girls, it had crumbled. How she wanted to hold that brave little body, to kiss her face, soothe her, tell her that everything would be all right, that she was worth more than a hundred of those girls, a thousand, a million.

"Will you be all right?" Lily asked, as casually as she could.

"Will you be here tomorrow?" Francesca asked, swiveling again.

"I'm not sure," Lily said. "But if I am I hope I see you again."

"OK," Francesca said.

"It was a pleasure to meet you, Tinker Bell," Lily said. "A real pleasure." And before she could disgrace herself and embarrass the child by releasing what felt like a lifetime of unshed tears, she turned and headed down the hill.

"*Ciao, ciao,*" Francesca called after her. "*A domani.*"

Until tomorrow.

Chapter 17

Daniel woke up on the tiny couch in his cramped hotel room, fully clothed and with an appalling hangover.

His neck hurt, his head hurt, his back hurt and the cloying scent of expensive perfume in the air led him to believe the blonde woman he'd met at the café was not far away.

He could not remember her name or how she came to be in his hotel room.

Daniel was not in the habit of picking up women and bringing them home. He, of all people, knew the peril in that, and he couldn't believe he would do something so loathsome now, when he was already in such a mess.

Bones creaking, he got to his feet and snuck a look at the woman, lying on her back in his bed, the sheet wrapped loosely around her, one arm curled around her head. She was sound asleep, also mostly clothed, and he saw that she was older than he'd originally thought, older than him. She'd not taken care of her body as well as Lily had; she'd spent too much time in the sun, perhaps, her neck showing the telltale signs nothing but a turtleneck could ever cover up. But she looked happy, even when she was sleeping.

He turned away from her and slipped out onto the little balcony, pulling the door shut behind him and lighting a cigarette as he watched a drugged-up zombie couple stagger down the cobbled road below. They zigzagged unnecessarily around the straight line of parked motor scooters that framed the curb and finally collapsed on the steps of the church opposite the hotel, like two deflating balloons.

Daniel blew a lazy smoke ring into the early morning air and thought about another body back in Montevedova; a perfect body really, if you liked that sort of thing, which he obviously did, if fleetingly. Now, in hindsight, he thought what he had mostly liked about that body was the ease in which the woman who inhabited it did so. She liked it herself and not in an obsessive way, but in a way that was just good to be around. She ate pasta and bread and pizza like it was going out of fashion and gorged herself on cheeses and salamis and all the things Lily didn't go near because they had added preservatives or hormones or were really dolphins or some other B.S. the green police had brainwashed her into. He suspected for Lily that it was mainly about not getting fat. Italian women didn't seem to care about getting fat. They thought curves made them sexier, and they were right, although it was the not-caring-what-anyone-else-thought that Daniel had originally found so sexy.

He stubbed out his cigarette. How could he have been so stupid? No, worse than that, so *ordinary*? That set of sexy curves and devil-may-care attitude had gotten his attention, sure, when he was at his lowest ebb. But to get so much more? It was such a cliché it made him sick. He was such a cliché it made him sick.

"Hey, Danny?" he heard the blonde woman call huskily from inside. Ingrid, her name, came tumbling back into his consciousness along with the embarrassing memory of telling her too much. They had done nothing but talk, and it had been him doing most the talking. And most the drinking. God, he was such a sap. A self-obsessed, boring, stupid sap. He tried to remember Ingrid's story, what she had told him.

She was married, he thought, to someone who was at a convention in Rome—or was it Milan?—and she'd always wanted to see Florence so had come here alone while her husband was convening.

"Oh, there you are." She smiled when she found him on the balcony.

She was wearing a fluffy white hotel bathrobe and she'd fixed her hair. He had no idea how she was going to be this morning, how he was going to be. He dreaded whatever was about to happen, felt the tension knot harder in his aching back and shoulders.

"Shall I call room service?" she said, and it was such an uncomplicated suggestion he nearly wept. "I don't know about you, but I'm desperate for coffee."

He started to shake his head but actually, when he thought about it, he was hungry. And he wasn't sure if he felt like being with Ingrid, but he also wasn't sure if he felt like being alone. He started to say that perhaps eggs were in order, and maybe a bloody Mary, but when he opened his mouth, something else entirely came tumbling out.

He was out of his depth, not just here in this hotel room but everywhere. In his life. He was drowning in his life and he had no one to blame but himself, and no hope of being rescued.

What he wanted to tell this woman, this Ingrid with the easy charm and the warm smile, was that breakfast was a great idea, but what he did instead was start to weep, desperately and uncontrollably, like a child. Like a baby.

Ingrid was not altogether taken aback. She had a good instinct for people and thought he wasn't a bad one. She was worried about him. And the weeping didn't bother her that much either; she was used to seeing grown men cry. She had three sons, now all in their twenties and all tending toward the "sensitive" side of the spectrum.

She reached for Daniel, led him back inside the room, sat him on the couch, wrapped her arms around him, and pretended he was one of them. It was what she would want someone to do for any of her boys if they were this unhappy.

Chapter 18

"What's going on in there?" Luciana asked as she stood behind Violetta, whose ear was currently pressed against the door into the *pasticceria*. "Can you hear what Lily is saying to the little girl?"

"No, I can't. Not with you booming like a foghorn behind me," complained Violetta. "These ears are nearly a hundred years old. They're tired, give them a break."

"Well, you could afford one of those thingamajigs that pick up even the smallest sound if you would just consider what I was saying about the *cantucci*."

"Pick up even the smallest sound?" Violetta spun around, furious. "Why would I want to do that? I barely want to hear the biggest sounds, especially when most of them involve you heckling me about our family business or that young whippersnapper Fiorella Fiorucci challenging my authority and asking lame-brained questions!"

"She's hardly a whippersnapper, Violetta: She's eighty-five. And she was only suggesting—"

"I'll tell you what Fiorella Fiorucci can do with her suggestions!" Violetta exploded. "She can put them where the monkey put the peanuts! She is trouble, that woman—short, fat, and practically-legally-blind-by-the-look-of-those-glasses trouble. We need to get rid of her, and soon. She's feeding conspiracies to the widow Ercolani like peppermints. She has the widow Mazzetti checking the rule book every five minutes on one trumped up charge or another. She is not one of us, Luciana. She is not!"

Luciana picked nonchalantly at the hem of her dress. "I think she is just what the doctor ordered," she said. "And she's fun."

"What the doctor ordered? *Fun*? Pah! What in the name of Santa Ana di Chisa has got into you?" She nudged her sister in the shoulder with her curled hand. "I can usually rely on you to back me up, but ever since that mouthy young trout showed up, you seem to have hitched your wagon to her caboose."

Luciana nudged her right back. "She only turned up yesterday and my wagon is hitched to your caboose, Violetta," she said. "It will be forever, but if I can stop your caboose from going off the rails and plunging down a deep ravine, taking me with it, I will."

The pain in Violetta's chest tightened its grip.

"Why are you doing this?" she asked her sister.

"Doing what?"

"Turning against me!"

"I am not turning against you, Violetta. I am trying to help you. Same as always."

"Same as always means you agree with me."

"Same as always means I say that I agree with you. It doesn't mean I actually do."

"You don't?"

"Not always."

"Then why say that you do?"

"Because I believe in you . . . that's what sisters do. And because it usually doesn't matter. But this is different. This time, you need to hear the truth."

"And what would the truth be?"

"That we can't go on the way we are, with the *cantucci* or, for that matter, with the League. We are old, Violetta. We are very old and getting older, we need to let some new light shine in or we could be snuffed out forever."

"We're not candles!"

"No, but if we were, we would be melted down to ugly little stubs and our wicks would only just be flickering."

"Nonsense! I could still burn down the whole of Montevedova if I wanted to."

"You could do it by mistake the way things are going."

"You're either with me or against me," Violetta said, the unsteady beat of her ancient heart clattering in her ears.

Luciana snorted. "Funny that. Mussolini said the same thing. And anyway, you know I'm with you. You've known that since . . ."

They both looked over at the pictures of their late husbands on the mantelpiece.

"I was right," Violetta said gruffly. "The thing is, I was right. It worked out. I knew."

"Yes, that's my point. You were right, and I was with you then and I've been with you ever since, so you should listen to me when I say that this time I am not so sure."

They were quiet for a moment, Violetta cursing the wretchedness of having her sister lose faith in her just when she had lost faith in herself. She could not go on without her. Not today. She would have to deal with this another time.

"Burn down Montevedova by mistake? Nonsense!" she said, attempting a halfhearted kick in the direction of her sister's shin.

"With me or against me indeed!" snorted Luciana, attempting the same maneuver.

"Watch out or you'll topple over and I won't be able to get you back up again, you silly old woman," warned Violetta.

"Well, watch out or I'll topple over and not want to get back up again," came the retort.

The sound of the bell above the door ringing in the bakeshop brought their quarreling to a halt. Lily was leaving the premises.

"Quick, wave your scarf at Ciacci. We need Del Grasso to stall her until someone remembers where Alessandro is this morning."

Chapter 19

Lily was hurrying past the Hotel Adesso when the little gray-haired woman she had seen hollering down the hall the day before scurried out of the doorway and grabbed at her arm.

"You want stay in lovely four-star hotel?" the old woman asked her.

"I tried to yesterday," Lily said, gently extracting her arm from the vicelike grip. "But there was a problem with the plumbing."

"Problem? There is no problem."

"The drains were blocked. There was a huge fuss."

"Oh, that," the woman said. "False alarm."

"False alarm? I could smell the drains from here in the doorway."

"There is no problem," the woman insisted, tugging at her arm. "I promise. You stay here. Is very nice. Four stars."

"The lady at the tourist office said it had no stars," Lily informed her.

"Lady at tourist office is like to drink too much."

Lily looked up at the hotel. It did look nice, and the awful smell had gone completely, but she'd already paid 500 euro to stay with Violetta, and anyway she didn't want to think about this now. She didn't want to think about anything.

"Thank you, but I'm fine where I am," she said, and after something of a tussle, she pulled away, continuing down the hill, cursing the cheerful ivy that draped elegantly over a garden wall, the faded turquoise of a shuttered building, the rustic charm of an ageing street lantern. Yes, Montevedova was beautiful. She got that. But what did she need with beauty?

She was almost back at her dry parapet when progress was halted by a slow-moving group of old women who all but blocked her path. So many old women! Where were they keeping the young ones?

No matter which way Lily stepped to overtake the shuffling group, they seemed to form a clump right in front of her, but just before she lost her patience and demanded that they either get out of her way or hurry up, they stopped, more or less delivering her like a pea down a slippery chute to the open door of Poliziano, a charming old-fashioned café with views out across the valley.

A grizzled old man was leaning on the counter sipping a glass of wine and Lily needed no further encouragement. She went in, crossing to a tiny Juliet balcony overlooking the view. It had room for just one table and so she sat down, ordered a coffee, and, after a pretence at hesitation, upon seeing it was almost eleven o'clock, a glass of prosecco. The coffee was good, but the prosecco better. Its tiny bubbles seemed to smooth away the enormous wrinkle that Francesca had made in her morning.

It wasn't the child's fault; she was—well, Lily didn't want to think about what she was. She was perfect. There it was. Plain as a pickle. Perfect. But why wasn't her hair being brushed? Why did her wings have holes in them? Who was taking care or, rather, *not* taking care of this tatty little Tinker Bell? Lily's missing certainty popped in for a brief visit as she sipped her drink. If Daniel walked through the door right then, she was certain what she would do. She would shoot him. In the heart. And then the head, and then the balls. And then she would feed what was left of him to the pigs.

She ordered a second prosecco.

This soothed her wounded heart a little more.

The balcony she was sitting on had a similarly splendid view to the one in her room, and, on reflection, Lily couldn't think why she had chosen it—it was a table for two: a hopelessly romantic spot to stare into a lover's eyes and be swept away in the magnificence of the surroundings.

Did Daniel bring his lover here, she wondered? Had they sat at this very table and gazed at each other while Francesca and her baby brother stayed at home taking care of themselves? Who was this man she had known so well for so long? A liar, a cheat, not even a good father.

She put her glass back on the table. She'd come to Tuscany because she wanted her husband, wanted to reclaim the love they once shared, wanted to get back what she'd lost. But now she saw what a fool's errand that was.

It was one thing to look at a photo and to rationalize a situation, even in a drunken my-husband-has-another-family-and-I-must-go-and-do-something-about-it way. But to see the results of that with her own eyes? To feel that little body pressed into hers? There was no going back from this.

She looked across to the grandfather clock in the corner. It was still not midday, but taking the time difference, jet lag, and her stewing emotions into account, Lily considered a third glass of prosecco. It was only low alcohol after all. Practically lemonade. Hardly worth counting.

But something about the way the waitress (finally, someone under thirty) looked at her when she came to collect her drained glass made her change her mind.

She paid the bill, leaving a generous tip, and, fueled by what little alcohol there was in those Italian bubbles, she decided to find an Internet café or a telephone to check in with Pearl.

The thought of work hinged her back to her old self a little. She knew where she was when it came to Heigelmann's—nothing had changed there—but she had taken only a couple of steps outside the café when she heard someone calling out to her.

"*Signora! Signora Turista!*"

She turned to find Alberto waving at her from outside his shop.

"Again," he called, "I am about to sit down to lunch! Bread, prosciutto, buffalo mozzarella, more tomatoes freshly delivered from my grandmother with instructions about a pretty blonde."

She laughed but shook her head.

"I'm sorry, Alberto, I'm just—"

But as she spoke an argument erupted from the doorway she had just passed. It was another bakeshop, more tacky than the Ferrettis', this window stuffed full of *cantucci* in a myriad of flavors and a brassy rainbow of fancy wrappings.

A curvy woman in a wraparound dress backed out of the store, almost bumping right into Lily. She was shouting in Italian at someone inside and came so close Lily could smell her. She was slightly lemony and very angry, her long dark hair flicking wildly from side to side like a horse tail swatting flies.

Lily could have reached out and pulled it. It was Daniel's lover, of course.

"Eh, Carlotta! Causing trouble again!" called a handsome young man from the *gelateria* opposite, and Daniel's lover spun around and unleashed a tongue-lashing on him as well.

"Carlotta, Carlotta," he repeated, shaking his head and backing into the ice cream store.

Carlotta! How dare she have such a turbulent, exotic name and cheeks aflame with such passion?

Another angry woman emerged from the tacky *cantucci* shop waving her fist at Carlotta, who started backing in Lily's direc-

tion. Desperate to avoid either winding up underneath her feet
or face to face with her, Lily spun on her heels and hurried toward Alberto who was still standing outside his shop watching
the commotion.

"You change your mind, no?" Alberto grinned. "My grandmother's tomatoes do this every time."

Lily stepped inside his little wine shop but again refused his
offer of lunch although it looked appetizing enough set out on
a white platter on his desk: the cheese pulled into chunks and
tossed with chopped fresh tomato and torn basil leaves, a crusty
loaf of sliced ciabatta next to it. But distress curdled in her stomach. Her head pounded. Carlotta!

"So what's the story with the woman in the street?" she asked.

"Crazy," Alberto answered with a disinterested shrug. "Nice
girl, good girl, but crazy. Whole family is crazy. She gets fired
from the Borsolini brothers once a week. But they crazy too. You
would like a glass of wine?"

She couldn't bring herself to ask any more, to ask if he knew
of Daniel, or Francesca, or that fat baby boy. For a start, she
didn't want to make a big deal of her interest, but also she was
afraid that if she started asking questions, she might never stop.
Did Carlotta know that Daniel had a wife? That her daughter's
dress was dirty? That you could be as crazy and as nice as you
wanted but that it wasn't right to steal someone's husband, someone's future, someone's dreams, someone's daughter?

If Alberto noticed she was distracted, he didn't let on, keeping
up a steady stream of chatter about his wines, the recent rain, the
local food, the bar he was going to later in the day to meet with
his friends, in case she was interested.

She wasn't, but she did get him to tell her a little about the
town and if there was much more to it than she had already seen.
The news was disheartening. Montevedova, Alberto told her, re-

ally only had two streets, the Corso and the lane that forked in the opposite direction at the parapet. In any case, the two of them joined up again at the *piazza grande* at the top of the village, where he was meeting his friends if she changed her mind.

There were back alleys and hidden pathways between the two main lanes, he explained, but pretty much what Lily had seen was what there was.

"Everybody must know everybody here," she suggested. "You must bump into each other all the time."

"You would think so," Alberto agreed, "but some like to keep to themselves. And the good thing about a small town is that you always know where everyone else is so you can *not* go there, you can go somewhere else."

This was a very good point.

Lily already knew where Francesca and Carlotta were and could only assume Daniel was not far away.

Inferring that she had already enjoyed all the sights Montevedova had to offer, she asked Alberto what she could explore farther afield. He suggested she head to one or another of the nearby towns, none of them as beautiful as Montevedova but all worth a look anyway. He then took her down to his basement and showed her out the back door, which was close to the bookstore. She bought a guidebook and headed to her car.

Chapter 20

All the widows dressed in head-to-toe black, as was expected of them, but as Fiorella pointed out in the League HQ while they waited for Violetta, in the height of summer it didn't make the slightest bit of sense.

"Although it certainly should help with all the sour expressions and the bad hair," she said. "As for the sweating that must go on! It's all right for me, I get a discount on deodorant at the pharmacy but for the rest of you—why stick with black, that's what I want to know?"

"It's slimming," the widow Ercolani pointed out although it didn't really work that way for her personally.

"It's the proper thing to do," announced someone else.

"It's what widows have always done."

"That's true," agreed the widow Ciacci, "although I have a little secret to tell you." With all the speed of a Sicilian stripper, she then whipped off her amorphous black smock to reveal a hot pink slip, clinging and quite low cut, with a fetching lace bodice. "It's La Perla," she said.

The other widows stared, slack-jawed.

"The color's called fuchsia," she added.

"Well, I wear witches britches," blurted out another widow. She undid her skirt, which fell to the floor with a thunk, such was the heft of its weave, and there she stood, in a pair of pale blue knickerbockers sagging at the crotch and not quite right with her flesh-colored kneesocks, but still, a riot of unexpected underwear.

"My brassiere is actually white," yet another widow admitted. "All my underthings are."

"I don't see why you should have to wear black at all," Fiorella said boldly. "I think you should wear florals and checks and polka dots and sequins. Who makes all these stupid rules anyway?"

"Actually that rule was also me," Violetta said. Only the widow Mazzetti had heard her knock on the door and had quietly let her in. "Our widowed mothers wore black, as did their mothers before them, and their mothers too. It's what we like to call respecting tradition, Fiorella, although I don't imagine you know much about that."

"We made it official in nineteen forty-nine," the widow Mazzetti said. "April the twelfth, I believe."

"We are a secret league, Fiorella," Violetta continued, "our purpose known to no one outside our ranks. As a group of silent black-clad individuals mourning our loved ones the way it has always been done in this country, we can disappear into the background in a way that would not work if we wore red stilettos and feather boas. If that's your preference, please feel free to do so, but not under our auspices."

Fiorella Fiorucci actually had a pair of red stilettos—her slut of a sister had sent them as a "sorry for stealing your husband" gift—but she sensed this was not the right time to bring this up.

And actually, she had worn them for a week both at the pharmacy and as she sat quietly in her own doorway staring at people, but nobody had noticed.

"Old dames like us disappear into the background no matter what we wear," she said. "I just thought it wouldn't hurt to live it up a little."

"This is a serious business," Violetta snapped. "We are trying to do something good here, so if you would all please get dressed and—where is the widow Del Grasso? She's supposed to be reporting on Lily."

"On Lily? Why? I thought Alessandro was the *calzino rotto*," Fiorella said.

Luciana reached for Violetta to stop her from clocking the widow Fiorucci upside the head.

"We know where Alessandro is," Violetta said between gritted teeth. "We have his schedule. We need to find Lily and place her in his way to orchestrate any progress. Without doing so, their paths may never cross and we will have another disaster on our hands."

Fiorella opened her mouth to say something, but the widow Mazzetti ran her finger across the base of her throat in the universal sign of "If you want to retain a body to go with that purple paisley smock, zip it now."

What she had been going to say was that she knew for a fact Alessandro did not keep to his schedule on Wednesdays, but piping up now was probably breaking some sort of rule, so she did as she was bid and zipped it.

Chapter 21

Pienza was one of the villages Alberto had recommended: an insanely compact and pretty town perched like another medieval crown on a hilltop half an hour away.

Looking at it was one thing but trying to get into it another; Lily circumnavigated the whole place what felt like a dozen times trying to find a parking lot and almost came to blows with Dermott over a certain nonexistent roundabout before eventually parking down a residential back street beneath the leafy canopy of an enormous tree.

The town was famous for having been the home of a fifteenth-century pope who basically invented the makeover, she gathered from the guidebook. This pope had not only spruced up the Pienza town square but built a stunning cathedral plus, while he was at it, his own lavish papal palace, which Lily paid ten euro to tour.

He knew what he was doing. The palace had a view over the surrounding countryside that was hard to beat, and he'd even thought to install a hanging garden through which to marvel at it.

Anything else Lily wanted to know about the pope and his leanings she gleaned from a pimpled teenager who was also on the tour, which would have been even more enlightening had it not been in German. She had missed the English tour, Rolf the spotty boy explained to her, but he could help her: to his mother's obvious consternation.

Each time Rolf translated anything for Lily's benefit, Rolf's mother shot her the filthiest of looks, and when he explained with enthusiasm about the little cupboard where the pope kept his lovers, Lily thought the woman might just explode.

She *was* interested in Rolf, but not in the way his mother assumed. Lily had imagined her own teenage boys looming over her ever since she'd first dreamed of having a family—initially with John Travolta, her poster boy in junior high. She thought she would have those sons by now. She thought one would be about Rolf's age. And she'd be a better mother to Rolf than this dour creature with her sour looks and disapproving guttural noises. Who called a kid Rolf, anyway? Hadn't the woman seen *The Sound of Music*?

But then Rolf's mother bade her good-bye with a sympathetic pat on the shoulder and such a compassionate smile that Lily crumpled afterward on the steps of the cathedral in the town's made-over piazza. Could she tell that Lily ached to have a pimpled son of her own? Was her desperation so obvious?

It was desperation of a different sort that eventually drove her from the sun-soaked steps of the duomo. The guidebook said that Pienza was known for pecorino—a local cheese made from sheep's milk—so Lily headed for one of the recommended restaurants tucked in a little square behind the piazza and ordered grilled pecorino with walnuts and honey.

She didn't, as a rule, eat cheese, so she proceeded to push the pecorino around the plate while she finished a half bottle of wine. But the pain that the prosecco bubbles had danced away so happily earlier on in the day showed no signs of subsiding quite as easily with the riesling.

As the moments ticked by in the little trattoria, thoughts of Francesca and Rolf and Baby Grace bounced in her mind like fat raindrops off the cobbled Corso. She kept trying to flush them away but no sooner had she gotten rid of one than another splashed in its place.

She shouldn't have taken the photo out of the shoe. She shouldn't have drunk-dialed Rose. She shouldn't have fallen foul of Tipsy Tourism. She shouldn't sit there and plough through another half bottle. If she'd not ploughed through the ones at home, she might still be meeting with Finance trying to decide who they could afford to let go and who they could afford to keep, where they could cut costs in the red-lit states of Maryland and Delaware, instead of sitting there wrangling walnuts and trying not to order more wine.

In the end, she decided to go somewhere else to do that, meandering across the other side of the main piazza until she found another trattoria that had an outdoor terrace showcasing yet another sumptuous slice of the Tuscan countryside. Through the soldier-straight trees that grew at the edge of the terrace, she could see sloping grassy pastures tumbling down to a patchwork of perfectly mown hayfields, their giant rolls of hay sitting evenly spaced and proud between the green of the neighboring grapes and olives.

Across the valley she could spot at least three other hilltop towns, their church spires and palazzos casually interrupting the horizon as though medieval fortresses and bell towers were perfectly normal, which, she supposed, they were. Did Tuscany ever get sick of being so ridiculously gorgeous?

She ordered more pecorino with walnuts and honey and more riesling. It would help her make her plan, which she now needed more than ever and which she promised herself she would have all done and dusted by the time the bottle was empty.

Obviously, when she found Daniel, she wasn't really going to shoot him. So what was she going to do? Without much experience in histrionics, it was hard to picture the scene. It would be unpleasant, that was hard to avoid, but it would not be loud. She would quietly demand a divorce, she supposed. Divorce. She hadn't honestly considered that up until now. Not honestly. But sitting here now, having met Francesca and not been a mother to Rolf, it seemed inevitable.

Or was it? She poured herself another glass. She didn't want to move out of the Seventy-second Street apartment. She loved the closets. Hers was perfect. She could find anything she wanted at just a glance. It was cost effective too, not that she needed to worry about that, lucky her, but being able to see all her beautiful clothes constantly reminded her of things she had forgotten she had, which meant she bought fewer new ones, or at least rarely doubled up.

Could she hold her marriage together for closet space? Stranger things had happened, she was sure. It was just that she didn't have a boring shoe collection like Daniel; she had a magnificent shoe collection. Hers were all color-blocked and shelved in individual cubbyholes. Never mind wearing them, it gave her a thrill just to see them. The question was, could she overlook the whole lamination issue just to keep them that way?

Anyway, if they divorced, Daniel would have to move out. She could still afford to keep the apartment. She would be in it by herself, but she was in it by herself a lot of the time anyway. She had never minded that. She had never minded Daniel being there and she had never minded him being away.

Being divorced might not change anything apart from giving her the opportunity to double her shoe collection, move into his side of the wardrobe.

Forget holding her marriage together over closet space, could she end it for the same reason?

She wasn't sure. And there was something wrong with that, there was something wrong with her not minding Daniel being there or being somewhere else. She had loved him with all her heart and soul, and although she wasn't sure if she still did, she knew she had never actually decided not to. So what the heck had happened? How had such an enormous change come about without her authority? No, worse than that, without her even noticing?

She had a lot to figure out and none of it was becoming any clearer, so she ordered another half bottle of wine, a dessert wine, and because it would seem inappropriate to not have dessert, she ordered one of those too.

"Tiramisu?" the waiter prompted her as she perused the menu a trifle blearily. She supposed that's what most Americans ordered.

"*Sí, grazie*," Lily answered with a curt little nod.

When the tiramisu arrived soon after, she pushed it away without even dipping her spoon in it and concentrated instead on the wine and her plan.

She could divorce Daniel or not, whatever she decided, and it appeared to not matter. This seemed hopelessly inconclusive. But as the afternoon light faded to evening across the hills, what finally became clear was that whatever she was going to do, she did not actually need to find Daniel to do it.

He was not a requirement in her immediate future.

She could just go back to her room at Violetta's, pack her bag, and fly straight home to New York. End of story.

Should she decide to keep the status quo, Daniel need never know she had been to Italy. Should she decide she wanted his closet space, she could see a lawyer before he got back and start the proceedings.

She need never see her husband again.

Lily left that possibility to fully sink in, but it seemed merely to skip across the glassy surface of her heart, only just breaking the surface, never plunging into its shadowy depths.

She tried to picture Daniel the way he used to be, the way he was when she couldn't imagine a minute without him, let alone a lifetime. He used to look at her as though she were the most beautiful woman in the world and he the luckiest guy. She knew this to be true, she'd seen that look a thousand times, but now, sitting in the back blocks of Pienza draining her glass, she couldn't imagine him that way, try as she might. All she could see was his Prada belt with a wide hip in front of it and a fat baby's striped leg attached to that.

A fat baby. Don't go there, she urged herself. Not now. Just don't.

"*Grappa, signora?*" the waiter asked, smoothly whisking away her empty wine bottle but leaving the tiramisu.

Lily looked at him in surprise. She could not believe she had finished the wine. It felt like she'd only just taken the first sip. She was as sober as a judge but still unbelievably thirsty. Insatiably thirsty. And she hadn't finalized the plan yet. She needed to finalize the plan. Grappa was a liqueur, she knew that, and while she generally steered clear of those, she thought it would round off her completely uneaten meal perfectly.

She smiled serenely. "*Sí, grazie,*" she murmured.

The grappa tasted like paint stripper. It was so strong her eyes watered when she lifted it near her lips and it was all she could do to sip it, although in the end she managed, and the second glass slipped down far more easily.

The good thing was that there would be no stigma attached to divorcing Daniel because nearly everyone got divorced these days. And there would be no stigma attached to staying with him because no one would know what he had done.

No one would feel pity for her, mumbling over the candles at dinner parties that there she was, the poor barren wife, working all hours of the day and night to keep him in style, while he was playing up in Italy, getting everything for himself that he had once promised her.

If they didn't know what he had done, life would go on as it had been. Daniel would have his pals and his golf and his trips to Italy, and Lily would have her wardrobe, her workouts, her sixteen-hour days at the office. This was the world she had built for herself. This was the world that still stood, that could stay standing, untouched by Daniel's betrayal, if that's what she decided was best.

She could keep living like that, she knew she could. But an image of a green-eyed, olive-skinned, leggy little girl popped into her mind. "What's wrong with you?" Francesca had asked.

Lily batted the image away and looked at the tiramisu. "Don't stay this cold, lonely person," it said to her, giving her such a fright she screamed.

The waiter dropped a tray of drinks on the nearest table and came running.

"Signora, is everything OK?" he asked, looking around, bewildered.

Lily stared at the tiramisu again, mouth agape, as the cream across the top shimmered. "It's not the real you," it said to her.

She sprang out of her chair and reeled back from the table as if the tiramisu was about to follow up its conversation with a physical attack.

"Is there something wrong with your dessert?" the waiter asked.

Was there something wrong with it? It had *spoken* to her.

"Did you see that? Did you hear it?" she asked him. "Don't you dare talk to me like that!" she said to the tiramisu.

"I'm sorry, signora? I just ask if there is something wrong with the dessert."

"No, not you," Lily said. "That." She pointed at the table. "That."

"Can I get you a glass of water, signora? Or perhaps a taxi?"

The waiter was no longer on her side, she could tell that. He stood back, irritated. Two couples sitting at another table dragged their eyes off her and started whispering among themselves. The tiramisu glistened in a smug fashion and stayed resolutely silent.

"Yes, you're right, it's time I left," Lily said, flinging far too much money on the table. "The cheese was too rich, I think . . . I'm so sorry. Thank you. Good-bye."

She stumbled out into the small square, down a curving alley, and emerged into the cool air of the emptying main piazza, where shock gave way to dizziness, confusion, embarrassment. She had to lean on the warm stone of the pope's palace to steady herself. That grappa!

Eventually she lurched over to a drinking fountain in a corner of the square and took a long slug of water. She should have been drinking water all day—what was the matter with her? Everyone knew that after a long flight you were dehydrated and needed to look after yourself. All that pastry for breakfast and plates of pecorino—never mind she hadn't eaten any of it. That wasn't the point. The point was . . . oh, hang the point. The point was beside the point. There was no point.

The tiramisu had spoken to her. That was bad. That was very bad. She'd drunk three half-bottles of wine (or was it four?) and some grappa and the tiramisu had spoken to her.

"I should have eaten the damn thing," Lily said to herself. "That would have shut it up."

"I'm sorry?" An elderly English gentleman who happened to be passing by with his wife thought she had spoken to them. "What was that?"

"It's nothing," Lily mumbled, horrified to hear that her voice sounded slurred. "Perfectly fine. Really."

The man protectively hustled his wife away, looking at Lily over his shoulder as he did so.

"I think she's had too much to drink, dear," Lily heard the woman say, to her complete mortification.

It was the grappa. She'd have been fine if she'd stuck to just wine. The grappa had been too strong and had unsettled her equilibrium. She just needed to find her car and get back to Violetta's to lie down on those crackling apricot sheets. She'd got carried away coming up with her plan and it had been foolish to accept a liqueur on an empty stomach. She just needed to sleep, then everything would be all right.

When she felt steady enough on her feet she retraced her steps and miraculously found her car, failing on the first few attempts to get the key in the lock, but finally opening the door and sliding into the driver's seat.

She got the key into the ignition but couldn't find the lights and as she hunched over the dashboard, stabbing at different levers and buttons, Dermott lit up like a Christmas tree.

"Please, please, I beg you, don't sweep this one under the carpet," he urged her in his Irish lilt. "Please, please, I beg you."

"You have got to be kidding me!" Lily cried, collapsing on the steering wheel, her arms flung around it, her head dropping on to them. It was too much. It was all just too much. Everyone was against her: Rose, Daniel, Carlotta, the tiramisu, and now even Dermott, whom she'd trusted with her life. Her life!

"I thought you were my friend," she told him tiredly. "You're supposed to be my friend."

He didn't reply but he didn't have to. Lily knew when she was beat. She closed her eyes and slept.

Chapter 22

Violetta sat back in her chair and wondered if she would ever be in a good mood again. Everything hurt.

"Tell us once more what happened," she said tiredly to the widow Del Grasso.

"I told you, Lily went to Poliziano and had two glasses of prosecco, then got caught up in Signora Borsolini firing someone again, but she ended up at Alberto's, just as we planned."

"Well, if she ended up at Alberto's just as we planned, why don't we know where she is now?"

"I waited outside for as long as I could," the widow Del Grasso said, "but nature called and I was only gone for a moment. I used the restroom at the souvenir shop, and then I suppose I, well, I got confused and then, I, then she . . . a person can only hold on for so long, you know."

"Yes, yes," Violetta said impatiently, who among them could not attest to how long, or otherwise, a person could hold on for these days. "It's all right, widow Del Grasso, of course it is, but widow Mazzetti, I wonder if we need a new rule to cover this business of going to the WC. It's not going to get any better."

"You and your rules!" chortled Fiorella. "How about a rule to stop having more rules? You can only eat *cantucci*, you have to wear black, you're not allowed to use the bathroom while you're snooping, and what else?"

"You must have known the true love of a decent man," piped

the widow Mazzetti, who took the question seriously. "That's actually the first one."

"Yup, I got that," said Fiorella.

"To benefit from the work of the League, to qualify as a *calzino rotto*, you must have a good heart and a clear conscience," continued the widow Mazzetti.

"A clear conscience? Hm. Tricky. Yes, but understandable."

"And our assistance is a special one-time-only offer," the widow Pacini added. "That one's quite new."

"What's that about?"

"That's about a lovely seamstress we found for pig farmer out near Aquaviva," the widow Mazzetti explained, "back in late November 1982, if memory serves me correctly, and it was an extremely good match. They would have been very happy, but he left the poor woman when she became ill and was advised to give up eating meat."

"Doctors orders," cried two other widows simultaneously. They lived in fear of the same thing happening to them.

"The pig farmer said there were some things on which he could not compromise," the widow Mazzetti went on, "and refusal to eat pork was one of them."

"He went straight back to being sad and lonely," Luciana added, "but started dropping hints left right and center to everyone he came upon about being on the lookout for another wife, but one with better bowels. It caused quite a stir."

Quite a stir, indeed. Two of the widows (the two most keen on swine goods, it had to be said) wanted to give him another chance, four more wanted to shoot those two, four others wanted to shoot the pig farmer, and the whole question of who deserved love and who didn't was debated hotly for weeks.

"The end result," explained the widow Mazzetti, "was that we voted on a regulation declaring that we would help the down-hearted once, but if they blew it, they were on their own."

"A separate clause," added Violetta, "mooted by Luciana, seconded by me, widely supported, and added as a note, was that love is all about compromise."

She looked at her sister, who looked straight back. They had barely spoken a civil word since their quarrel about the *cantucci*. Just what Violetta needed: another lump in her throat.

"What if she'd just chosen to not eat meat?" Fiorella asked. "The Aquaviva pig farmer's wife. Would we have had more sympathy for the pig farmer then?"

"Yes, of course," said half the women in the room.

"No, not at all," said the other half.

Another spirited debate was about to break out, and not in a good way, so Violetta called the group to attention with a single bellow.

"It would behoove us all to remember," she went on, quite menacingly, glowering at Fiorella in particular, "that when a single sock goes missing, it is sometimes never found. This is a catastrophe for the sock that remains. We have just let such a sock slip through our net, so now is not the time to stand around causing trouble and nitpicking. Now is the time to remedy this disaster."

The widow Del Grasso took this opportunity to sneak off to the bathroom and have a good cry. It was her eyes, her pesky, cloudy, failing eyes. She'd sat on her glasses the month before and couldn't afford new ones. The truth was that after she'd been to the restroom, she had thought she was following Lily out of Alberto's wine shop but was practically inside one of the washing machines up at the Laundromat on the other side of town before she realized the person she was following was actually much younger, much shorter, and had much more gingery hair than Lily.

It was the white pants. She had simply followed the white pants and it had been her undoing.

Back in the main room, the door from behind the baptismal font burst open and the widow Ciacci bustled in, red-faced and wheezing. She'd spent the past few hours looking for Alberto, her grandson, and had finally tracked him down to a poker den behind the *piazza grande*. Of course he knew where the *bella* blonde was headed, he proudly told his grandmother.

"She's in Castelmuzio," she reported breathlessly to her friends. "Or Montefollonico. Or Pienza."

"My sister lives in Castelmuzio," spoke up one widow. "I could make a few discreet inquiries with her."

"I know the baker in Montefollonico," said another. "I could try him."

"My cousin's a waiter in Pienza," the widow Del Grasso said, entering the room again, red-eyed but hopeful she could undo some of the damage she had caused. "His wife's a bit of a battle-axe and won't like it if I call this late, but I can try anyway."

Chapter 23

Ingrid and Daniel sat across the table from each other at an outdoor table in the Piazza della Signoria. They had both ordered grilled tuna with asparagus sauce, but only Ingrid was eating.

"You know, I think Florence might just be my favorite spot in all the world," she said, taking a sip of her wine. "What about you?"

"I'm not sure," Daniel answered, pushing his food around the plate. He had no appetite for anything.

Ingrid eyed him, weighing whether she should stick another oar into his murky waters or leave him to it. His earlier emotional outburst had ended without explanation. He'd simply stopped weeping, excused himself, and emerged a half hour later looking perfectly normal.

Still, in her opinion, Daniel Turner was a study in a broken man doing an almost OK job of holding himself together. He had a good heart, she could tell that as easily as she could tell an avocado was ripe just by squeezing it. But he was in trouble.

Part of her, the vacationing part, just wanted to enjoy having lunch with a handsome man and then wander across the Ponte Vecchio to the Boboli Gardens like a normal tourist. But another part of her, the mothering part, wanted to know what had happened to him and to see if there was anything she could do to help.

She remembered a day from a darker part of her past when she had abandoned her little boys at home untended and run to a nearby park where she hid on a bench, sobbing, until her elderly neighbor happened upon her. She'd have left them forever, she thought, if not for Mrs. McArthur's sage advice that sometimes getting to the end of the day without killing anyone was as good as it got—but that was still pretty good.

They'd held hands, she and her ancient widowed neighbor, until Ingrid felt the return of a little fault line of love for her noisy children and her distracted husband. Then the two of them had gone home, and Mrs. McArthur had helped her feed and bathe the little boys and put them to bed.

Sometimes, thought Ingrid, all you needed was someone to tell you that not committing a heinous crime was a major achievement.

She put down her knife and fork and leaned across the table to take Daniel's chin in her hand, lifting his eyes to meet hers. "Look at me," she instructed. "I'm not interested in making anything difficult for you, so you can just relax, OK? I'm meeting my husband, whom I adore, back in Milan when his conference finishes and you'll never see me or hear from me again, but in the meantime I'd like to enjoy my outrageously overpriced lunch in this sensational part of the world so just indulge me a little, will you?"

"I'm sorry, Ingrid," Daniel said, pulling his face out of her grasp. "I really am. I'm just not good company at the moment."

She thought about asking if he wanted her advice but decided she would just give it to him anyway.

"You are a charming, good-looking man in your prime, Daniel. You should be the best company there is. Do you want to tell me whatever it is that's wrong? Fifty-three years on the planet, thirty of them happily married to the same flawed but lovable individual, I know a thing or two. Maybe I can help."

He liked that she told him her age because she certainly didn't look fifty-three. He smiled, and as his face relaxed, so did some other part of him.

"You say you're happily married yet you're here in Florence with me," he said, half joking.

"I'm not 'with' you in a way that would worry my husband," Ingrid said. "I'm worried about you. And I didn't say my marriage was perfect, I don't think any marriage is, but mine is definitely happy. How we get there is our own business. I have my ways and no doubt Richard has his, but the point is, we do get there."

Daniel could so easily picture Ingrid and her doctor husband, laughing over a bowl of pasta and a bottle of red in their big, warm Boston house, their sons dropping by to visit their old rooms, bringing girlfriends, laundry, stories of life outside the nest. He envied her. He envied all of them.

"My wife could not have children," he said. "We tried for years, but for whatever reason, it was not to be."

"I am sorry to hear that," Ingrid said.

"We tried to adopt," Daniel continued. "Privately, through an agency. Through three, actually. For a few years there, every time the phone rang, I swear . . ." He stopped, remembering the look on Lily's face when the call would inevitably be about something other than a pregnant woman wanting them to be the parents of her unborn baby.

"She wanted to be a mom more than anything else in the world and it just never happened," he said.

Ingrid pushed aside her plate, thinking of the ease with which she had produced those three sensitive boys.

"I can't imagine how difficult that must have been," she said.

"It gets worse," said Daniel. "The phone call finally did come one day. Brittany, from Chattanooga, Tennessee, had seen our file and chosen Lily and me to bring up her baby, so a month later we headed down there, drove straight to the hospital and met our newborn daughter, Grace."

"Oh, Daniel!" His smile broke Ingrid's heart.

"Just watching Lily pick up that little bundle," he said. "Seeing that she finally had what she'd dreamed of for so long and tried so hard to get—Jesus."

He broke off. Shook away the memory.

Ingrid thought about reaching across and taking his hand but instead stayed silent, ready to listen.

"We visited her, the baby, over the next couple of days in the hospital and then we were able to take her ourselves to this little place Lily had rented, all cute and homely, you know, with a rocking chair and . . . anyway, she was such a natural, my wife, you'd have sworn she'd had a tribe of kids already. It was incredible to watch, it really was. I was in awe of her. It was like looking at a whole new person. She was just made to be a mom."

She'd had six-day-old Grace in a papoose slung around her front when the phone call from Brittany's lawyer came. Daniel was making a snack in the kitchen and Lily was out in the garden.

According to Tennessee law, on the sixth day of a baby's life, the new parents could become legal guardians, the first step toward adoption. Daniel and Lily were headed to the attorney's office to sign the papers that afternoon.

But on the sixth day of a baby's life, the birth mother could also change her mind, and that's what Brittany did. She changed her mind.

As the attorney explained, Brittany's maternal grandmother had been kept in the dark about the pregnancy but had somehow gotten wind of it and then made a visit to her granddaughter, putting the fear of God into the twenty-two-year-old about abandoning her "issue" to total strangers.

Brittany lived in a trailer with her unemployed boyfriend, who was not Grace's father. She had told Lily she wanted to go to college and become a teacher, but that she couldn't do it with a baby, and she wanted her baby to have a better life than she'd had.

Still, she'd changed her mind.

Daniel could not even begin to think of this without seeing his wife curled around that papoose, the noise coming out of her soft, so as not to frighten Grace, but from so deep within her, it still made the hairs on the back of his neck stand up.

Lily had wanted to take the baby and run, to go to Mexico or Australia or somewhere, anywhere, where she could keep what she had found in her week of being Grace's mother.

Daniel had said little, knowing that this was an impossible solution, knowing also that however she felt right now, his wife would not ultimately deprive Brittany of her own shot at motherhood.

Eventually, he figured, she would hush up and let him take Baby Grace to the lawyer's office so they could hand her over like a neatly wrapped parcel being returned to a store.

He was right. Lily's tears dried, she packed up all the baby's things, and they drove in empty silence across town to the ugly little building where Brittany was waiting. The grandmother was there, scowling and looking dangerous, while Brittany's face remained as blank as milk as she took sleeping Grace awkwardly in her arms.

"Keep her safe," Lily said, and that was all.

They got in the car and drove, again in silence, straight to the airport, stopping once for Lily to throw up, and a second time for her to dispose of the car seat they'd brought with them and used twice: once to bring Grace home from the hospital and once to deliver her back to who knew what.

Lily put it carefully in a Dumpster outside a fast-food restaurant.

"We won't be needing that," she said when she got back in the car, and she didn't say much else for the rest of the journey. Or the day. Or in fact, the next week.

She hushed up all right. And she stayed that way.

Chapter 24

Lily woke up at dawn with the Fiat emblem from the middle of the steering wheel engraved on to her cheek and a crick in her neck no osteopath in Christendom would be able to fix without removing her head from her shoulders, one of which was frozen in a hunch up by her ear.

Her bladder was so full it hurt. The inside of her mouth felt like a tenement doormat that had never been shaken, let alone cleaned. Even her hair hurt.

These were her current physical problems, but they were not, in the cold light of day, her biggest.

That honor would go to the fact she had drunk so much she had argued with a custard dessert and started a relationship with her GPS.

She felt so ashamed she could not imagine feeling any more so, until she heard the *rat-a-tat-tat* of someone knocking on her window and looked up to see with abject horror that it was once more Alessandro, the linen-shirted Italian of whenever it was she had arrived in horrible, hideous, hateful Tuscany.

Instinctively she ripped Dermott's power source out of the cigarette lighter to keep him quiet and at least managed to get the window down without incident.

"So, you never did find Montevedova," Alessandro said with a smile. "Perhaps you should have followed me after all."

Lily opened her mouth to speak but her tongue was stuck to the roof of it.

"Perhaps I can be of some assistance now?" Alessandro offered.

Her tongue stayed where it was as her brain tried to shuffle her options.

She could once more assert her independence and drive off, leaving Alessandro in a cloud of exhaust. He was a stranger, after all, and she had her dignity to consider.

A small but boisterous burp escaped her.

She closed her eyes and felt the world spin.

Her dignity, she had to admit, was currently beyond consideration.

She had no plan, a bird's nest for a hairdo, and her formerly cool exterior was now decidedly hot and sticky. She gave up. This handsome Italian was offering assistance and the easiest thing to do was accept it.

She opened her eyes again and looked into his, seeing this time what that intensity was she'd had trouble putting her finger on when she first met him. Sadness. Buried deep under the smooth surface of his olive skin, but as obvious to her at that moment as if it were a sheepskin coat.

"I did find it, as it happens, Montevedova that is," she croaked, managing a woeful smile. "But I'm afraid I seem to have lost it again. A case of too much vino and not enough pecorino, I fear."

"Aha, well then, Alessandro D'Agnello, at your service," Alessandro said again, with a deferential nod of his head.

"Lily, Lillian, in need of it," Lily said and held her hand through the window for him to shake. At some point in the night she had tried to take off her bra underneath her long-sleeved T-shirt, and it was poking out of her sleeve, bunched at her wrist.

They both looked at it, she with horror, he with amusement.

But Alessandro was nothing if not impeccably mannered.

"We're not far from my villa," he said, shifting his eyes to hers and keeping them there. "Would you care to join me for coffee? I brew an excellent cup and I'm in need of one. I've been on something of a goose chase this morning."

"A wild goose chase," Lily suggested.

"A strange goose anyway," Alessandro agreed. "I had a call very early this morning to meet a courier driver, I think she said, at an address in this street, but there's no one here. No one but you," he said, and smiled at her.

She smiled, wanly, back.

"So, can I convince you to join me for an early morning espresso on your way back to Montevedova?"

"Actually, yes, you can," she said. "That would be lovely."

"Excellent," said Alessandro. "Just follow me. And if you get lost, pull over and I will find you again. I seem to have a knack for it."

"Don't you say a word," Lily said to Dermott as she pulled out into the road behind the black Range Rover. "Not a word."

Back nearer to Montevedova, Alessandro's villa sat nestled into a copse of trees at the end of a white stone-chip driveway.

"I like your place," Lily told him when she extracted herself from the car. "Been here long?"

"About five hundred and seventy-six years," Alessandro answered, guiding her toward the front door. "The house that is, not me. It belonged to my father's family but was lost some time in the nineteenth century, and I bought it back a few years ago and have been restoring it."

"It was lost?" Lily asked as they made their way into the grand entrance, then through to a surprisingly welcoming kitchen at the rear. It had state-of-the-art appliances glistening wherever she looked, yet the countertops were full of bowls of fruit, vegetables, and herbs, and there was a tart of some sort on a stand, freshly dusted with confectioner's sugar. It was a space that looked well-used and much appreciated.

"Yes, my great-great-great-grandfather got in a fight with a villainous neighbor over a horse," Alessandro answered her, "and in the ensuing vendetta, lost his house, two of his daughters, and, eventually, his mind."

Lily laughed. Villainous? Now that was a word she didn't hear very often. Her laughter petered out, however, when she saw the look on Alessandro's face.

"I'm sorry, I don't mean to be rude. It just sounds so dramatic—villains, vendettas, madness. Like a Shakespearean play. No disrespect to your ancestors."

Alessandro raised an eyebrow and nodded, but remained silent as he busied himself in the kitchen, so Lily asked if she could look around and walked through the dining area into a sunny living room. This whole rear section of the house faced out on to an enormous swimming pool surrounded by yew trees in oversize terra-cotta pots. Behind it, the undulating grounds stretched for miles, populated haphazardly with gnarled stands of ancient, arthritic-looking olive trees.

It was yet another preposterously beautiful view.

"Actually, I think it more likely that Puccini would write an opera about it, my family history," Alessandro said, coming up behind her, his good humor restored. "A tragedy, I think, for that's what it is."

"But you have the house back again now and that was all so long ago. Shouldn't the family feud be laid to rest?"

"You have not been in Italy long," he said, smiling, "so you may not be aware that we treasure our past here much more than you Americans—and with it our feuds and tragedies. We do not find it as easy as you do to extricate them from the present, for some reason. It is difficult."

She was about to challenge him, but then she thought of Rose, her only sister, whom she adored but had been feuding with for what felt like hundreds of years.

She looked across at Alessandro as he gazed out across his property and it struck her again, his deep, silent sadness. She wondered what other tragedies from his past he was treasuring and thought it an odd concept, that these rivalries would be cherished, but hadn't the heart to argue any further. She was on the back foot, after all, in his house, clearly the worse for wear and desperate for coffee.

"Espresso?" he suggested, right on queue. "Machiatto?"

"Is a machiatto the small one with just a splash of milk?"

"It is, yes."

"Then I will have one of those, thank you," she said, following him back to the kitchen. "I don't suppose you have soy milk?"

"I don't suppose anyone has soy milk," Alessandro agreed. "We're surrounded by cows."

"Yes, but are they organic? I get the impression organic has yet to take off over here."

"We don't have the modern obsession with it, that's true," Alessandro said. "But then in Italy we don't eat as much nonorganic food, if that's the right word, in the first place. The milk I have in my refrigerator, for example, comes from cows that live two valleys away from here. You can see them from the corner of the pool by the loggia. I grow my own vegetables, some fruit, get nuts sent up from a friend in Puglia, and have oil made from my own olives. Signora Benedicti, my housekeeper, makes my bread from flour milled near Lucca and I get my meat or chicken from the butcher in San Quirico where my family has been going for hundreds of years, in good times and bad. I know where everything I eat comes from, and to me, this is better than organic, and this is how we have always done it in Italy. True, that's changing, but it is how it has always been done up until now."

"Well, I come from a city of more than one-and-a-half million people covering an area about the size of your farm," Lily said, "so you'll have to forgive me if I don't grow my own olives. I'm lucky there's room to stand up."

"You live in Manhattan?"

She nodded.

"I've been there. Yes, New York, a magnificent city. Expensive, for me anyway, but still, magnificent. So you would like a machiatto with ordinary fresh cow's milk?"

She nodded again.

"And you must have a slice of this tart," he said, cutting a large wedge out of the pie on the counter. It had a pastry base and a berry jam in the middle, just the sort of thing in which Lily had absolutely no interest.

"Not for me, thank you," she said, holding up her hand, but Alessandro would not take no for an answer.

"Signora Benedicti is famous for her *crostata di more*," he insisted. "I ask her to make it all the time but usually she ignores me. Today, though, here it is!"

He pushed a slice of the dark, toffee-smelling pie across the breakfast counter to Lily and to her surprise, her mouth watered at the sight of it.

"I'm sorry but I don't really do desserts," she said.

"But it's breakfast!"

"Well, I especially don't do desserts for breakfast"

"Lily, if you are going to stay in Italy, you need to appreciate that we eat desserts all day long."

"Well, I can appreciate that without eating it," she laughed.

"But why wouldn't you?" Alessandro was genuinely perplexed. "Signora Benedicti has made it, for once, and there it is right in front of you. Half the population of Montevedova would give their right eye to be in your situation."

"All right, all right." Lily could see he was not going to let it lie, so she carved off the end of her piece of tart with a fork and plopped it in her mouth. The sweet blackberry jam combined with the tart fresh berries piled on top of it exploded on her tongue.

"Mmmm, delicious," she said, then helped herself to another mouthful.

Alessandro laughed.

"You are not the first person to find Signora Benedicti's *crostata di more* irresistible," he said.

"Irresistible? It's practically addictive. Maybe she laces it with cocaine," Lily joked.

"Well, she's just your average little old Italian widow," Alessandro shrugged, "so I would be surprised, but you never know."

Lily watched Alessandro polish off the rest of his slice of tart, then another one, and finally what remained of hers. It was obvious how he acquired his girth, but he held himself well, regardless of the extra pounds, she thought, as he covered the remainder of the tart in layer upon layer of plastic wrap to keep himself, he told her, from finishing the whole thing off before lunchtime.

It seemed a strangely intimate thing to do, watch a man tidy his own kitchen.

"You live here alone?" she asked.

"Since my wife died," he answered, and she could see the tension hike up his shoulders as he spoke.

"I'm sorry, Alessandro, I don't mean to pry."

"You do not pry. It is just . . . difficult."

So here, then, was the root of his sadness. It was raw; no wonder he still wore it on the surface. Lily smoothly excused herself to freshen up and restore her bra to its rightful position then, when she came back, asked to see the rest of his property.

Outside in the vegetable garden she developed a thumping headache but still did a good job of feigning interest in how he got his tomatoes to grow so well and his beans so straight. He grew apples too, he told her, and grapes, from which he had a neighbor make his own wine, and there were the olives of course, much better than the Spanish and far superior to the even worse Greek ones, which according to him made oil that tasted like aviation fuel.

Inside his barn though, her hangover was momentarily chased away when he pulled open the doors and there, like a huge whale carcass, spanning almost the length of the building, sat a gondola.

It was unfinished, but even someone who has never been to Venice knows a gondola when she sees one. And even someone who has never been to Venice knows that the reason gondolas are so popular there is that there is a lot of water and no roads.

Tuscany, on the other hand, had no water and a lot of roads. Steep ones. Even if the whole place flooded, a gondola would be of absolutely no use whatsoever. None.

"Alessandro, it's . . . well, it's . . ."

"Incredible, no? I am building it from scratch in the traditional style, not that there is much of a tradition anymore; gondola building is a dying art, like just about everything else."

He picked up a hand planer and started smoothing the sides of the incomplete vessel. The sun was streaming in through the open barn doors, casting a golden light on the boat and Alessandro, whose handsome brow was furrowed in concentration.

Lily looked out across the miles and miles of lush dry land, and then back at Alessandro, working carefully on his boat.

"I know I don't have the best navigational skills in the world," she said, "but aren't we a long way from Venice?"

He stopped, rested his arm on the side of the boat, wiped his forehead.

"No one cares for tradition anymore," he said, and he seemed sad about that too. "No one cares that the gondola builders are dying and no one is replacing them and one day there will be no more traditional gondolas."

"But do they need to be traditional? Couldn't there be a modern version that maybe makes more economic sense to build?"

"Some things can change with the times and still be true to their purpose, yes, I believe this, but you modernize a gondola and it is no longer a gondola. Not everything *needs* to be traditional, but some things do. If we do not cling to our traditions, then what? If there is no tradition, there is nothing. We are just the same as everyone else."

"And what's the matter with that?"

"Ah, Lily, I keep forgetting, you have just arrived here. In Italy, the people of Montevedova consider themselves a world away from the people of Montalcino, who we can see from our bedroom windows. We can sneeze and hit them but they are like aliens in so many ways. We eat different food, we drink different wine, we have different customs. We like being different from each other, we thrive on it, and it is our traditions that make us different—otherwise we are all just a bunch of stupid people living in an increasingly corrupt country whose economy is going to the dogs."

Lily knew little of Italian finances or politics so was ill-equipped to offer an opinion. Her headache was back. It was time she said good-bye.

"Just so you are clear," she told him as she got into her car, "I am not the sort of woman who just follows someone to his house and eats his tart."

"Of course, yes, I understand, especially as you barely touched the tart," he answered, and those sad brown eyes tugged at the wasted maternal part of her. "Maybe next time you will stay a little longer, hm? Eat a whole slice."

"I'm not sure how long I will be here, but maybe. And thank you, Alessandro."

"My pleasure," he said. "And if there is anything else I can help you with, please allow me to do so."

Chapter 25

"Oh, well done, Violetta! Well done!" The widow Ciacci's head bobbed up at the sisters' open window.

Violetta nodded, as though she was as pleased with the way the Alessandro business was turning out as anybody else, but she was not. Her stomach was in knots and her indigestion wasn't helping.

News that Lily had been found and reunited with their *calzino* had put the other widows in fine spirits, but Violetta, with her instinct still stuck in her sternum, felt nothing but fear and ill humor.

Lily had taken to drink and passed out in her car. These were not the actions of a woman born to heal Montevedova's favorite son. Yet when Violetta and Luciana negotiated the narrow secret stairway to the church basement, the rest of the widows gathered there had worked themselves into a fever of excitement. They buzzed like bees in clover.

"Did you hear? Alessandro rescued her."

"He may as well have ridden in on a white charger!"

"She went back to his villa."

"She ate the widow Benedicti's *crostata di more*."

"Oooh, that *crostata di more*. Mmmm, if only we had some of that here. It's just what I feel like. Those blackberries."

"What do you add, Benedicti, to get that extra piquance?"

"Oh, Violetta! You have done it again!" The widow Pacini

grinned from ear to ear as the Ferretti sisters made their way into the room. "This is a good one. This is a really good one."

"My Alessandro is finally going to get the happiness he deserves," trilled the widow Benedicti, extra puffed up because her *crostata* had once more been admired. "Our greatest triumph yet. Dear, dear, dear Alessandro."

Nearly every woman in the room sighed, a sound that Violetta found so irritating, it was all she could do to keep herself from slapping someone. They really were quite silly when it came to Alessandro.

To her surprise, Fiorella Fiorucci seemed as unmoved by the adulation as she was. She just rolled her eyes and pulled an iPod out of one pocket, fitting the earphones in her ears as though she didn't want to hear any more.

"What's the problem?" she asked when she saw Violetta staring at her. "Don't tell me there's a rule about no music. Next thing you'll be saying a person can't undo the top button of her skirt when she's had three helpings of *ribollita*."

The widows' collective mooning over Alessandro ground to a halt. *Ribollita* was a soup made with beans—a *lot* of beans. It was a well-known fact, especially in a secret basement with limited ventilation, that a lot of old women and a lot of beans were not a good combination.

"Yes, anyway," one of the widows said. "What next, Violetta? For our lovebirds?"

"The widow Benedicti says a cup of coffee was as hot as it got," someone else said. The widows approved of a decorous courtship but liked to know that fireworks were around the corner.

"Are we going to lure Alessandro into the *pasticceria*?" suggested someone else.

"Get Lily back to his villa, pronto?"

"Have them both stranded somewhere in between?"

"Stranded, yes. That worked with that pretty florist and the potter, didn't it?"

"Or was that the little hatmaker and the barber?"

"Yes, yes, Violetta. What about a stranding? Or do you have some other clever trick left up your sleeve?"

But Violetta's sleeves were empty.

All she had tucked away anywhere were enormous doubts and stabbing pains.

"Will you just leave me be!" she snapped at her friends. "This constant pestering is enough to give me hemorrhoids."

"Speaking of which," Fiorella said, turning to the widow Ercolani. "How is that cream working out for you? Or are you using it on your eyes. They do that in Hollywood, so I hear."

The widow Ercolani looked at a spot on the floor as though it might open a portal to a catacomb beneath and swallow her, but before that could happen Fiorella moved her attention to the widow Ciacci.

"And you, feeling chirpier?" she asked. "You'd be amazed how many people in this town are taking those pills. It's a wonder the lot of us aren't singing and dancing every hour of the livelong day."

The widow Ciacci wilted into a chair.

"And as for you," Fiorella said to the widow Mazzetti, "I hope you've got your knitting needles sharpened. That youngest granddaughter of yours is in the family way."

"But she's not married," insisted the widow Mazzetti. "Oh! That little madam!"

"Oh, hang on," Fiorella said. "No, I have that wrong. Stop knitting. It's not the youngest, it's the second-to-youngest and she'll never be in the family way if she keeps taking those contraceptives."

"But she *is* married! Oh, that little madam!"

The collective spirit in the room was suddenly not so fine.

Chapter 26

Lily woke early the next morning, the sweet smell of baking *cantucci* drifting up the stairs and lightly tickling her taste buds. It was a delightful way to greet a new day and put her in an upbeat mood that her circumstances didn't otherwise warrant.

She sat on her windowsill drinking in the glorious view and wondering which piece of her broken-down life she should start picking up today, but those rolling hills, those jewel-like rooftops, that hazy blue sky over distant green horizons . . .

A day perched on top of such a stunning vista could only be so grim.

The vista that met her in the mirror was nowhere near as pleasing: Lily's dark roots needed urgent touching up and that, at least, she knew how to fix.

She followed her nose downstairs to the kitchen, pushing open the door to find the two sisters hunched over the refectory table covered in flour once again.

"No rest for the wicked I see," she joked at which Luciana dropped the bin she was holding with a *clang*, sugar spilling like paint across the stone floor.

Violetta gave her sister an earful, which Luciana robustly returned, then they both looked miserably at the mess on the floor and just as miserably up at Lily.

With a deep sigh, Violetta attempted to sink down to ground

level but didn't get farther than the mildest of knee bends. Luciana then leaned on the table for balance but winced with the pain of putting even a fraction of her weight on one wrist.

"Hang on there," Lily said. "Neither of you is going to get anywhere near the floor without a crane and a trampoline and possibly the local fire brigade. Here, let me do it."

She took the dustpan and brush that she saw Violetta heading for and started to sweep up the mess.

"I may already have mentioned," she said as she cleaned, "that I am not really a kitchen person. My sister, Rose, is the domestic one. She would have this cleaned up before it even hit the ground. And I'll tell you something else, if Rose were here, I bet her biscotti, I'm sorry, I mean her *cantucci* would be perfect. I've never seen anything come out of her kitchen that wasn't."

She found the trash can and poured the spilled sugar into it.

"Mind you," she continued as she crouched to sweep the floor again, "if Rose were here we wouldn't be speaking to each other because she thinks I'm turning into an abusive alcoholic like our mother, and I think it's not fair she got to have all the children."

When she stood up again, Luciana was holding an egg in the air.

"Oh, will you look at that," Lily said. "An egg. But seriously, I am the original person who can't even boil one."

"*Uova*," Luciana said, pointing at it with a curled finger. "*Uova*."

"*Uova*?" Lily repeated.

Luciana nodded, holding the egg even higher. "*Uova*."

"*Uova*," Lily said again, putting the dustpan back in its place. "Oh! *Uova*. I get it. Egg! *Uova*! How about that? I feel just like Helen Keller with the water. *Uova*. A comfortable bed, a beautiful view, and an Italian lesson as well. Thank you, ladies, it is very much appreciated, but now, if you will excuse me, I will leave and let you get on with it."

"*Burro*," Luciana said, holding up a saucepan of melted butter. "*Burro*."

"Yes, *burro*," agreed Lily. "Butter. Thank you. I'm sure it is but look, I really need to go."

Luciana poured the butter into the mixture on the table. "*Mescolare*," she said to Lily. "*Mescolare*." She turned to Violetta, who seemed deeply unimpressed although it was hard to tell; she always looked a bit like that. "*En inglese?*" Luciana said to her sister. "*Mescolare?*"

The smell of the sugar, the fresh eggs, and the warm butter wafted in invisible tendrils around Lily's face, unlocking a secret door in her memory so sharply she could almost hear a key turn. She couldn't for the life of her tell what lay inside but for a moment was overwhelmed by an indescribable flood of something warm and delicious. And happy, really happy.

"Oh," she said, her hand on her chest. "Goodness."

"*Mescolare*," insisted Luciana. "*Mescolare!*"

"Look," said Lily, "you will just have to excuse me for my lack of *Italiano*, but I don't want cooking lessons or language lessons. I'm not a real tourist, you know. I never even wanted to come to Tuscany until I found out my husband had a girlfriend and two children here."

This time it was the bowl of hazelnuts in Violetta's hands that fell to the ground. The bowl broke in two and the nuts bounced cheerfully to the four corners of the room.

"*Santa merda!*" Violetta whispered.

"*Santamerda?*" Lily echoed as she got to the floor once more to pick them up. "*Santamerda, santamerda, santamerda*," she repeated as she chased the nuts around the kitchen floor.

"It's all just getting too strange for words," she said from beneath the table. "The thing is, I was trying to lay low while I worked out a plan, but then yesterday—was it yesterday?—yes, then yesterday there she was, his daughter, standing in your shop staring at me with his great big green eyes."

She scrambled under the dresser while above her Violetta—somewhat shakily—sought more hazelnuts from the pantry.

"Those *santamerda* sure know how to move," Lily said, spotting a coven of them over in the far corner.

"What I wouldn't give for that little girl to be mine," she continued, putting the last of the spilled nuts in the trash and moving out of Luciana's way as she took a pan of *cantucci* logs out of the oven. They were perfectly cooked, if a little kookily shaped.

"Francesca," Lily continued, absentmindedly moving back to the table and plunging her hands into the mixture in front of her, folding it between her fingers and slowly blending in the new hazelnut supply as the elderly sisters looked on.

"Who wouldn't want a daughter like that? I mean, she's perfect. And the totally crazy thing is that I can't even bring myself to hate him, to hate Daniel, for having that gorgeous little girl, and I know that I should and I know that deep down I really, really must. And I certainly feel the occasional wave of something dark and possibly ever-so-slightly murderous, but mostly what I feel is envious. Envious! You see? That's crazy. It's pathetic. It cannot be normal. Can it be normal?"

Beneath her hands, the mixture was emerging as a smooth dough bubbled with round brown nuts.

"And now there's this other guy," she said as Luciana began cutting the cooked logs into sliced biscotti-shaped discs and laying the discs on another baking pan.

"Oh, so that's how it gets to be *cantucci*—you bake it again," Lily said as she halved the mixture she was working on, then halved it again. "Anyway, this guy—I won't even mention his name because you just might recognize it—this guy is the sort of man you dream about showing up to give you a helping hand and he seems to keep doing just that, and if I can be honest with you, which I think I can since you don't have a clue what I am saying, I've never really been given a helping hand like that and it's not all bad. In fact it is pretty darn good."

"I have a clue," Violetta said, but Lily, not expecting her to be speaking English, did not hear it that way.

"I went to his house, for heaven's sake," Lily told her. "I went to his house in the middle of nowhere without telling anybody and ate some tart, some really good tart."

"I know about tart," the little old woman insisted, fixing her with her dark beady eyes.

"No need to look at me like that, Violetta, it was only a few mouthfuls," Lily said.

"Why so much fuss about a *crostata*?"

"So anyway, will you look at this! Here are your *cantucci* logs all ready for baking, and quite smooth and even, too, if I may say so myself. Did I really do that? So, listen, this has been fun and I'm glad I could help, but my roots are showing and I'm missing my standard hair appointment at home so I am going to go find a hairdresser and there's no point asking you, not that there's anything wrong with a bun at a certain age, but I think I'll be getting down to the tourist office to see who they can recommend. Good luck with the finished product. *Ciao, ciao!*"

She left the old women having what sounded like the rumblings of a humdinger of an argument and headed down the Corso but stopped in her tracks when she considered that Carlotta could well be reemployed at the bakery down the hill by now.

Rather than risk running into her again, she decided to take one of the tiny alleyways leading away from the main street, up toward the *piazza grande* and the other lane on the opposite side of the hill.

She could bypass Carlotta's bakery that way and still make it to the tourist office. However, the first thing she saw on the Via Ricci after winding through a handful of the little lanes to get there was a hairdressing salon, its window full of faded pictures of 1980s bouffy blonde hairstyles.

In New York, she had her roots done every three weeks at great expense in a salon on Fifth Avenue where caviar blinis were served with ice-cold Veuve Clicquot.

This did not look like a blini-and-Veuve Clicquot establishment, but her roots needed attention—she would not let standards slip just because of her current predicament—so she went in and explained to the frumpy woman at reception what she would like. The frumpy woman did not speak English but seemed to understand her anyway, pointing at her own parting, then at a picture in a magazine of a beautiful blonde with perfect highlights.

"*Sí, sí.*" Lily smiled and was shown to a seat. The frumpy woman then called out something in Italian to whoever was in the room at the back of the salon, said "*Uno momento*" to Lily, and shuffled out the front door.

A scented oil was throwing out a pleasant, grassy aroma in the corner while gentle, classical music played at just the right level. Lily was starting to relax into an Italian fashion magazine when her hairdresser emerged from the curtain behind reception bearing a tray of dye and brushes.

She sank into her chair as deeply as she could.

"*Buongiorno,*" the hairdresser said limply and looked at her in the mirror.

Take me now, Lily silently pleaded to whatever cosmic ghoul was in charge of punishing her so harshly. *Take me now.*

The hairdresser had the thin lips, the mistrustful smile, the same long mane but without the swish. How could Lily have been so stupid? Carlotta was not the woman in the photo, this was the woman. Sisters!

The hairdresser was curvier than Carlotta, and she definitely had hips: They were currently straining the lower buttons of her dress, and her dangerous look, while not just then in evidence as much as it was in the photo, still seemed not far away.

"*Mi chiamo* Eugenia," she said, in a tired voice. "My name is Eugenia. You want your roots done, no? Not a cut? Some inches off the bottom?"

She held Lily's hair out and made a snipping gesture.

Lily, the famous problem solver, could not for the life of her figure out the solution for this.

If Eugenia knew who she was, she was in a very vulnerable position. The woman could render her bald with just a few toxic drops in the dye solution or could bring out the shears and give her a mohawk.

If Eugenia didn't know who she was, Lily could just get up and leave, which might create a fuss, but still, it was the better option. However, as she started to rise from her chair, she felt the cold tingle of the blonding solution on her scalp.

"Is all right?" Eugenia asked, confused, the plastic bowl of bleach in her hand.

Lily waited, but a cold tingle was as bad as it got. She settled stiffly back in the seat. Her hair, for the moment, was safe, and she had no choice but to sit there and watch in the mirror as Eugenia worked slowly and methodically on her roots. Eugenia (not a red-hot seductress name by any stretch) was not the siren she had imagined. She wore little or no makeup, the hem was falling down on one side of her dress, her high heels were worn on the outsides, and she chewed nervously on her lower lip as she applied the solution to Lily's thick hair in neat sections.

When she was about halfway through, her cell phone rang. She snatched it out of her pocket, said "*Scusi*," and hurried into the back room. Lily strained to hear the conversation, but it was over too quickly and Eugenia soon came back, even more disheveled than before.

She did not look anything like a happy, confident, husband-stealer. She looked like a wreck.

She applied more dye to Lily's roots, which was when Lily noticed that her hands were unsteady.

"Are you OK?" she asked carefully.

Eugenia nodded violently.

"Fine," she said. "Truly, is fine."

But she did not seem fine. In fact, she seemed to be unraveling before Lily's eyes. "Really, is nothing," she insisted, and applied yet more dye. "Is nothing, absolutely nothing," she repeated, almost angrily, and plunged the brush she was using back into the bowl, stirring it viciously, so viciously that little bits of blue solution slopped onto the floor, onto her dress, onto her foot.

Lily's shoulders were back up near her ears. Where was this heading? Suddenly, though, Eugenia stopped, her whole body collapsing into a slump, and she shook her unhappy head.

"Is not nothing," she said.

Trapped inside that plastic cape with a scalp full of blonding solution, Lily felt her heart pound, felt the blood thunder through her thighs, her forearms. She was ready to spring to her feet and run.

"My boyfriend . . ." Eugenia began.

Lily's hands gripped the arms of the chair.

Her *boyfriend*.

This was going to be bad.

She looked at Eugenia's image in the mirror, but the wretched woman wasn't glowering with rage, she was just standing there, hunched over, looking at the floor, shaking slightly. She did not look like she was going to dump all the dye on Lily's head and throw in a cup of acid for good measure. She did not seem inclined to grab the shears and give her a buzz cut.

In fact, she collapsed on the chair next to Lily and burst into tears.

"My boyfriend is run away!" she cried. "He is run away from me!"

Her husband's mistress clearly needed comforting, but as Lily sat there, her hair standing out Smurf-like from her head, she couldn't bring herself to do anything but shift uneasily as Eugenia's weeping drowned out the music.

"You are very upset," she eventually said. "I'm so sorry, this must be a very difficult time for you, but perhaps we should wash this dye off and I could come back another time?"

"Sorry, sorry," Eugenia sobbed, her tears falling like the week's earlier rain. It was impossible to not feel sympathy for her, but she was still the woman who was stealing Lily's husband, and she just couldn't sit there and counsel her, even if she had known what to say.

"OK, well, I think I will just start doing it myself if that's OK with you," she said, moving over to the basin and turning the faucets on.

"Sorry, sorry." Eugenia sobbed even harder as she watched her client rinsing her own hair. "I am so sorry."

"I'm sure he hasn't run away," Lily said, applying shampoo. "He's probably just gone somewhere on business."

"One week he is gone," Eugenia said. "One week he is not wanting to see me."

One week, thought Lily, upside down and rinsing as she calculated when she had left home. She'd assumed Daniel was staying longer in Italy because of the mistress and children, but if he wasn't with them, where the heck was he?

"How long have you had this boyfriend?" she asked as casually as she could, rubbing conditioner into her hair.

"A long time," Eugenia answered. "We have a child. We have children. But he is a bad boyfriend. Very, very bad!" And she was off again, weeping.

The children! They had all but escaped her mind. This nervous wreck who could barely dye half a head was in charge of Daniel's children.

How could he leave her like this? Her Daniel, known for his kindness, his understanding, his lovely character, and endless patience? It was bad enough that he was cheating on Lily and leading a secret life somewhere else, but to be botching that up too? Had he walked in right then she would have mohawked the living daylights out of him.

But he didn't. And Eugenia was clearly not expecting him to. The weeping woman reached into her pocket and shook a couple of pills out of a prescription bottle.

As Lily dried and styled her own hair, Eugenia stayed slumped in her chair, crying.

"My purse," Lily said when she was done, pointing to her bag, which lay at Eugenia's feet.

"Sorry, sorry," she wept as she handed it over. "You have lovely hair. Come back tomorrow and I give you free blow dry."

It was all Lily could do to mumble an apologetic good-bye and flee, leaving poor Eugenia collapsed in front of the mirror, rocking back and forward, and chewing through the Kleenex.

Chapter 27

"Are you going to tell me what is going on?" Luciana asked after Lily left the kitchen. "You look as though you've been run over by a horse and cart. What did she say?"

Violetta sat down. Her head was spinning. "What was that? With getting her to help make the *cantucci*? You think anyone can make our *cantucci*?" she asked.

Luciana raised her spindly eyebrows. "You can talk. What was that with getting her to round up the '*santamerda*'?"

"You know, I'm getting mighty sick of you questioning every single thing I do, Luciana!"

"Well, I'm getting mighty sick of it too. If you'd just answer my questions perhaps we would both be happy!"

"You can't just let anyone come into our kitchen and make our *cantucci*. It doesn't work like that."

"No, it works better! Did you see how she mixed the dough? She was a natural. Those beautiful strong young hands. Look at these smooth straight logs, Violetta. She did that in no time at all while thinking about something else. What on earth are you so scared of?"

"I'm scared of what little we have left going straight down the drain and taking us with it," Violetta argued, but that wasn't the truth.

"I know my memory's going but I'm sure you used to be more fun than this," Luciana retorted.

"And you used to be six foot tall," her sister barked back.

"Well, if I was six foot tall now, I would pick you up and throw you out the window."

"And I would roll down the hill and not stop until I hit the coast where I would set up another *pasticceria* in competition with your one and squash you like a tiny little cockroach."

"A tiny little six foot tall cockroach. Good luck with that!"

They bickered like this for a couple more hours as they baked Lily's dough and grumpily made more of their own in nowhere near the time or fashion.

Then the widow Ciacci's head poked up at the window.

"I have a report to make," she trilled. "No need for a meeting as it's only an update."

"Get on with it," snapped Violetta.

"Burn the *cantucci* again, did we?" the widow Ciacci asked cheerfully. "Honestly, there isn't a molar left among the lot of us, you may as well try your hand at marshmallow."

"I said get on with it!"

"Well, I've just been to the bank to—oooh!" She disappeared from the window. "*Allora*! Not again," they heard her say from the street below. Her chair had seen better days, that was for sure.

Luciana poked her head out the window but her neck was too stiff to look downward.

"I'm OK," the widow Ciacci called up, and eventually there she was again. "Serves me right for using flour and water instead of going to the *alimentare* for glue. Anyway, as I was saying, I had to go to the bank to get money out because I lost thirteen euro playing pachesi with my sister-in-law. She's quite the whiz, could make a fortune in the back streets of Palermo let me tell you. But anyway, when she came to meet me to pick up the cash—first time she's ever turned up anywhere on the dot as far as I know—

she told me that she'd nipped away from her job at the salon on Via Ricci while a 'pretty blonde American,' that would be our *calzino's amore*, was having her roots done. Fancy that! Her roots! Do you know what this means?"

"The salon on Via Ricci?" asked Violetta.

"She's not a natural blonde!" crowed the widow Ciacci.

"I don't think anyone is a natural blonde," said Luciana.

"Did you say the salon on Via Ricci?" Violetta asked again.

"Yes, yes, Via Ricci."

Violetta turned to her sister. "Didn't you tell her to tell the widow Ercolani to recommend any salon *other* than the one on Via Ricci?"

Luciana looked puzzled. "I think I did, although you didn't bother to tell me why. Or did I?"

"Yes, yes, you did," assured the widow Ciacci. "but she didn't go to the tourist office in the end. The widow Pacini saw her cutting across just up the hill here. She found the salon on Via Ricci all on her own, but I wouldn't worry too much if I were you, Violetta. Eugenia Barbarini may have her problems, but she's a very good hairdresser, according to my sister-in-law, as long as she remembers to take her pills. Or is it if she doesn't take her pills?"

"Eugenia Barbarini," Violetta echoed.

"Yes, Eugenia Barbarini, you know—strumpet daughter of the late loony Maria, sister of crazy Carlotta, mother of the peculiar kid who was in your store yesterday."

"I know who she is," Violetta said, her mind whirring as the widow Ciacci's chair gave way a second time. "*Allora!*" they heard again, then Violetta poked her head out the window.

"Get the town perimeter covered and when you find Lily try to keep her contained. Don't ask why, just do it. And get widow Del Grasso to head straight to Poliziano and tell her to use the restroom first this time. If Lily turns up and stays for more than two glasses of wine, I want to hear about it, pronto." Then she shut the window and pulled the curtain.

"What on earth is going on?" Luciana asked her. "You look like the same horse and cart has come back and run you over a second time."

Chapter 28

Whatever Lily had thought she might achieve by coming to Tuscany, she felt a long, long way away from it.

In the space of forty-eight hours she had been talked to by a tiramisu, berated by her GPS, sought refuge from a total stranger, and nearly relieved of her crowning glory by the unhinged mother of her husband's secret love children.

The truth was, she thought, after half an hour of being lost in the back alleyways between Eugenia's salon and the *pasticceria*, she felt a long, long way from anything.

But when she finally emerged back onto the Corso, she found herself in a familiar spot, right beside the little *gelateria* she had seen the day before when Carlotta was out in the street being fired.

The same handsome man was standing in the doorway and lavished her with a beautiful smile. "Signora," he said, "can I interest you in a gelato?"

He was short, shorter than she was, but had the most gorgeous big brown eyes. Italian men really knew what to do with that unusually seductive part of their anatomy. If Alessandro's eyes were deep pools of sadness into which, nonetheless, a person still felt like diving, the gelato man's were a bubbling Jacuzzi: just as inviting but fizzing with energy.

"I'm sorry, I'm not much of a gelato fan," Lily said, smiling back at him.

"No!" he cried, holding up his hands in mock horror. "There is no such thing I think as 'not much of a gelato fan.' You obviously haven't tasted my gelato. Come on, come on, just try some. Just a little bit?"

She shook her head, but before she could scuttle away, he walked over to her, holding out his hand.

"Mario Cappelli," he said as she shook it. "Come on in, I'll give you one on the house. I will not be able to rest thinking there is such a beautiful woman right here in Montevedova who is not much of a gelato fan."

Up close he looked almost edible. His skin was like slightly burnt caramel and those eyes so chocolatey they made her feel hungry. Although a glass of wine would be nice, she thought, as she allowed him to lead her to the glass-front freezer where his gelati were glistening.

There were a dozen or so flavors, but it was the three different sorts of chocolate, at varying levels of decadence, that caught her attention.

Three glasses of wine would be even better, Lily thought, eyeing up the triple chocolate.

"If you are going to go *cioccolata*, you are barking up the right alley," Mario said. "This is my own favorite: chocolate gelato with chocolate drops and chocolate *crema*. My grandmother and I make it all right here, *fatto a mano*. The best in the whole town, if not all of Toscana."

It was wrong, Lily thought, to be looking at *triplicare di cioccolata* but to be wanting wine instead. It was wrong to want to drink wine at all after disgracing herself so horribly in Pienza. The thought of what had happened there still made her skin crawl and conjured up a picture of her mother asleep at the dining table while Lily and Rose chomped silently through burnt macaroni and cheese.

"Well, I guess I'll have the triple chocolate," she said suddenly. It had been years since she'd eaten ice cream, but she didn't particularly have any place else to be, only places she particularly didn't, and this wasn't one of them, so why the heck not.

She sat at the one table in the window of the store while Mario scooped out a huge helping of the delectably glossy gelati and put it in front of her. She was just lifting the first spoonful to her lips when Francesca, still wearing her tatty wings, poked her head in the door.

Lily's heart jumped—she had so much of Daniel in her! It was truly extraordinary. It wasn't just the eyes, the cheekbones, the chin; there was a slight reticence that was uncommon in good-looking people, the opposite of arrogance. It made the likes of Francesca and her father all the more appealing.

The little girl's face lit up, but Lily wasn't sure if it was at the sight of her or the gelato.

"This is really too much for one person," she said to Mario. "I don't suppose you would have a second spoon?"

She waved Francesca over and she flew to the seat opposite, fizzing with excitement.

"Why aren't you at home?" Lily asked when they'd made a decent inroad into the ice cream.

"My mamma came home from work," Francesca said. "She need quiet in our house."

"Where's Ernesto?" Mario asked from behind the counter.

"With Aunt Carlotta," Francesca told him. "Forever, I hope."

"You don't like having a little brother?" Lily asked.

"Sometimes it's OK but mostly he likes it with Carlotta," Francesca explained matter-of-factly. "At home, my mamma cries, he cries, everybody cries, and it is very loud."

"I'm sorry to hear that," Lily said. She looked over at Mario, who gave a noncommittal shrug.

Lily felt the gelato slide cold and heavy in her stomach. She had assumed that Daniel had betrayed her for an idyllic life, but that was clearly not the case and she couldn't decide if this was better or worse. She'd imagined him in a love nest here, his adoring mistress draped in clinging wraparound dresses and constantly smiling at him as she cooked his meals and took care of his children. Instead, Daniel himself was missing, the mistress was a train wreck, one child was fobbed off to an aunt and the other one had been kicked out of the house and was roaming the streets. Luckily there were only two of them to roam.

"What do you do for your job in America?" Francesca asked.

"I'm vice president of Logistics for a big company in New York," Lily explained, taking welcome refuge in her Heigelmann's persona. "That means I'm in charge of transporting our product from its factory bases on the Eastern Seaboard all around the rest of the United States. We move more than eighteen million units a month, so it's very important that everything gets to where it's going on time so our customers can buy it and we can meet our budget forecasts. That's up to me."

"Oh," Francesca asked, licking her spoon. "What's a unit?"

"A unit is one of our products. We have more than 185 different products and they're all coded, contained, and shipped out separately."

"But what are they?" Francesca persisted.

"They're a single item," Lily continued. "A single product item is what we call in English a *unit*. If we made spoons like the one you are holding, it wouldn't be called a spoon in any meetings we had about it, it would be called a unit."

"*Allora*, English is complicated," the little girl said. "I still don't understand. *Capito*, Mario? *Io non capisco*."

"I think she wants to know why you don't just call it a spoon," Mario said.

"I haven't explained it very well, have I? We don't actually make spoons so I'm confusing you."

"But what do you make? That's what I mean," Francesca asked.

"Well, we make a lot of things but they are all basically some sort of premixed or premade consumer comestible," Lily explained, losing faith in her Heigelmann's persona, which was proving to be of little help in present company.

Francesca stared at her a moment, then turned to Mario.

"Is she speaking a different language?"

He shook his head. "I don't think so, but I don't know what she's talking about either," he said. "What's a comestible?"

"I suppose it is a different language," Lily said. "A comestible is something you can eat."

"Oh! What is premix?" asked Francesca.

"Premixed is where we have done most of the work in the factory and all you have to do at home is just tip it out of a carton or a package and finish it. So if you want to make a cake, for example, you buy a packet of our cake mix instead of having to buy all the separate ingredients like flour and sugar and . . ." She thought of the painstaking torment Violetta went to in making her *cantucci* and wondered if perhaps baking mixes hadn't taken off in Italy.

"Or, you might buy your biscotti, your *cantucci* dough, premade in a tube and frozen, and all you have to do is slice it up, bake it again, and then you have your *cantucci*."

"You make *cantucci* in America?" Francesca asked, finally grasping something. "Like you do at Violetta's shop?"

"I'm not making *cantucci* at Violetta's shop, sweetie, I'm just staying there, and anyway, at home we call them cookies and they come in all sorts of different flavors like chocolate chip or peanut butter or lemon cranberry—that's new by the way. But I certainly don't make them myself there, either."

"But that's your work!"

"No, no, no, my work is in an office, really, just organizing and arranging things and going to meetings and actually probably not very exciting at all to a little girl like you."

"But I would like to make the cookies with you, Lillian. That would be exciting! Would we do that? In the Ferretti sisters' kitchen? Would we?"

Lily laughed. "No, sweetie, I don't have any of the cookie mix with me and even if I did . . ."

She felt that little door in her mind swinging open and closed again. What was behind it?

"But before you had this product of the units with the premix you must have made them with the natural ingredients, no?" Mario asked. "With flour, sugar—you know, all the old-fashioned things?" He had gone a bit sour on her, Lily thought, which was perhaps not so surprising since everything here was *fatto o mano*. But at home, well, that was the way the world had gone with Heigelmann's pushing it every step of the way. Mixes were cheaper and quicker, and statistics had told her, had told everyone, that nothing beat cheaper and quicker.

Francesca was next to Lily now, fairy wings trembling slightly as she pleaded at her elbow. "Please, please, please, Lillian Watson, can we make the American cookies together?"

"I don't know how," she told Francesca. "I just don't know how."

"You never made them when you were a little girl like me?" Francesca asked.

Lily looked into the little face turned up at her now and saw that it might have borne Daniel's features, but it wore Lily's own girlhood longing; for love, for attention, for everything to just be normal.

Francesca's mother was locked in her house popping pills and crying over a doomed romance with the wrong man. Wasn't that Lily's own history? Her mother slapping, cursing, crying . . . there it was again—that unexpected pleasant sensation wafting into her consciousness, the same one she got from the ceiling in her room and the smell of the Ferrettis' kitchen.

A glimmer of light shone through the door in her memory. Could it be . . . ?

"Yes, I think I maybe did make them when I was a little girl like you," she said gently, unable to keep herself from reaching out and stroking the smooth brown skin on Francesca's cheek. "Oatmeal cookies. They were my sister's favorite."

"I wanted Ernesto to be a sister," Francesca said. "But he turned out a boy."

"Well, I'm sure you will love him anyway, just like I love my sister," Lily said, and she had never felt more like a coward and a fake.

"Maybe does your sister know how to make the oatmeal cookies?" Francesca asked. "We could get her to show us."

"She doesn't live here, honey. She's in America."

"But you could call her," Francesca insisted. "Or you could e-mail her or SMS her."

"I could," Lily said, softly. The modern world made it very difficult to not get in touch with people. You just had to want to.

"Well?" Francesca asked. "Can you? Ask her? Pleeeease? Can we make the cookies together? Pretty please?"

Making cookies was the last thing Lily felt willing or able to do, but the truth was that a woman could not spend half a lifetime dreaming of having a small child beg for her company and then, when she found one, turn her down.

"You know what?" she said. "Of course we can. I'll find the recipe somehow, and then you and I will make oatmeal cookies."

The smile on Francesca's face was worth all the mess she

could ever make in the Ferrettis' kitchen—and even a medium-size but perhaps controllable fire.

A less controllable fire was the one she was in danger of igniting by getting so close to Francesca's mother and aunt.

"You want me to check with someone that it's OK for you to come by?" she asked.

"I can do that," Mario said, to Lily's relief. "With Carlotta I mean. She will appreciate the help, I am sure. You know when you can do this?"

"Let's say eleven, tomorrow, unless I let you know otherwise. Carlotta won't be worried that she doesn't know me, that I'm a stranger?"

"You are not that strange, signora. You should see some of the other people who have stayed at the *pasticceria*. And you're good with her," Mario said, nodding at Francesca. "That's all Carlotta will care about."

He was a little sweet on Carlotta, Lily thought, trying not to swell with pride at being "good" with this child who was so close to being hers—yet also so far away.

"I'm going to make cookies!" Francesca hooted. "American oatmeal cookies!" And she danced out the door and up the street.

Chapter 29

With every step Violetta took across the *pasticceria* in the direction of the next meeting of the Secret League of Widowed Darners she felt her confidence drain and collect at her swollen ankles like wrinkles in her stockings.

The League had given her so much to live for over the past decades; all those broken hearts patched up and sent on their way. So many futures! So much hope! And now, this spectacular failure with Alessandro was going to bring her to her knees—the very ones currently clicking and clattering like the useless giant knuckle bones they were.

Lily was not the one for Alessandro, that was now painfully plain as day. Violetta should have confessed when Luciana's toe first throbbed that her itch was nowhere to be found. She should have admitted there was no orange blossom.

Then Alessandro would have talked to Lily at the side of the road without the slightest thing being made of it, and this poor wretched woman could have proceeded to find her cheating husband and sort out whatever mess she was in.

Instead, Violetta's foolish pride had placed Lily in the way of the widows' favorite prospect, and when they found out, they would skin Violetta alive and make garter belts out of her for it would look to them as though she herself had broken Alessandro's heart all over again.

"You have the face of a fish that's been passed up on market day," Luciana said as they approached the secret shelf and worked together to push it aside.

"Will you shut up and leave me alone!" exploded Violetta. "You have no idea how much I have to worry about right now. There's Alessandro, there's the *cantucci*, there's your bones and my chest and everyone's ears and eyes and Santa Ana di Chisa knows what else! You're all very happy to leave everything up to me but when there's a problem, I'm on my own and I'm sick of it. I'm thoroughly sick of it."

With this, the shelf slid open and she stepped into the darkened recess, shaking with rage and fear.

Luciana, startled at her sister's outburst, was slow to follow, so Violetta grabbed her by the sleeve and pulled at her. But on stepping over the threshold Luciana stumbled, her foot twisted sideways on the narrow top step, and her weak wrist did not have the strength to hold on to the slippery handrail or keep her upright against the wall.

In front of Violetta's eyes she toppled silently like a sack full of soft potatoes to the landing six steps beneath them.

"No, no, no!" cried Violetta, scrabbling down as quickly as she was able behind her. "Oh, no, no, no!"

Luciana lay in a still heap. She looked so small. They were disappearing, the two of them, but she wasn't ready to disappear yet, and she was even less ready for Luciana to.

She creakily lowered herself to the landing floor, sat beside her crumpled sister, and with trembling fingers, turned her face. Luciana's eyes were closed, her face motionless. It was impossible to tell if she was breathing.

"Please don't die, Lulu," she begged, stroking the papery skin on her face. "Please don't shut up and leave me alone. I can't do it without you. I just can't."

Her sister lay unmoving, no rising of her lumpy little chest, no flicker in her wrinkled eyelids.

"We're in this together, Lulu," Violetta said, taking Luciana's warm, limp hand. "We always have been. And we've lived through worse, my dear little sister. We've lived through much worse. We lived through our darlings being taken away from us. And before that we lived through me getting our darlings mixed up, which you let me fix, my little sweetheart, and which you forgave me for all those years ago. So many years ago! We decided then that sticking together was more important than anything else in the whole wide world and I'm sorry about the *cantucci*. I'm sorry if I've been stubborn. I'm sorry if I haven't been listening to you. I'm scared, that's all. I'm scared of what's happening to me, of what I'm losing, of the life that seems to be draining out of me with every breath I take. I'm scared of not being wanted, of not being useful, of not being here. But more than any of that, I'm scared of not having you, Lulu. Of not having you. So please, please, please wake up. Please."

And Luciana, who even when she was unconscious really did just want to please her big sister, obligingly woke up.

"We need help, Violetta," she croaked. "We need help."

Chapter 30

Despite the recent embarrassment in Pienza and the bowlful of triple chocolate gelato, the lure of Poliziano proved too strong. Lily slid into the light-filled café, avoiding the romantic table, and ordered a glass of prosecco.

Daniel, Eugenia, Francesca, Rose—the complications of her life sat around the table with her like ghosts, their backs to the green, fertile valley falling into the distance behind them.

She drained her drink so quickly, she barely tasted it. Baking cookies? What hat was she going to pull that out of? She blinked away her invisible unwanted guests and looked around.

The café was all but empty, just a couple of tourists sitting in a far corner looking through the photos on their camera and one fidgety old lady at the next table.

"Another prosecco, *per favore*," Lily ordered when the waitress came to fill her water glass, but when she returned, it was not with a drink but, to Lily's horror, with a glass dish full of tiramisu.

Lily reared back from it. "No, no, no, this is not mine," she said, pointing to the old woman sitting near her. "It must be hers."

The waitress looked confused, then rattled off something in Italian to the old lady.

"She says you can have it if you want it," the waitress said, but Lily was on her feet already, moving toward the door.

"No, thank you, I'm good," she insisted, not waiting for her check but flinging money on the counter next to the cash register. "I'm good."

Another tiramisu incident she did not need, so it was with some relief that she soon pushed open the door of the *pasticceria* and stopped for a moment in the quiet coolness of the dark sweet-smelling room.

The familiar bowls of old, silent *cantucci* sat on their thrones, soaking up the light through the store front window.

"Eeoooooh," the big blue bowl directly facing her said. "Eeeeeeooooh."

Lily jumped back, heart thumping. She had only one glass of wine. How could this be happening again?

"Eeooooh," she heard again. And again. And yet again. But that was it. No admonishment, nothing she recognized as a life instruction, just a distant call. She took a step closer to the bowl. The noise continued, but it wasn't coming from the *cantucci* itself, it was coming from behind the counter.

Gingerly, she stepped farther forward and peered over it. There was nothing there.

"Eeeeeoooh," she heard again, but now that she was closer, she realized it seemed to be coming from the dusty shelves against the back wall.

She slipped around the counter and inspected them more closely.

"Eeeeeoooooh! Eeeeeoooooh!" It was coming from behind the dusty shelves.

Lily had little time for hauntings or Hogwarts. It had only been one glass, she reminded herself. There would be a logical explanation. She was not making this up. It was really happening. "Hello?" she called out. "Hello!"

"Lily!" came the reply. It sounded like Violetta. Stuck behind the shelves?

"Yes, it's Lily," she shouted at the wall. "Where are you?"

"Slide! Slide!"

"Slide?" Lily repeated, wondering what that meant in English. "What do you mean?"

"Slide! Slide the shelves. Across."

Lily pushed her shoulder against the dusty shelves and with hardly any effort, sure enough they slid across and revealed a tiny dark stairway.

"You speak English?" Lily asked as her eyes got used to the dark. "All this time you've been able to . . ."

Violetta was sitting on the landing below, gently patting what looked like a pile of rags.

"She is hurt," the old woman said. "Luciana is hurt."

"I'll call an ambulance," Lily said, turning away.

"No! We must lift her," Violetta said. "Upstairs. To the bed."

"Seriously, you shouldn't move her. It could make her worse."

"She does not want ambulance. She wants the bed."

"I really think I should—"

"Please! Help me," Violetta pleaded. "Lift."

There seemed no point in arguing further, and once she'd negotiated the awkward task of picking up the crumpled old woman in the tight space, it was easy to carry her up to the kitchen and put her carefully on the bed.

"She weighs next to nothing," Lily said. "I think I should call the ambulance now, Violetta, really."

"I will take care of her," Violetta insisted.

"You might not be enough. She needs expert help."

"I am enough!" Violetta argued angrily, but as she picked up Luciana's limp hand and rubbed it, tears fell down her crinkled cheeks. "Please, please wake up, Lulu," she said in Italian. "Please, please, wake up again."

Lily did not need to understand what she was saying to get the picture. She put her hand on Violetta's small, shaking shoulder.

"I can see you love your sister very much," she said gently. "And I know you want what's best for her so I'm going to call an ambulance now."

Violetta opened her mouth to protest—ambulances only went to the microwave and that was more often than not a one-way trip—but as she started to speak she felt Luciana squeeze her hand, feebly at first but then more firmly.

"You promised me," her sister croaked, eyes still closed. "You promised."

Violetta looked up and nodded, at which Lily ran to the Hotel Adesso where she told the hotel receptionist what had happened and ensured that an ambulance was called.

When she returned to the sisters' kitchen, Violetta was still sitting on the side of the bed holding Luciana's hand, but her bedside manner had taken a turn for the worse. She was shouting at her sister in Italian.

"Violetta, please!" Lily urged. "The poor woman's taken a terrible fall!"

"She should watch where she is going! This is what I am telling her."

Luciana opened her eyes then and limply muttered something, which her sister responded to with another robust chastisement.

"Perhaps you could quarrel with her when she comes back from the hospital," Lily suggested. "She's weak now. She's had a shock. She could be badly hurt. Now is not the time for arguing."

Violetta narrowed her eyes. When she came back from the hospital? Hah! "At our age, there might not be another time," she said, but still, her voice caught.

"Isn't that all the more reason not to argue now?" Lily suggested.

"But if we do not argue, how do we know what the other one

is thinking?" Violetta asked. "We argue for nearly a hundred years and this is noisy, yes, but there is never confusion. She knows how I feel. I know how she feels."

The rare sound of a motor vehicle approaching filled the room, and moments later two paramedics entered. Under Violetta's cantankerous supervision, they maneuvered Luciana onto a stretcher and carried her out into the street—which looked to Lily only an inch wider than the ambulance.

Indeed the vehicle was so small that when Violetta tried to get in the back, the paramedics waved her away, saying there wasn't enough room for her and she should meet them at the hospital.

This did not go down at all well.

"I'm sure they will take very good care of her there," Lily said helpfully, moving closer to the little woman as the ambulance drove off down the hill at a perilous speed considering how close it was to the walls on either side.

"Pah! Good care? This is not what our hospital is known for," Violetta said, and although she sounded angry, her wrinkled cheeks were wet with fresh tears.

"I am lost without her," she said, and a sob escaped, although it sounded a bit like a teaspoon going down the garbage disposal. "I am lost."

Her words echoed around Lily's tightly squeezed heart.

She took Violetta's hand and led her inside, sat her at the kitchen table, and got her a glass of water, unsure what to do next until a neighbor popped up at the kitchen window obviously wanting to know what was going on.

"She will take me to see Luciana," Violetta explained to Lily at the end of the conversation, her face smaller and paler with every word.

The elderly neighbor seemed happy to be in charge, and her

landlady thus taken care of, Lily went upstairs and sat in her picture window, breathing in beautiful Tuscany, mulling over the chaotic events of the day and slowly letting the door in her memory open long and wide enough for her to see what lay behind it.

Chapter 31

Ingrid and Daniel meandered away from the river up the Via Tornabuoni.

It had moved her, almost unbearably, to hear him talk about the nightmare of returning his almost-adopted baby, but he himself seemed a little distanced from it. There was more to this sad story, she was sure.

"So what happened?" she asked as they slowed down outside one of the designer shops for her to admire the window display. "Your wife fell out of love with you after she gave up on having children?"

"She fell out of everything," Daniel said. "I think I was just included in the package."

"You think she was depressed?"

"No, I don't think so. She just got more involved in her work—she's a VP at Heigelmann's—started exercising a lot, being at home less. Keeping busy, I guess, until we seemed to be living almost separate lives. It's not as though we argued or anything. We just stopped being together."

"Were you trying?"

"I don't know."

"What do you mean you don't know?"

"It's complicated."

"Well, maybe it doesn't have to be. I mean do you still love her?"

"Ingrid, I still love her so much I can hardly get out of bed in the mornings knowing how badly I've screwed it all up."

Aha, thought Ingrid. *Here it comes.*

"Oh? And how did you manage that?" she asked lightly, dawdling in front of the next sumptuous window display.

"I made a mistake."

"Well, you wouldn't be the first person to do that."

"It was a colossal mistake."

"How colossal?"

"I met someone."

"Well, that's hardly—"

"She got pregnant. I have a six-year-old daughter and to all intents and purposes a two-year-old boy in Montevedova."

This stopped Ingrid in her tracks.

"You want to slap me, I know you do," Daniel said. "And I deserve it, but the truth is, it couldn't make me feel worse than I already do. It is the worst betrayal, the greatest deceit, the lowest of the low. I know all this. Trust me, I know."

They stood there, looking at each other for a few frigid moments, then Ingrid raised her arm, but not to slap him. Instead she held a cool hand against his cheek. It burned as though she had struck it. He was perhaps the saddest man she'd ever met.

"The woman in Montevedova," she said.

"It was nothing—a weak moment."

"But the children make it difficult."

He nodded. "It's complicated, but I can't abandon their mother, and because of that, I can't be happy with my wife."

"Are you sure about that?"

"I have everything that Lily wants only I have it with someone that precludes her from having anything to do with it. I've tossed the options up in my head a thousand times, but I still don't know what to do."

"What's wrong with things the way they are?"

"Eugenia is what's wrong with things the way they are. She's given me an ultimatum—shape up or ship out. I've wanted to ship out since the very beginning, but once Francesca came along . . . Eugenia has problems. She is not robust. She needs a lot of help."

"So what are you doing here in Florence?" Ingrid asked.

Daniel had nothing left to hide.

"I'm running away," he told her.

"Now I could slap you," she said as the crowd rippled and flowed around them. "Running away never solved a problem for anyone, you know that. I think you know exactly what you have to do, you just need someone to agree with you."

He thought then how lucky her three sons were to have her for a mother.

"Come on," Ingrid said. "Let's go get a drink and make a plan. You need to go back and sort your life out."

Chapter 32

Thankfully there was no one in Montevedova's only phone booth, because Lily needed just the slightest excuse for her courage to abandon her, but once inside the dusty little box she quickly dialed Rose's phone number and held her breath as it rang.

"Hello, Harry speaking," a youthful voice tinkled down the line from across the ocean.

"Hello, sweetie, it's your aunt Lily here," she said, unable to keep the tremor from her voice. "How are you doing?"

"Good," he said. "I can read almost as fast as Jack now, but he's much better at soccer."

"I'm so happy for you, honey. That is such great news. You're such a big boy now! Hey, is your mom there?"

She heard the phone drop to the floor and Harry roar into the background that Lily was on the phone, that he'd told her about the reading and the soccer.

Rose was there in a moment.

"Lily? Is that really you?"

"It is, yes, I'm in Tuscany."

"Oh my God, I can't believe it! You sound like you're just around the corner. AL! TAKE THE KIDS OUTSIDE AND DON'T COME BACK UNTIL I TELL YOU TO, I'M ON THE PHONE TO LILY IN ITALY. YES, ITALY! So what happened? Did you find Daniel? What's it like? How are you?"

"I'm fine but I didn't find Daniel. He's not here."

"Not in Italy?"

"I'm not sure, but he's not in the place where I thought he would be, where he usually is, where I am now."

"And what about the floozy?"

"Well, she's here, but to be honest, she hardly fits the floozy bill. It's a long story but I think Daniel has run out on her as well."

"You're kidding me," breathed Rose. "Are you sure?"

"Yes. No! Actually, I don't know. I have absolutely no idea. I'm just not—God, Rose, I just can't believe this is Daniel we're talking about. My Daniel. What happened? One minute we're just us, an ordinary happily married couple, and the next it's like being in one of those awful dreams where everything just keeps getting worse and worse but I can't even wake up. I'm stuck in this. I'm completely stuck."

"Oh, honey, I can't imagine what you're going through," her sister said, and the truth of that burrowed into Lily's untapped loneliness so swiftly it floored her.

No one knew what she was going through. No one ever had. Other people might have suffered the same sorts of losses as she had, but other people weren't her. They did not know what it had done to her. They did not know how hard it was, how hard it always had been, to manage her survival. She was so tired of it.

"Those babies, Rose," she whispered. Those beautiful lost babies. Little slips of hope and prayer that had almost delivered her everything she dreamed of.

Survival? The world she'd built to keep from pining for those lost babies crumbled inside that phone booth right then and there—and Lily with it. She slid down the wall, collapsing on the dirty floor.

"I'm so sorry, Rose," she sobbed. "It's all my fault. Everything is my fault. I just couldn't bear to see you being so happy with your children when I couldn't even have one of my own. I'm so sorry, I really am, and if I could turn back the clock I would, but I've missed you so much. I really have and I'm so sorry."

Her head in her hands, she pushed the phone to her ear as though it were Rose herself.

"Oh, Lily," her sister said. "Please, I'm sorry too. I could have fixed it myself, you know, but I didn't. You're the one who fixes things and so I left it to you, but I shouldn't have, so we are both at fault. And I might have all these kids, but the truth is I've envied your life too. I SAID OUTSIDE, AL, ALL OF YOU! I've envied your beautiful clothes not covered in spit, your varicose vein–free legs, your tiny little figure, all your sleep, the quiet. Seems you never want exactly what you have, no matter what that is. And the way I feel about Al right now I'd give anything for him to run away with someone else, only I wouldn't even go looking. I'd move houses so if he ever brought his sorry ass back home again, he wouldn't find me."

Lily sniffed. "You are joking, I hope."

"Honey, sometimes all you can do is joke. Don't worry about us, we'll be fine as soon as these kids grow up and get scholarships to good universities and leave and never come back. It's you we need to worry about."

"I need you, Rose," Lily said. "I really need you. Without Daniel there isn't a single soul who gives a damn about me."

"I give a damn, Lily, and you only need one single soul that does. That's all any of us needs—just one person who'll walk on hot coals for them."

"I thought it was him!"

"I know you did, sweetie. I know you did. And it was, too, but right now it's not. It's me."

"But you're there and I'm here!"

"That doesn't matter. It's not like I have to tie your shoelaces. I just need to be rooting for you wherever you are; that's what you told me when we were kids and you were going off to middle school. Remember? I can help you from here, Lily. I can help you from anywhere. Just tell me what's your plan?"

"I don't have one," Lily cried. "At first I thought maybe I'd find him and make him come home, then I thought I'd just come home without him and either file for divorce or pretend nothing had ever happened. But then I met his daughter, Rose, and now I don't know what to do. Her name's Francesca, she's nearly seven and she looks so much like him, you wouldn't believe it. And she's great, she's really great, but the mother—the floozy who isn't really a floozy—is a total mess and Daniel's missing in action so . . . oh, it's all screwed up."

"Oh, brother," Rose breathed. "I could kick his polo-shirt-wearing ass!"

"You don't like the polo shirts?"

"I don't like them now!" Rose exclaimed. "I don't like anything about him now. You must hate him. You must want to snap his neck in half or take to him with a pick axe."

"I can't even find him," Lily protested. "I'm not even sure I'm looking for him. And I know about the pick axe and maybe I will feel like using one when I see him, but before I can hate him I just need to know why he would do this to me, why he ruined everything and why he's still ruining it. If that seems weird and not evil enough or whatever—it's just that if you could see Francesca, you wouldn't want to kill her father either. She's so young and, I don't know. This could really mess with her. Look how having our so-called father hardly ever there messed with us."

"Lily, it wasn't not having a father that messed with us. It was having our mother."

"But Francesca's mother is a wreck too! And if Daniel abandons those kids . . ."

"Listen, Lily, don't jump the gun too much. We might not have led the life of fairy-tale princesses, but we actually turned out OK."

"Well, you can say that now, but you know how horrible it was back then and it's just that Francesca is so—I can't explain it, Rose. She's just at that age where she could be anything she wanted but she could also be crushed."

"That's every kid in the world, Lily. They're all fragile little eggs whose shells can be broken."

"Or not, Rose. Or not. I guess she reminds me of me, of you and me. Actually, she's sort of why I'm calling. She wants me to teach her how to make oatmeal cookies." A hard ball of something indescribable rose up from somewhere below Lily's heart, squeezing it as small as it could, then pushing its way past to her throat. "We used to make them with Mom, right?"

"Oatmeal cookies? With Mom? Yeah, right!"

"The thing is, Rose, I keep having the strangest feeling, this weird sort of half a memory."

"Half a memory is generally enough in our case, Lily. The woman was a monster. Especially to you. A monster. Don't go there."

"Rose, she had an apron. It was pale blue and it had little yellow and mauve flowers on it with greeny sort of ivy winding around them. Do you remember?"

There was a long silence. "No, I don't."

"Before he left for good, Rose, before the drinking and the hitting and—"

"And the kicking," Rose butted in. "Don't forget the kicking."

Lily blinked as a tiny torn piece of memory fluttered into a corner of her mind. It wafted from side to side before settling long enough for her to grab hold of it. She saw Rose's chubby legs in Mary Janes standing on the kitchen chair. She saw the footstool next to it.

"Before all of that, Rose, she had this pale blue apron with little yellow and mauve flowers and she bought us our own special spoons and you stood on a chair and I was on a foot stool and we made cookies with her."

"I don't remember," Rose whispered.

Lily pushed away the memory of ice clattering into a glass, the crackle as warm gin hit the frozen cubes, the jangle of her mother's bracelets as she lifted the glass to her bright red lips again and again and again.

"Before all that, Rose," she said, shutting her eyes against the pain of the hair being pulled from her head, the welts on her legs, the bruises on her arms.

"Before all that, we made cookies with her, I remember, and she was laughing and dancing around the kitchen and she kept kissing us, Rose, and telling us how pretty we were, and she was beautiful. And happy. She made frosting and we were allowed to eat it in spoonfuls out of the bowl. And I think she loved us then, Rose. I think then she really loved us."

"I'm crazy about frosting," Rose said, crying softly. "I've always been crazy about frosting. And she must have at least really liked us. You don't bake cookies with kids unless you really like them. I know this. They make such an unholy mess of the kitchen."

Lily laughed—an impossibly light, unfettered sound that seemed totally unfamiliar to her. "We did turn out OK, didn't we?"

"It's going to be all right, Lily," Rose sniffed from across the world. "Everything is going to be all right."

Chapter 33

It was a small subdued collection of widows waiting in the church basement when Fiorella made it there at the end of the day.

"I just passed Lily in the phone booth by the piazza," she said. "Should someone have been snooping?"

"Luciana's had a fall," a white-faced widow Pacini reported. "She's in the microwave and Violetta's in there with her."

"That will be the end of her," the widow Ercolani added. "That will be the end of both of them."

"What was Lily doing in the phone booth?" the widow Benedicti asked. "Was she talking to Alessandro?"

"Never mind that," said the widow Pacini, "it's the Ferrettis we need to think about now. If they don't make it out of the microwave, what will happen to the League? Violetta has always made the big decisions and without her . . . well, it hardly bears thinking about."

"At least no one will have to eat their *cantucci* anymore," Fiorella said. "That stuff is the pits."

"How dare you!" The widow Ciacci rose to her full height of just about five feet tall and pointed a shaky finger at Fiorella. "How dare you waltz in here and start criticizing the Ferretti *cantucci*. It has been eaten by popes, I'll have you know. By popes! It is the best in Tuscany and it always will be and for you to suggest otherwise when poor Luciana is in that place and may never come out again, well, it's disgusting. You should be ashamed. Poor Violetta, if Luciana goes, she is sure to follow. And then where will we be? Where will any of us be!" She collapsed on a chair, her face in her hands, and the widow Mazzetti shuffled over to put an arm around her shoulders, glaring at Fiorella.

"Sorry, sorry, sorry, didn't mean to offend," Fiorella said, pushing her glasses up on her nose and sniffing. "Boy, sure smells musty down here," she added, by way of a diversion.

"She can still smell?" whispered one widow to another.

"Yes, you're right, it is musty," agreed a third.

"We should buy some of those air fresheners that girl with the thick legs and the moustache sells," the widow Ciacci said. "You know the one. She and her mother and grandmother still have all their husbands and that tiny little boutique the English people go crazy for just behind here. Make everything themselves."

"Please, ladies!" cried the widow Benedicti. "Enough! What of Alessandro?"

"Yes, quite," agreed Fiorella. "Lily wasn't talking to him on the phone."

"How do you know?" asked the widow Del Grasso.

"I speak English," answered Fiorella. "I learned it on the Internet. German too."

"So who was she talking to?" asked the widow Benedicti.

"Her sister in America," Fiorella reported. "I think they have had some sort of a bust-up, although it's not like the sister ran away to Naples with her husband or anything, but there seems to have been a *rapprochement*. That's French, by the way. I speak *un peu* of that too."

"She is a pain," the widow Ercolani mouthed to the widow Pacini, pointing at Fiorella.

"I heard that," said Fiorella, although in fact she had seen it reflected in the screen on the League's long-defunct TV screen.

The widow Ercolani buttoned her lips.

"So, she was talking to her sister in America," the widow Benedicti interceded. "What does that have to do with Alessandro?"

Having clearly heard Lily speak of a cheating husband and his Italian daughter, Fiorella was putting two and two together regarding Lily and Alessandro, but she knew enough to know that now was not the time to elaborate.

"She was talking about baking cookies," she said. "That's what Americans call biscotti. It's English. Maybe she's going to help out the Ferrettis while they're indisposed."

"Indisposed?" scoffed the widow Ercolani. "Being disposed of, more likely."

One lot of tongue-holding was enough for Fiorella. "You know, you've got it all wrong about that hospital," she said. "I had my hip done last year and look at me."

She did a little waltz around the room, ending with a jaunty kick ball change. "And you know something else? The food in there was delicious. Three meals a day brought to you in your bed and every single one *squisito*."

"You were in the hospital?" the widow Ciacci asked. "And you came out again?"

"It's like a four-star hotel," insisted Fiorella. "I wanted to stay longer but they made me go home."

"Don't listen to her," the widow Ercolani said. "She's trying to get rid of us all."

"Well, I can imagine wanting to get rid of you," said Fiorella, "but I kinda like the rest of them."

Before this could develop into anything more vocal, the widow Benedicti stepped into the middle of the group and held up her hands. "Never mind all that," she said. "Our thoughts and prayers—take pity on us Santa Ana di Chisa—are obviously with the Ferrettis right now, but we must not forget Alessandro. We need to get him and Lily together again as soon as possible. It's what we are here for. It's what Violetta would want."

"I'm not so sure about that," Fiorella said, but the widow Mazzetti made her "zip it" gesture, the widow Ercolani balled her sizable hands into fists at her side, and the widow Ciacci made the sign of the cross and put her face back in her hands.

"I can get Alessandro into the village for a couple of hours tomorrow around, say, midday," the widow Benedicti said. "All I need to do is send him to Alberto's to get some nonexistent liqueur for my *crostata*. So if a couple of you tail him, and a couple more tail Lily, we should be able to herd them together and let nature—and true love—take its course."

Benedicti looked pleased with herself. It wasn't so hard what Violetta did after all. But the other widows looked doubtfully at each other.

Who among them could last long tailing anyone these days?

Chapter 34

Oatmeal, it seemed, or more specifically, rolled oats, had never made it as far as the hilltop towns of Tuscany. Nobody in Montevedova knew what Lily was talking about, or could find an Italian word to help her further seek it, and she was inept when it came to miming what an oat was. For a start, she didn't really know what an oat was.

Finally, a charmless supermarket in an industrial strip mall outside a neighboring village coughed up the requisite bowls, measuring devices, and most of the remaining ingredients but still, no rolled oats.

At least there she bumped into an English woman who said she had lived in Italy for the better part of twenty years and had never found anything resembling them.

"So what do you use instead?" Lily asked.

"When in Rome . . ." laughed the English woman. "I used to have oatmeal for breakfast and now I have a pastry like everyone else."

Lily pondered this until she came to a quirky little collection of discounted bits and pieces piled in a torn carton between the cheese graters and the oven mitts.

She was in Rome herself, wasn't she, she thought, as she picked through the box, finding something that brought a smile as wide as Francesca's to her own face. She would make Italian cookies—with an American twist.

Back at the bakeshop there had been no sign of Violetta since she had gone to the hospital, but Lily could not imagine her having an objection to the kitchen being used. She busied herself getting the ingredients ready and at eleven on the dot heard the bell above the *pasticceria* door ring.

When she emerged into the store, a fierce-looking Carlotta was standing there clutching Francesca's hand. The little girl still had her tatty wings on, but her hair had been brushed and she was wearing a different dress, a little too big for her, but clean.

Lily smiled but she was nervous, not so much about the baking—although she had every reason to be—but at putting herself deliberately so close to Daniel's lover's sister.

"Hello, sweetie pie," she said to Francesca, her smooth corporate charm kicking in as she thanked Carlotta for bringing her.

Carlotta chewed her lip, then said something to Francesca, who shrugged and looked up at Lily.

"She says she knows who you are."

"I'm sorry?" Lily was unsure whether this meant she knew from Mario that she was the cookie maker or knew some other way that she was Daniel's wife. "*Non capito?*"

Carlotta spoke again to Francesca who impatiently translated: "She says she knows who you are and that my mamma is very sick and she doesn't want any trouble."

The two women locked eyes and it occurred to Lily that what she had initially taken for aggression in Carlotta could actually be something less threatening. She had brought Francesca to her, after all.

"Tell her I don't want any trouble either," Lily said. "Tell her we are just going to have some fun and make some cookies, and we won't be bothering your mamma at all."

Francesca repeated this as Carlotta and Lily continued to hold each other's gaze.

She is just worried about her sister, thought Lily. *She is doing whatever she can to help her even if it means leaving Francesca with me.* It could just as easily be Rose fighting for Lily. This fiery Carlotta was not fierce, she was frightened.

Lily smiled and a secret sort of understanding passed between the two women.

Carlotta bent down to say something to Francesca and gave her a kiss.

"She says could you bring me to her place when we are finished," the little girl repeated, wriggling out of her grasp and skipping behind the counter with Lily. "I'll show you the way."

"But the baby," Lily asked Francesca, thinking suddenly of those fat striped legs at home with Eugenia. "Can you ask her what's happening with the baby?"

"He's not a baby," Francesca said, sulkily. "He's nearly three."

"Well, could you ask for me anyway," Lily urged and she duly did so, reporting back that Ernesto was none of her concern.

"None of my concern?" Lily repeated, looking at Carlotta, whose brown eyes stayed just as troubled as she shook her head and repeated: *"Non è il suo interesse."*

"You should be glad," Francesca said. "He cries almost as much as Mamma. And he smells."

"I don't understand," Lily said, but Carlotta just repeated what she had said, then, with a toss of that wild head of hair, bustled out the door and up the Corso.

Lily had set everything up in the kitchen just the way Rose had recommended to make it easy in case she got flustered or anything went wrong, which was what she fully expected. The old Italian sisters might just pull things out of the pantry and plunk them on the table, but Lily was not going to go quite so *alle naturale.*

At first she tried mixing the flour and sugar together with a handy little wandlike electric gadget, but the dry mixture flew out of the new bowl with alarming ferocity, making Francesca shriek and spreading flour as far as the walls. Next time, they mixed it the old-fashioned way, with a spoon.

"Now, we add the *uova*," Lily announced with more confidence than she felt.

Her first attempt at breaking an egg ended up with most the shell in the mixture and at least half the egg on the table. Her second one was not much better. The third time, she handed the chore over to Francesca, who at first refused to have anything to do with it, then reluctantly tapped the egg with exaggerated care on the side of the bowl, only for the whole thing to smash and explode across the table and slither toward the edge, an evil yellow alien. At this point Francesca pounced on it to stop its progress but knocked the rest of the carton of eggs onto the floor as well. Eight of them landed upside down and splattered on the stone and the ninth plopped rudely onto one of Lily's shoes and oozed across her toes into a brilliant yellow puddle.

Francesca leapt away from the table, her hands held aloft, and Lily would have laughed but immediately saw that this was not a comic turn. It was not mischief in those pale green eyes; it was something else altogether, something that struck a chord in her own long-lost seven-year-old self.

Francesca was looking at her with dread. "I'm very sorry," she whispered, on the verge of tears. "I didn't mean to. I'm very sorry, Lillian."

Lily's heart sank to the tips of her egg-dipped loafers.

In that instant, she understood something monumental. Not about herself or Daniel or their marriage or his girlfriend or her mother or her own hidden fears and buried secrets. Not, in fact, about anything in the past, hers or anyone else's. What she understood was about the future—that the future could be changed if only someone knew that it had to be. "You only need one person who will walk on hot coals for you," her wise, warm, precious baby sister had only just told her. Just one person.

"Oh, these pesky *uova*," she said to Francesca, picking up a fresh egg from a new carton. "Don't you just hate it when they do that? You know, it's almost like they do it on purpose because they know we are beginners, but we can show them a thing or two. Oh, yes. We can show them who's boss, that's what I think. Do you know, when I was younger I used to be able to juggle?"

"Juggle?"

"Yes, you know, like a clown."

"With great big shoes and a red nose?"

"Oh, I can manage the red nose every now and then, but mostly I just do it like this."

With that she picked three eggs up and threw the first in the air, followed by the second and the third, but instead of catching them in her other hand, she just let them fall—*splat, splat, splat*—on to the floor.

"There! Take that, you wicked eggs," Lily berated the mess. "I'll only catch you if I feel like it and don't you forget it."

Francesca stared at her in wide-eyed disbelief.

"Wanna try?" Lily asked, holding a fresh egg out to her. "We have plenty more. And it feels really good."

Gingerly, Francesca took an egg, then another, and threw them both in the air at the same time. Then she stood back and hid her face, screeching when they exploded at her feet.

Nearly two dozen eggs later, Lily's old hand-eye coordination skills were all coming back to her while Francesca had given up tossing the eggs in the air and was working out how to gently crack them against the side of a smaller bowl and extract the contents neatly from the shells.

The kitchen looked like an omelet festival gone horribly wrong, but the atmosphere was otherwise one of contained triumph.

"You know what, I think we have shown them a thing or two, don't you?" Lily stood back, trying not to beam too proudly, as Francesca neatly broke another egg into the bowl.

The little girl nodded, a modest smile tweaking the corners of her mouth.

Having mastered the art of egg-breaking, they moved on to mixing in the hazelnuts and rolling the dough into neat, even logs, rounder and fatter than the ones the sisters had been attempting—but this was for a reason that would become clear later on, Lily explained.

When the tray of logs was finally in the oven, they turned to the mess around them and started to clean.

They were both under the table sweeping up the broken bits of shell and scraping away the drying yolks when, protected by the dim light and the forest of wooden legs, Francesca's sweeping came to a halt, her dustpan dropping to the floor.

She knelt there, perfectly still, her wing tips brushing the underside of the table.

"She doesn't mean it," she said, not looking up. "She only does it because she is sad."

Lily's heart was thumping. *This was me*, she thought. *This was me!*

"I understand," she said softly. "Your mamma is not well. But just so you know, it's not right. And I don't know exactly how just yet, but I will try and help. OK?"

The dustpan stayed still a moment longer, then Francesca gave a quick nod and started sweeping again. Lily longed to hold that child her in arms and never let go. The sight of that little backbone bent over beneath those bedraggled wings made her want to weep. She could help Francesca and she would, but not all wrongs were hers to right. She had to be careful what she promised.

"It smells so good," Francesca said, climbing out from under the table, back to her old self. "Come on, Lillian, let's see what we have done."

When Lily took the *cantucci* out of the oven, the logs looked as good as they smelled: golden brown and glorious—not undercooked or overcooked or flattened or exploded or any of the things she had expected to go wrong.

When they had cooled, she took out the sharp knife as she had seen Luciana do and sliced the logs into thin discs, laying them flat on another pan and only then pulling out the cookie cutter she had found in the bargain bin at the market.

Under Francesca's watchful gaze, she pressed the cutter into the first disc to make a perfect heart shape.

She held the cookie up and the radiant smile on the little girl's face when she saw what it was, in that moment, almost made her own heartbreak worthwhile.

Francesca took the cookie cutter and pressed out dozens of heart shapes, her smile never fading, which then went back into the oven for their second baking.

"What will we do with the outsides of the hearts?" Francesca asked, gathering the remaining bits of half-baked cookie in a pile and nibbling at them. "They taste just as good even though they don't look like anything."

"Don't worry, we'll think of something." Lily smiled and the two of them started to mix up a second batch of *cantucci*, this time with lemon and, in the absence of cranberries, dried cherries.

Finally, when the hazelnut cookies were baked a second time and cooled enough to eat, the two of them sat on either side of

Violetta's table, took one heart each, and at the same time, on the count of three, took a bite.

"Francesca, you make really out-of-this-world divine cookies," Lily said.

"Yes," Francesca grinned, eyes glistening. "Out-of-this-world divine."

Chapter 35

Luciana woke up after a night in hospital to find that she was almost her old self, except with a few extra cricks and creaks. But really, what were a few extra cricks and creaks at her stage in the proceedings?

The painkillers she had been issued for her badly sprained ankle had given her a more restful sleep than she'd had in years, helped no doubt by a mild concussion, so she was in good humor, and had color in her cheeks for the first time that year.

Violetta, on the other hand, looked like she'd just been unearthed from the ruins of Pompeii. She'd not changed her clothes nor slept a wink since Luciana had tumbled down those stairs.

"Looks like we should swap places," Luciana said, when she saw her sister sitting there, slumped in the uncomfortable visitor's chair like a pile of secondhand coats.

"I have something to tell you," Violetta said.

"Am I missing a limb?" Luciana asked, feeling for her arms, her legs, her nose.

"No, I've hardly let them near you," Violetta said. "It's not about you, it's about me. It's about the League. It's about this match."

"I won't mind if it's my spleen, you can live without a spleen," Luciana said. "I don't think I've ever even used my spleen."

"It's not about spleens! Listen to me, Luciana. I don't have a clue about Lily and Alessandro. I never smelled the orange blossom, I never felt the tingle, I never sensed anything special. My sixth sense is gone. Completely gone. Lily is the wife of poor sick Eugenia's American benefactor. You know, the wine man. Francesca's father. Lily is his wife! She's come to find him and I have instead pushed her into the arms of a man whose heart has already been shattered and will now be shattered all over again and it will be my fault, all my fault. It's the very opposite of what the Secret League of Widowed Darners is supposed to do. It's like I have taken a sock with the tiniest hole and ripped it to shreds. No, worse. It's like I have taken two socks and done that. I am a fraud and a failure and I deserve to be torn limb from limb."

"Well, you're in the right place if it's missing limbs you're after," Luciana said, struggling to sit up a little higher in her hospital bed.

"This is not a joke!" cried Violetta. "This is the end!"

"Calm down, sister, calm down," soothed Luciana. "It is not the end or anything like it. Oh, the difference a good night's sleep can make! Listen to me, will you? Let's just ignore for a minute the orange blossom and the tingle and the sixth sense and regard just the way things have turned out."

"They've turned out to be a catastrophe!"

"Possibly for Alessandro, yes, but not for everybody."

"Well, if he's the *calzino rotto* then he is all that matters."

"Exactly! But what if he's not the *calzino rotto*, Violetta? What if Lily is the *calzino rotto*? Maybe it's her heart that needs mending. Maybe Alessandro has nothing to do with it."

"Lily, the *calzino rotto*?"

"We already established she's no more foreign than anyone else."

"But Lily and who else? Alberto? Mario? It doesn't make sense."

"Well, what about the husband?"

"But he's hardly a decent man, he's a cheat."

"He has taken care of Eugenia and her children when most men in his place would have run for the hills years ago. Haven't we all thought there's more to that scenario than meets the eye? She can be wayward, and he doesn't even stay with her when he's here."

"So?"

"So, need I remind you, Violetta, that sometimes cheats can be stupid and decent all at the same time."

Many, many years earlier, when the sisters were engaged to their twin fiancés, Violetta had slipped into what she thought was her sweetheart's bed, only to discover two terrible things: one, that the man in the bed was not her sweetheart and, two, that he should have been.

"It took just one kiss," Luciana reminded her, "for you to realize you were engaged to the wrong man, but you knew it, just like that. Just one kiss, hm? And you did something about it even though you risked so much. You told him, you told me, you told Silvio. You could have lost us all but you believed in true love, you believed in yourself, and we believed in you, Violetta. We all believed in you. And you were right. Everything turned out just as it should have for us all. Imagine if you had been too frightened to make that move? Imagine if we had both ended up with the wrong husbands?"

"But you said it yourself, it was a mistake."

"Yes, to begin with it was a mistake. But everyone makes mistakes. It's being able to recognize them and having the courage to fix them that makes you special."

"I'm not special, that's what I am trying to tell you."

"You are special, Violetta, that's what I am trying to tell you. You knew who belonged to whom way back then and you did what had to be done to make it right. And it will be exactly the same this time. You are special and I still believe in you."

Violetta was silent for a moment as she considered this.

"Santa Ana di Chisa," she whispered, eventually, rising slowly from her chair and standing straighter than she had in months. "Oh, Santa Ana di Chisa, I have just had the most monumental realization!"

She looked at Luciana.

"It's you," she said. "It's you. You are my sixth sense. I haven't lost it at all! It's you! Nurse, call the ambulance!"

"Violetta, you are already in the hospital."

"I know that, but I need a ride back to town and they owe me one. Don't look so sour, I'm not leaving you here on your own. You look perfectly fine to me right now, so it's all downhill if you stay put. I'll help you get dressed and then we are going home."

Chapter 36

Lily was walking across the magnificent *piazza grande* holding Francesca's hand and only half-listening to her chatter when she saw her husband across the square.

Her heart skipped an old-fashioned beat.

He was waiting in the shade of the well opposite the *duomo*, one leg crossed over the other, hands in his pockets, sunglasses hiding his eyes.

He wore one of the polo shirts she'd given him, a fact that caught and twisted in her chest with a dagger's vengeance.

He looked so much like himself, that was the thing: so much like the man she thought he was, the man she thought she knew. She had expected him to look different now that he was not her perfect husband but a stranger, a liar, and a thief of the future she'd assumed they had together.

But there he was, looking just like the man she'd fallen so easily in love with all those years ago, and had she not been in Montevedova's *piazza grande* holding the hand of his secret love child, she would not have believed he could ever be anything else.

They'd lost pace, Lily's limbs suddenly so heavy she could barely drag one foot in front of the other. Francesca stopped her chattering to see what was slowing them down, but then spotted Daniel.

"That's my papa," she cried, letting go of Lily's hand. "I didn't think he would be here." She ran toward him, each smack of her sandals on the piazza's cobbles burning like a slap on Lily's cheeks.

She could not have planned for this, she realized. She could never have calculated the effect that seeing him would have. For all her executive expertise in navigating hiccups, absorbing variations, avoiding pitfalls, she felt nothing then but clueless. This was not boxes of cake mix and spreadsheets. This was flesh and blood and those other impossible ingredients, love and history.

She could not sink into the safe reliability of a supply chain flowchart now. She could only sink.

She watched as Daniel caught sight of Francesca, and the look on his face as he opened his arms to his little girl twisted the dagger in her chest even deeper.

Grief. The word rang in her head as clearly as the church bells she heard throughout every day she'd been away. Grief. That was what she felt and oh, the pain, the emptiness of it. Everything they had wanted together, Daniel had. There it was, nestled in his arms. He kissed the top of Francesca's head and Lily wondered how she could keep breathing, living, caring, hoping; how she could keep doing anything after that.

And then he saw her.

All the precious control she'd spent years perfecting abandoned her, squeezing tight her heart, tearing apart her skin, leaving her raw and exposed in the searing afternoon sun.

Her shoulders started to shake, her legs trembled, and she pressed both hands over her mouth to stifle whatever was trying to get out. She didn't want to live through this. It was too much to ask, too much to bear.

She started to sink to the ground, but as her knees buckled an old woman pushed past her, bumping into her and dropping her shopping bag, from which bounced out a hundred marbles. Marbles? They danced around Lily's ankles clicking and clacking as the old woman thrust her out of the way and tsk-tsked while she chased them, as though it were Lily's fault the marbles had been let loose in the first place.

"*Scusi, scusi, scusi,*" the old woman said, slapping at Lily's legs, forcing her to step from side to side, and just like that, the hysteria was sucked right out from under her and rolled away as though it too were an escaped marble.

When she looked up, Daniel was frozen beneath the elaborately carved archway over the well, Francesca clinging to him as he stared out at his wife being shunted this way and that by a grizzled old woman in black.

Francesca looked over at her and waved, jumping on the spot with excitement.

Lily fought to contain herself, swallowing a howl of despair, breathing deeply, and reaching once more for that single glimmer of certainty: that whichever way it went, no matter how wicked the turmoil and how high the cost, Francesca deserved to have a father who loved her and showed it.

If this was about that precious child, not her tattered heart, she could do it. She took a step forward. Daniel lifted his hand to his sunglasses and pushed them onto the top of his head.

She took another step, and another, willing herself to keep walking calmly toward him, concentrating on keeping her face as neutral as possible.

He did nothing, remained frozen on the spot until she was so close she could see the fear in his eyes, the sleepless bruises below them, the gray of his skin lingering just below his shallow tan.

"This is Lillian," Francesca said.

Lily could see the vein in his neck throbbing, the one she used to kiss and tease him about. How long since she had done that?

"Your daughter and I have been making *cantucci* together," she said evenly, looking at Francesca, who beamed back at her. "You have a very special little girl here."

Daniel looked down at his daughter and then at Lily, his tired brain still struggling to take in the combination.

"You made *cantucci*?" he asked his wife. It was a ridiculous question to ask, given how many others there were, but it made perfect sense to Francesca.

"We were going to make oatmeal cookies from America," the girl said, "after her sister gave her the recipe on the telephone, but then Lillian could not find the oatmeals so she decides that we can make *cantucci*, only a new sort in the shape of a heart!"

She fished excitedly in the pocket of her dress where she had stashed some of the cookies while Lily wasn't looking, but the first one she pulled out was broken, as was the second, and the third.

The smile slipped off her face and she came to Lily's side, shy suddenly, taking one of Lily's hands, her hips twisting, their two arms swinging in unison.

"Carlotta's been looking after us," Francesca said to her father, squinting into the sun. "Mamma is going *pazzo* again."

Daniel appeared then the way Lily felt before the old lady's marbles hit the ground, like he couldn't bear it, like he wanted to collapse and let the piazza absorb him through the dusty cracks in the warm cobbles, like he couldn't go on breathing.

"I know," he said. "I know, baby, and I'm sorry."

He looked at Lily, his eyes clouded with secrets and shame. "I am sorry," he said again. "I don't know what else to say. But I am sorry, you must know that."

"Yes, well, all that can wait," Lily said stiffly. Logistics, she was thinking, logistics. Insure safety of product, being Francesca; then broach breakdown in supply chain, being their life; and after, consider repair strategy, being God knew what.

"I think you need to take your daughter home, Daniel," she said briskly. "Or to Carlotta's. That was our arrangement. Francesca needs to know that everything will be OK. And everything will be OK," she added, softening for the little girl's benefit. "I'm not here to make trouble, believe me."

"But—"

"But how about we discuss this later? Perhaps we could—"

A thought occurred to Francesca then and she turned pleadingly to interrupt. "Can I come and stay with you, Lillian? Please! Please, please, please! No one will mind. Not Mamma anyway. Papa can tell her and then she won't mind. Please!"

Lily kept her tone as playful as she could manage. "Sweetiepie, you need to go home and tell your mamma all about your *cantucci*. And give her the ones you made especially for her." She held up a small paper sack stuffed full of their handiwork. "Isn't that right, Daniel?"

"That's right, pumpkin," he said, holding out his hand. "Let's go."

"You can come back and make more *cantucci* another day, remember," Lily said.

"But I want to come now!"

She was angry, flustered, and it was a side of her that Lily had not seen before but she thought she understood. When a little girl's home was not her sanctuary, she would rather do anything than go back there.

"I'll be good! I'll clean up! I will not make any noise. I can stay with you above the *pasticceria*. I will have a bath and clean my teeth and . . ." Daniel put a hand on her shoulder and Lily bent down to sweep the hair from her face.

"It's all right, Francesca," she said, her arms itching to wrap themselves around her. "Papa will take care of you."

This is what it would have been like with Grace, she thought.

Daniel and I together, soothing her, looking after her, making sure she knew she was safe, that her world was in order.

She looked at Daniel and wondered if he was thinking the same thing or if he ever thought about Grace now that he had his own daughter.

She felt it then, the need for a pickax, her missing rage. He felt it too.

The strangely gentle uncertainty between them switched instantly to tension. She could almost hear it crackle and hiss.

Francesca seized the awkward opportunity the adults' distraction provided and wriggled out of Daniel's grasp.

"I'm not going home!" she shouted. "Never!" And she took off, running like a bat out of hell across the piazza.

Daniel and Lily, both slightly dazed, were too slow to follow and before either of them could get close to her, she had disappeared down the alley between the bell tower and the town hall, and by the time they got to the top of it, there was no sign of her.

"You go down toward Via Ricci and Piazza San Francesco," Lily ordered, "and I'll go down Via del Teatro toward the Corso."

"How long have you been here?" Daniel asked.

"Daniel! Go after your daughter!"

Lily left him there, bolting down the alleyway, straining her ears to see if she could hear the slap of Francesca's sandals in the lanes and hidden stairways on either side of her.

The town of Montevedova was small, but it contained more hidden nooks and crannies than Middle Earth. Lily shouted into doorways, scuttled down dimly lit passages, even lifted a waterlogged tarpaulin from a pile of abandoned building supplies— but there was no sign of Francesca.

After half an hour of searching, she limped back to the *piazza grande*, and ten minutes later, Daniel appeared in the far corner, holding up his hands in a hopeless gesture.

"Where could she have gone?" Lily asked him. "She wouldn't go home, so what about Carlotta? Would she have gone there?"

"You know Carlotta?"

"Daniel, pull yourself together. This is hardly the time to synchronize address books. I've been here a week. I met Francesca straight away by pure chance and Carlotta soon after. Eugenia did my hair. I'm staying above the Ferrettis' *pasticceria*. Anything else you need to know?"

"Well, hell, Lily, yes. What are you doing here?"

"Are you kidding me? I'm your wife, Daniel. Remember?"

"Remember?" he echoed, running his fingers distractedly through his own hair as they started back down the alley Francesca had first disappeared into.

"Yes, remember! Love at first sight? The best thing that ever happened to you? For better or worse? Is any of this sounding familiar?"

"Of course, Lily. Jesus, it's just that—"

"We were made for each other?" It's what everyone said, and she had believed it; even through the tough times, she had believed it.

"It's true," Daniel said desperately, still flailing for the right words. "It's true."

"If it's true, then perhaps you would be so good as to explain the golf shoe."

"The golf shoe?"

He looked so mystified that for a moment she thought maybe she had got it all wrong, that there was some logical explanation, that there would be a happy ending to their story.

But then the look on his face changed to utter dismay. He stopped.

"Oh, Lily. My God, I'm so sorry. That's how you . . . ? I'm just so . . . Ah! Listen, it's not what you think," Daniel said.

"It's not what I think? Oh, there's a refreshing response. So what is it then?"

"Well, it's complicated," he said, "and I'm not sure—"

"It doesn't seem that complicated to me, Daniel. Is Francesca your daughter?"

"Please, Lily, I can't just stand here and—"

"Daniel, I'm asking you one thing: Is Francesca your daughter? It's a yes or no question."

"Nothing is yes or no, Lily. I wish it was but nothing is yes or no."

"Just answer me! Is she your daughter? Have the guts, will you, to at least tell me the truth to my face instead of hiding and lying and cheating and continuing to betray me. I've been through enough, for God's sake. I've suffered enough. Don't do this to me. Don't you dare do this to me."

She was shouting, her angry words bouncing off the dark stone of the crooked buildings on either side of them, ringing in her ears.

"I know you've suffered," Daniel said, his voice also raised. "But I've suffered too, Lily. I've been through it too. I was doing it right there beside you."

"No, you weren't," she cried. "You were here doing it with Eugenia!"

"It wasn't like that, Lily. It was a mistake," he shouted. "A huge, huge mistake."

"A mistake? Nothing's a mistake, Daniel. Nothing. We choose what we do. I chose you. I could have had anyone. I could have married anyone. I never went a day without a man who loved me my whole adult life, but I chose you to be my husband—my lawfully wedded husband, my for better or for worse husband—over everybody else because I loved you and I trusted you and I thought out of anyone in the world you would never, ever, ever do anything to hurt me like this."

"Oh, Lily, I know. I screwed up! I didn't mean to hurt you, please believe me. That's the last thing I would want. I love you. I've always loved you."

"Well, I hate you!" she cried. "You've ruined everything. I hate you! I wish you were dead, Daniel. I wish you were dead!" She flew at him then, beating at his chest, wishing she had the strength to hurt him as much as he had hurt her, deliberately or otherwise. It didn't matter, the pain was still the same.

Daniel caught her flailing wrists, held them still, then slowly lowered them. He had tears in his eyes.

"If it makes you feel better, a lot of the time, I wish I was dead too," he said.

Lily pulled her wrists away from him.

The hiss of a nearby cappuccino machine threaded up the alley between them. A pigeon flapped above their heads. A clump of chattering boys on a group outing passed the gap in the alley that opened on to the Via del Corso.

Then there was silence. The anger beat a whipped retreat.

"Am I supposed to feel sorry for you now?" Lily asked him.

He reached for her again, stricken, but she stepped away.

They both saw Francesca skip past the alley at the same time.

"You go," Lily said. "She's your daughter."

Chapter 37

The widows were crowded around the table in their underground HQ staring at Lily and Francesca's heart-shaped *cantucci*.

"Well, are we going to stand here gawking or are we going to eat them?" Fiorella asked, her mouth watering.

"They're not the right shape," one widow said.

"They're not the right color," added another.

"They're not made by Violetta and Luciana," pointed out a third.

"Oh, please," Fiorella scoffed. "This *cantucci* looks good, it smells great, and we know for a fact it was baked this morning, not some time in the 1970s, so what are we waiting for?"

Her age-spotted hand reached toward the fluted bowl she'd brought down the stairs, hovered briefly—mostly for dramatic effect—and clamped down finally on a heart-shaped *cantucci*.

"Santa Ana di Chisa! It's sensational," she said after devouring it in one gulp like a fairy-tale wolf. "I think the shape makes a difference. Sweet and spicy all at the same time. Could be dipped in *vin santo*—well, couldn't everything?—but could be eaten just the way it is. Like *cantucci* but with extra *amore*. *Amorucci*! Come on, you scaredy-cats. What are you waiting for?"

It didn't take much more encouragement for the other widows to dig in, and the general impression was that the heart shape indeed made the cookies taste even better, and that Lily and

Eugenia's little girl—what a strange combination that was!—
had brought Ferretti *cantucci* back from the dead, or at least the
inedible.

Their licking of lips and picking crumbs out of cleavages was
interrupted, however, by the widow Del Grasso staggering into
the room, entirely hot and bothered and wheezing so hard she
could hardly speak.

"Lily . . . the piazza . . . that little girl . . . oooooh, *cantucci*."
She shoved a heart-shaped cookie into her mouth and chomped
cheerfully, trying to get hold of her breath again. "It's *delizioso*."

"It's *amorucci*," said one widow. "It's new."

"What were you saying about Lily?" asked another.

"Yes, oh, just one more *amorucci* and then, mmm, yum . . .
much to tell. Oh, those cherries! Anyway, well, I was following
them across the piazza and they were mooching along happy as
larks, but then something happened, something strange, something that made me think that this love match with Alessandro is
perhaps not working out quite the way it should be."

"Oh, really?" Fiorella asked. "And why is that?"

"Well, it's to do with the little girl, Francesca. Or more to the
point, her father," the widow Del Grasso said. "You know, the
American, the wine guy who comes and goes."

"Ye-e-e-s," they all said.

"Well, Lily saw him," she said.

"Ye-e-e-s," they all said.

"And I saw her see him.

"Ye-e-e-s," they all said.

"And, she, well, there's no other way to put it, but I'm afraid
to tell you that she went quite weak in the knees."

The widows had worked out years before that this wasn't just
an expression, women often did go weak in the knees—but only
for their true *amore*.

"She went weak in the knees for the American wine guy?" the widow Benedicti asked. "Well, that can't be right."

"I intervened, of course, just like Violetta would want me to," the widow Del Grasso said. "I happened to have a bag of marbles on me that I'd confiscated from my grandson for feeding them to his neighbor's dog—the results of that, let me tell you, are not to be stepped on—and so I let the marbles go on the ground beneath Lily's feet."

"Good thinking," agreed the widows.

"She soon got control of her knees again so I followed them. Well, I followed all of her—thank Santa Ana di Chisa for my sister-in-law's spare spectacles—but then I lost her but then I found her again, I found both of them. They were up the alley just past your place, Mazzetti, and they were having a blazing row."

"About what?"

"Well, I don't know exactly because they were screaming bloody murder in English, but I did pick up one word I know."

"Ye-e-e-s?" the widows said again.

"Husband," pronounced the widow Del Grasso with a big smile. "I think the American wine guy is Lily's husband."

There followed a stunned silence.

"How could Violetta have got it so wrong?" the widow Mazzetti finally asked.

"We've fluffed before, but never this badly," added the widow Ciacci.

"What have I been trying to tell you all this time?" the widow Ercolani exclaimed. "Violetta is far too over-the-hill for this kind of carry-on."

"I most certainly am not," announced Violetta, surprising them from behind. "I turn my back for one minute and you leave the door unlocked? Who was the last one in?"

"That would be me," confessed Fiorella, even though the

widow Del Grasso was entirely to blame. "'Born in an igloo,' my *nonna* used to say. I didn't even know what an igloo was till I was forty-seven. They're made of ice, you know. They don't have doors."

Violetta's mood darkened just at the sight of her. "You know, ever since you arrived here there has been nothing but—"

"Never mind that," the widow Mazzetti interjected. "You've got it all wrong about Alessandro."

"His heart! Our poor darling's heart!"

"Broken again, because of us."

"Shattered, just like that."

"Stamped on for a second time."

"So, how's your sister?" asked Fiorella, surprising Violetta by taking a different tack.

"Good," answered Violetta. "She's upstairs. Intact but a little wobbly on her feet. Listen, about Alessandro, it's not as bad as you think."

And then she noticed it: the most wonderful smell. It filled her nostrils and she pointed her little snout in the air and sniffed and sniffed and sniffed. Orange blossom! Today of all days!

"In fact, it's even better than that," she exclaimed with the nearest thing to glee she could manage.

Fiorella Fiorucci, who was really very sharp, saw her sniffing and started to get a bad feeling.

"The truth is, I got it wrong, indeed I did, but not completely. It is not Alessandro who is our *calzino rotto* at all, it is Lily."

The widows broke out into a babble of disagreement. Alessandro was a village son, his heart was broken, and it was he who needed mending, not some foreigner in a sordid love triangle.

"I'm right, I know I'm right," said Violetta. "You have to trust me but to prove it, as if I need proof, now that everything has become quite clear, or perhaps that is why it has, there's orange blossom in the air. I can smell it as plain as if it were sitting right in front of me."

"That's funny," said the widow Mazzetti. "So can I."

"Me too," agreed Del Grasso.

"Me three," said Ciacci.

"Well, I'm not surprised," said the widow Ercolani, holding up the air freshener someone had bought and put on the mantelpiece above the hearth. "It *was* sitting right in front of you. There's practically an orange blossom factory underneath your shop, Violetta. This is what you've been smelling all these years. Air freshener."

Chapter 38

Lily stood in the alleyway not knowing what to do with the unhappiness roaring inside her. She didn't want to go back to the *pasticceria*, she didn't want to go to Poliziano, she didn't want to go anywhere—she didn't want to be anywhere.

She headed down the Corso, clinging to the walls of the leaning buildings, replaying the horrible fight with Daniel. She should have stayed in New York. She was better off not knowing, not hearing, not seeing.

She should have put the stupid picture back in the shoe and just gone on with her old life; that's what she should have done.

"*Buonosera*, Lily," Mario called out from behind his glistening ice creams as she passed the *gelateria*. "Come in for a gelato! I have your triple chocolate here waiting for you!" She waved back but sped up as if she were expected somewhere else.

Farther down the hill, Alberto beckoned to her over a customer's shoulder, then hurried out to his doorway. "A glass of wine, Lily? A prosecco?" She managed a tortured smile but could feel the tears this squeezed into the corners of her eyes as she hurried past.

"*Fragoli?*" the stout old woman in the *alimentare* near the half-renovated church offered her, stepping into her path bearing a tub of strawberries. "Fresh. *Oggi*."

Lily shook her head and kept scurrying, slamming to a standstill only when she bumped slap-bang into a middle-aged man dressed in expensive but crumpled linen. He had stopped in the middle of the Corso to scrutinize a tourist map with his wife.

"Oh, I'm sorry," Lily said, checking to make sure he was all right.

"Thank heaven, you speak English," smiled the wife, trying to pull her suitcase out of the way of other pedestrians. "Perhaps you can help us."

The husband wiped his sweating brow with a spotted handkerchief. "You wouldn't happen to know where we would find the Hotel Adesso, would you?"

"Actually, I would," Lily replied, surprised that her voice sounded normal. "You've a way to go, I'm afraid, but it gets shadier once you turn off to the left at the top of the hill. Then there's about another ten-minute walk and it's on your right."

"There you are, darling," the wife beamed. "I told you someone would stop and help."

"Thank you," her husband said. "It's been quite a day."

"But it's beautiful here, isn't it?" said the wife, her face a picture of blissful vacationing. "We thought Florence was to die for, but this place just takes the cake. It's precious! Just precious!"

The husband smiled at her, then reached out and touched her shoulder, as if just to thank her for being so thrilled. She smiled back up at him and it was so tender a moment that Lily looked away, a lump in her throat.

They thanked her, then struggled onward and upward, leaving her standing there, looking after them. The sun was shining, hitting the faded shutters and windowpanes on one side of the street, throwing a darker shade of Tuscan stone on the buildings opposite.

Everyone around her seemed to be laughing, even the geraniums in a pot on the windowsill beside her seemed suddenly impossibly perky. Some smoky jazz tune wafted in the air from a third-story window above. Through a peekaboo slice in the buildings, she could see distant trees being tickled by the gentle breeze that danced across the valley. Coffee was being roasted nearby, a couple of lovestruck teenagers murmured sweet nothings to each other as they sat on the steps of the church, their arms and legs entwined like tree roots.

How could the sun shine and the flowers bloom when the lovestruck man her own arms and legs had once been entwined around had turned out to be little more than an illusion—smoke and mirrors?

It should be raining.

It was Lily's turn now to get jostled by a bustling pedestrian whose unintentional shove spun her round almost full circle until she found herself almost in the arms of the shover.

It was Alessandro. Despite reports to the contrary, Montevedova really was a town where you bumped into everyone you knew.

"I am so sorry for meeting you like this," Alessandro said, a wide grin splitting his handsome face, "but I am also very happy for meeting you like this." He paused, his smile fading. "But are you all right, Lily? You look lost."

"I guess you could say I'm not having the best of days," she said.

"Me too," agreed Alessandro. "My housekeeper has sent me on another strange goose chase. I have been waiting for a bottle of liqueur to arrive at the wine shop for nearly two hours now, but I give up. It's such a beautiful day—too good to waste."

Actually, she was glad she had bumped into him too. He was a breath of fresh air just when she needed one.

"Have you had lunch?" Alessandro asked, at which Lily shook her head.

"Would you care to join me?"

"In Montevedova?"

"Anywhere you like," Alessandro smiled.

"Anywhere that isn't Montevedova," Lily answered.

"I know just the place. It's something a little different from here and I think you'll like it."

"*Fragoli?*" The woman in the doorway of the *alimentare* called after them as they headed out through the ancient city portal toward the parking area. "*Fragoli?*"

The "something a little different" proved to be something quite breathtaking: a nearby town called Bagno Vignoni where the *piazza grande* was not a cobbled square, but an ancient water bath contained by a stone perimeter around which the rest of the tiny village nestled.

Alessandro chose a table at the café closest to the water and Lily sat down beside him, gazing across the mirror-still surface through the gaps in the houses that surrounded it to yet another ridiculously comely, perfectly symmetrical hilltop town perched on the horizon in the distance.

"This is just the most beautiful spot," she said.

"It is," agreed Alessandro. "I used to come here often with my wife."

He smelled delicious, she could not help but notice, sort of fresh, like limes, or something more exotic—passion fruit perhaps.

"I'm so sorry, Alessandro," she said. "About your wife. You must miss her very much."

"Yes," he said. "I do."

"Do you want to talk about it?" she asked.

"It does not make for good conversation."

"Well, I'm not much in the mood for good conversation, if that makes any difference."

The waitress came and took Alessandro's order, a Campari, and Lily paused—fearful of ending up with her bra sticking out of her sleeve a second time—but then ordered the same.

"When did she pass away?" she asked when once again it was just the two of them.

"Two years ago," Alessandro answered. "Just a little more than two years ago." He was staring across the bath water, the nail of one thumb scratching at the knuckle of the other. "Something wrong with her heart that we did not know about. She was driving to Pienza and . . ." he broke off, shaking his head. "It was very sudden. She would not have suffered. This is what they tell me. She would not have suffered."

The wife, Lily thought, had the better part of the deal by far. It was her surviving husband who was doing the suffering.

"You had been married a long time?"

"Almost twenty-five years. We were at school together, university together, we traveled together, we did everything together."

"She liked to travel?"

"Yes." He smiled, the reminder of happier times pushing away her loss. "We both did. Around Italy at first: Sicily, Puglia, Umbria, Venezia. She loved Venezia."

"Venezia?"

"Venice."

"Oh, so the gondola . . . ?"

"Yes, a special memory. The day I asked Elisabeta to marry me."

"Romantic."

"Yes."

His mood seemed to darken.

"I'm sure you will find romance again," Lily suggested, as softly as she could.

He looked at her. "I want to, but this is hard. I don't know what to do without her, how to be without her. I wish she was here. I wish that a lot. Just that she was here and that it could be the way it was before."

"I'm sure she knew how much you loved her," Lily said. A man who felt like Alessandro did about his wife must have been telling her so every minute.

"That is nice for you to say but I am not sure that she did," Alessandro said. "We were not the sort to tell each other all the time, 'Oh, I love you, I adore you, I couldn't live without you,' because I assume she knows this. But now I wish we had spoken of it more often because this is the truth."

"I'm sure she still would have known."

"If I had my time again, if she had her time again, I would tell her every day so that if she was suddenly taken away from me, she would be certain—" he turned away, his pride keeping him from showing Lily his tears.

It was then she knew she was going to sleep with him.

She suspected she had known it when she first saw him through her wet window on the road leading into Montevedova, the rain splattering his white linen against his olive skin.

She was heartbroken in Tuscany, after all, confused about everything except this sad, kind, lonely person whom destiny seemed determined to push into her arms. He smelled good and she wanted to make him feel better. She could do that.

She invited herself back to his villa and he accepted the invitation.

It had nothing to do with Daniel, she told herself, with what he had done to her, with what had transpired earlier in the day. It had to do with Alessandro. Sad, sexy Alessandro and the way he made her feel like she had something he wanted, he needed.

The barn doors were open when they pulled up outside his villa and she could see the gondola sitting there, shipwrecked in Tuscany. Her heart ached for the memories it held.

Inside the villa she excused herself to put on fresh lipstick, check her hair (Eugenia had actually done a good job), and spray a little perfume on her wrists. It had been a long, long time since she had seduced anyone, but she figured men hadn't changed that much in the past twenty years. And she had felt whatever was between she and Alessandro as plainly as if she could see it. Chemistry, possibility, heat; it was all there.

The moment she walked into the kitchen where he was making coffee, Lily realized seduction was not going to be necessary. Alessandro was feeling all the same things, she was sure of it. The look in his eyes when he saw her, the slight tingle in the warm summer air, the little soupçon of electricity that flickered and sparked between them; she and Alessandro were going to fall together as easily as she and Daniel had fallen apart.

She relaxed. Everything was going to be just fine.

He took their coffees into the living room and put some music on—opera, something Lily had heard before but couldn't name. He opened the doors out to the pool and the valley beyond, then stood there with his back to her as the sheer linen drapes on either side fluttered in the breeze.

Finally, he turned, smiled his mournful smile, and Lily simply moved to him, dreamlike, and could not keep herself from doing so. It seemed inevitable.

Her arms ached to hold him, to push away his grief. She knew what it felt like, how lonely it was, how deep the hole inside could get when it had been emptied so thoroughly and nothing else seemed to fill it.

She turned her face up to his and kissed him, tasting the salt on his lips, feeling the shudder that ran through his body at her touch.

If he was surprised at her boldness, he didn't show it. He dropped deep into that kiss and Lily dropped with him.

He pulled her closer, one hand on the back of her head, the other on her hip, and kissed her neck, her ear, the collarbone he had admired the first day he met her.

She threw her head back as she felt some of the pain melt out of him, heard a little groan of ecstasy, moved closer, her hips fused to his, an insatiable hunger burning its way from her toes all the way up through her body to her lips.

When they again found Alessandro's, waiting, desperate for more, Lily tasted salt once more, but this time, it was different. These tears, she realized, were her own.

Chapter 39

The League's headquarters had never been so silent.

Violetta blinked and waited for someone to say something. No one did. Although the widow Ciacci put the air freshener back on the mantelpiece.

"I thought . . . all this time . . . it's just . . ." Violetta started to age before their very eyes, her face falling, her shoulders sinking, her glee evaporating into the thin, quiet air. "Love," she whispered. "I thought I knew. Luciana was so sure. How can this be?"

It was Fiorella who came swiftly to her rescue. "Oh, for the sake of Santa Ana di Chisa," she said, eyes rolling, of course. "What does it really matter?"

"What does it *matter*?" breathed the widow Mazzetti. "Violetta's our spiritual leader! We trusted her. We followed her!"

"But isn't the reason you do that so you can mend broken hearts?" Fiorella charged her. "I just can't for the life of me work out why it matters so much *how*. It's great that you see signs that lead you to the people who most need your help, but actually, you don't have to look far to find someone in that boat. Walk down the Corso and you can spot a half dozen broken hearts between here and the *gelateria* if you're looking for them. They're everywhere! A tingle here, an ache there, maybe that has had something to do with it, but the point is that most other people don't give a rat's butt. Bottom line, there are fewer broken hearts out there thanks to you noticing them in the first place, so can't we just take that and move on?"

"But poor Alessandro . . ." started the widow Ciacci.

"Oh, poor Alessandro, my elbow," pshawed Fiorella. "There's no escaping he's a looker, and a nice enough guy to boot, but there is the whole daughter issue."

The widows muttered that this had been much discussed and was considered to be a work in progress, therefore not an impediment to his candidacy for their assistance.

"Well, what about the fact he's been schtupping the pharmacist's wife for the past eighteen months?" asked Fiorella. "And while that doesn't make him a total creep, he's been slipping it to her sister in Montechiello as well, although not on such a regular basis owing to her husband not being hopped up on goofballs all the time—although he does drink lot. Alessandro? Clear conscience? I think not."

The widow Benedicti looked ready to explode, her face purple with rage as she pointed a shaking finger at Fiorella. This seemed to happen to her a lot.

"That's a lie!" the widow Benedicti hissed. "That's a bald-faced lie."

"Your boss sneaks off somewhere around three on Wednesdays and comes back smelling of Aquolina's Pink Sugar perfume, am I right? It's a little heavy on the musk if you ask me but it's our most expensive scent—the guy's not cheap, I'll give him that."

"He's mourning his wife, for heaven's sake," the widow Benedicti insisted. "He is kind and generous and polite and good and, and, and . . . tall!"

But she had noticed the smell of Pink Sugar wafting about him on a Wednesday evening. She knew it for sure because he'd given her a bottle of the stuff for her birthday. And there was the receipt for the slinky nightgown that she'd found in his pocket while doing the laundry. It was from a shop in Montechiello, as she recalled.

"I have my suspicions about the woman pruning his olive trees, too," Fiorella said. "Usually when two people get mosquito bites that bad at the same time in the same place it's a no-brainer, that's all I'm saying."

The olive pruner had had her hooks into Alessandro from the moment she first clapped eyes on him, the widow Benedicti had seen that. And she'd seen her fair share of scratching soon after, but she'd just never put two and two together.

"I can't believe it," she said in a way that indicated she could perhaps believe it just a tiny bit.

"Look, I'm not saying the guy's a total waste of space," Fiorella said, "but he has issues. Sure he's sad, he's super sad, but the ladies love that, don't they? I just don't think he's the guy for Lily."

"So you agree Lily is our *calzino rotto*?" Violetta asked.

"I think she's as good as any other, and then there's that little girl to think of. The one with the wings."

"The cheating husband's love child?" The widow Mazzetti was amazed. "Well, now I've heard everything. What does she have to do with it?"

"Hello! She has everything to do with it. That kid needs a mother and our *calzino* needs a daughter. What more do you need to know? Hearts can be mended in a hundred different ways, you know. Maybe this hole is going to be darned with a different-colored thread." She actually stopped to wink at Violetta. "It gets the job done every bit as well, just looks a bit peculiar from the outside."

"But that little girl already has a mother," said the widow Del Grasso.

"A mother who isn't all there."

"Yes, but . . ."

"Yes, but nothing. She wants a month or six at the funny farm that one and—"

"They're not called funny farms anymore," the widow Mazzetti interjected. "That's politically incorrect."

"We don't have politically incorrect where I come from," Fiorella said.

"And where is that?"

"Italy! What are you, asleep?"

"Now, now, ladies!" Violetta had some of her old chutzpah back and called the group firmly to order. "Let Fiorella finish."

"All I'm suggesting is that blondie stays here in Montevedova and maybe helps the cheating husband be a father to those children. They're good people, those two, you can tell, despite the mistakes they've made. And who here hasn't made a mistake? Oh, that youngest kid isn't his, by the way. Anyone remember that Scandinavian hunk came through a couple of years ago? Chlamydia, the stories it can tell. Anyway, how about this for a plan: Eugenia can go off to the politically correct institution of someone-in-a-better-position-to-decide's choice and with a bit of TLC should come right, then she can come back and find true love with someone else, because she doesn't love Lily's husband and he doesn't love her and when everybody's done the math and worked it all out they should all end up in the right arms, plus in the meantime those kids are taken care of. Does it really matter who does it as long as it's done?"

The widows looked at each other. Most of them were a bit confused, but not Violetta—she was looking at Fiorella as if she was a giant gelato in her long-forgotten favorite flavor.

"That's a lot to ask of poor Lily, isn't it?" someone asked.

"Any ninny can see she likes the kid, and do we care if she's stuck here making heart-shaped *cantucci* until Eugenia gets her wits together? No, we do not."

"She made heart-shaped *cantucci*?" asked Violetta.

Fiorella wiped some crumbs off her dress. "We call it *amorucci*," she said. "You could whip some Borsolini butt with that stuff, let me tell you."

"It's still a lot to ask of poor Lily," said the widow Del Grasso.

"Well, nobody said it would be easy," Fiorella pointed out. "Love's a messy business, after all. You must have worked that out by now."

"She just comes in here and tries to tell us what to do," the widow Mazzetti said to the room. "There are rules for this sort of—"

"Oh, please!" Fiorella threw her hands up. "Don't give me rules. What do rules have to do with love? No, it's not fair; yes, it's complicated, but look at me: I was tricked into marrying a total dope and had to watch the man I loved die of a broken heart and I turned out all right."

"That's a matter of opinion," the widow Mazzetti muttered quietly, but not quietly enough.

"Well, let me tell you this, Signorina Rule Number Six, Clause B, Addendum Two Point Five," said Fiorella, turning on her. "I would go to Montevedova Hospital right now and have every limb removed and my eyes and my ears and my nose as well if it would give me just one day back with my Eduardo. I don't care how hard that would make the rest of my life. If all I got was a minute, a single minute, of being with him again, it would be worth it. That is love, you nitwits. You're supposed to be experts. You don't remember how hard it is? Well, you are in the wrong game. Shame on you. Shame, shame, shame."

The essence of mass mortification filled the room, giving the air freshener a run for its money.

"I would go to Montevedova Hospital and have my legs chopped off for another moment with my Antonio," sniffed the widow Del Grasso into the embarrassed quiet.

"Me too," whispered the widow Benedicti.

"And my ears," sobbed the widow Ciacci.

"To be in my sweet one's arms again? Oh! They could take everything!" wept even the widow Mazzetti. "Everything!"

Into the middle of these sniffling nonagenarians stepped the tiny Violetta.

"I think Fiorella has reminded us all of why we are here and how precious our mission is," she said, but was interrupted almost immediately by the widow Pacini bustling in, her chest puffed with pride, and the rest of her quite puffed as well.

"Success, success, success," she crowed. "Del Grasso, your grandson couldn't get her into the *gelateria* and Ciacci, yours couldn't get her into the wine shop, but right outside my *alimentare* over today's freshly picked strawberries, our *calzino rotto* met his match!"

"What happened?" a chorus of voices asked.

"They drove off into the sunset," the widow Pacini reported triumphantly before noticing something was amiss. "Why the long faces, isn't this what we wanted?"

"How long ago did this happen?" asked Violetta.

"A couple of hours ago, I suppose. Maybe longer."

"And you waited all this time to come and tell us?"

"I had to close the *alimentare* and stop at Poliziano for a celebratory cannelloni or two. I know they're Sicilian but they're perfect for such an occasion. Why? What's going on?"

"There's been a change of plan," said Fiorella. "We're swapping horses."

"Swapping horses? Violetta, is this true?" The widow Pacini was aghast. Violetta was the person least likely to swap horses, after all.

"Yes, it is," Violetta confirmed. "It most certainly is."

Chapter 40

Lily had forgotten the all-consuming drama of that first deep kiss.

There was nothing else in the world quite like it—that moment of everything else in the universe, troublesome or otherwise, being swept away.

The fine linen curtains billowed into the room on a theatrical gust as Alessandro moved Lily toward the plush sofa, graceful for such a big man, his hands on her so delicate she might have been a prized antique.

He took his time, a practiced lover, slowly unbuttoning her shirt and admiring her body as it was gradually revealed. He spoke in Italian and she could have listened to him forever. With his hands on her neck, her breasts, her ribs, her stomach, her hips, her thighs, it was impossible to think of anything else other than the feel of him, the sound of him, the smell of him.

Her lips burned where Alessandro's touched them, her skin quivered, her hair fell out of its tidy knot. She felt free, impossibly free, as though she were soaring weightlessly in the blue Tuscan sky miles above the sordid wreckage of real life.

It was bliss.

Afterward, she didn't plummet back down to earth with an immediate thud. She stayed floating in Alessandro's arms as he told her how beautiful she was, how lucky for him he had met her, how sometimes destiny delivered the right souls into the right arms, and how he felt happier than he had in a long, long time.

She wanted to stay there forever, suspended in the heavenly simplicity of it all: two wounded adults enjoying each other's bodies, each other's warmth, each other's comfort. She tingled from head to toe in a way she could not remember ever tingling before.

But destiny, as it turned out, did not want Lily to stay where she was. Destiny had other plans and they involved Alessandro's aged housekeeper appearing in front of them, a look of horror contorting her reddened face. She was holding a metal bucket full of soapy water, which she promptly dropped to the floor with a clang.

Lily, beyond mortified, although thankfully partly clothed by then, sprang away from the sofa, buttoning her shirt, swiveling her skirt around the right way, snatching at her underwear, which was sticking out from underneath a cushion.

Alessandro, only recently re-trousered, looked in bewilderment as the clearly flustered Signora Benedicti then held aloft, like a weapon, a feather duster.

"I am come to clean," she announced, and pushing Alessandro out of the way, she picked up the cashmere throw that had been cast on the floor and started to straighten the cushions where the lovers had just been lying.

"Signora Benedicti, what are you doing here?" Alessandro, remarkably calm under the circumstances, asked in Italian. "I thought you cleaned the house this morning."

"I am," she answered in English. "But is still very dusty. See?" She brought the feather duster down on the nearby sideboard with such an almighty thwack that Lily, now at least appropriately buttoned and zipped, jumped with fright.

"But I don't understand. We said good-bye. I saw you leave."

"And does the dust take such close notice of this activities?" the housekeeper answered. "If you would wish your lady friend to get the allergy and create a big nose and water eyes, I will not arrive, but to keep the beautiful face is necessary for my work to have done and now."

"You know, I think I should be going," Alessandro's lady friend said.

"Not at all," said Alessandro. "I would be very sorry if you left now. Please, just give me a moment. If I've upset you, Signora Benedicti, I am sorry," Alessandro said, switching back to his native tongue, "but this is really none of your business."

"I don't have a business," she answered, also in Italian. "Just a lot of dust to get rid of, your ironing to finish, the kitchen floor to mop, and something that smells very unpleasant to locate in your refrigerator and dispose of. I work very hard for you, Alessandro, much harder than that olive pruner you always make such a fuss about, but no matter how hard I work it never seems to satisfy you. Never!"

Alessandro was astounded. Such an outburst was totally out of character.

"Signora, are you feeling all right?" he asked her.

She looked at him for a moment or two—he really was a kind man, if overly randy—then said that actually she was feeling very poorly and could he please take her into the kitchen and make her a nice tall glass of fresh lemonade with a sprig of mint from the patch growing wild beneath the olive trees, the unpruned ones, out behind the barn a few hundred meters.

"Please, Lily, I apologize but if you could just excuse us for a little longer," Alessandro said escorting the widow out to the kitchen.

Lily stood there for a moment, trying to shake her embarrassment. The housekeeper and her soapy bucket and feather duster had certainly put her feet back on the ground. The dreamily fluttering linen drapes now made an annoying flapping sound, the open doors had welcomed a trio of buzzing flies, it was too hot. Her skin didn't tingle anymore. She had the beginnings of a headache.

She tried to recapture the floaty, free feeling, but it was gone.

A photo on the sideboard that Signora Benedicti had just been dusting caught her eye. Half a dozen other framed pictures had been left lying facedown, but there was one left standing at the front. Lily picked it up. It was a younger Alessandro and his wife, she assumed, Elisabeta—a petite beauty who gazed up at him adoringly—but nestled between them was a teenage girl, the image of her mother, looking shyly into the camera.

Alessandro had a daughter?

She had never asked him if he had children, she hated the question so much herself, yet this kid looked so much like him there was really no doubting it. Had she died too? It was so strange he had never mentioned her.

He was thinner in the picture and his hair was shorter, but mostly what struck her was the lightness about him. He stood taller, somehow, and his shoulders did not bear the weight of his current grief. His eyes, his smile, even the way he held his head radiated happiness, contentment.

They were a happy family, she thought, comparing the photo with the one in Daniel's shoe.

Daniel.

She sank into the sofa, the photo falling from her hand onto the seat next to her, her head thrown back on the cushions as she gazed blankly at the ceiling.

Her husband and Alessandro were opposites in every way. Daniel was fair where Alessandro was dark, chiseled where Alessandro was soft, reserved where Alessandro was impassioned.

She could not see Daniel getting wound up about some ancient enemy stealing the family seat a thousand years ago. He forgave his own parents far worse crimes.

He did not hold grudges, Daniel. He preferred smoothing the waters to making waves. Shouting at her in the alley was as angry as she'd ever seen him.

What had happened to the husband she knew so well? She had thought he looked the same as always when she first saw him in the piazza, but in the alley with his harsh voice, his hooded eyes, and his obvious fury, he seemed a different man. Older. Older?

Today was Saturday. It was Daniel's birthday.

Lily closed her eyes and felt a tear trickle down her face toward her ear.

A lifetime ago she had planned to spend this afternoon with her husband having lunch at the Museum of Modern Art and meandering around the collections.

Instead she had spent it betraying him in the same way he had betrayed her.

Alessandro, having finally extracted himself from his sickly housekeeper, swept back into the room.

"Please forgive me," he said. "But I think Signora Benedicti is recovered now. At least she says she can start cleaning again, although I have instructed her to take a rest for an hour or two."

He stopped when he saw her tears.

"You are upset, I am sorry," he said, coming to her.

"No, I'm sorry," she said.

He looked at the photo in her hands.

"Ah," was all he said.

"You have a daughter," she said, holding up the photo.

"Yes."

"You never told me about her."

"There is not much to say."

"Well, how old is she? Where does she live?"

He seemed angry and she thought for a moment he was going to storm out of the room, but he didn't. Instead he came and sat down beside her, picking up the photo.

"She is twenty-one and she lives in Pienza."

"How often do you see her?"

"I do not see her." He paused. "Sofia."

"That's a beautiful name, Alessandro. For a beautiful girl."

"She is lost to me," he said.

"I can't believe that."

"It is true. She has been lost to me for some time. Remember when I told you of the family that cheated us out of this house? She married one of them."

"But that was hundreds of years ago!"

"The same cheating poison still runs in the Mangiavacchi blood," Alessandro said. "This is no secret and she knows it yet still she marries him."

"Well, that is what we call cutting off your nose to spite your face where I come from," Lily said. "She's your daughter, Alessandro. And she has lost her mother. She must miss you so much and surely you must miss her."

She could tell from the set of his jaw that he was about to fight for his position, to defend himself, but in the end he didn't. He slumped back farther into the sofa and sighed.

"Yes, I miss her," he said. "Of course I do. And now she has a son, my grandson, but . . . I have never met him."

"Alessandro, that's so sad. Not just for her but for you, and for that little boy. Can't you kiss and make up?"

"I am waiting," he said. "I am waiting until I am no longer so angry with her."

"And how long do you think that will take?"

"I don't know how long it will take, Lily. I did not think it would take this long."

"You have to find a way to forgive her, Alessandro."

"I know this, Lily. I know this. Please, can we talk about something else. What of you? Is your face also missing a nose?"

"Not quite," said Lily. "But I do have a husband."

"I see." He didn't seem that surprised.

"He has a girlfriend and two children and I only just found out about them, so I came here to find him."

This he was surprised by. "In Toscana?"

"In Montevedova."

"And have you found him?"

"Well, he's there," she said. "I saw him today."

"Ah," Alessandro said. "And then you saw me."

Lily supposed it really was that shamefully obvious. "You must think I am a terrible person," she said.

"I think you are beautiful and I think you are sad," Alessandro said. "I have thought that since the moment I saw you."

She managed a smile. "That's funny. I thought the same thing about you."

"We are a good pair for this reason, perhaps?" suggested Alessandro.

"I think that we are not a pair," she said. "I think that what happened just now, between us, was a mistake. A very nice mistake. But still a mistake."

Alessandro fixed her with his baleful brown eyes. "You still love your husband, no?"

He did not know the Lily who had built a fortress around her heart's darkest chambers, so she let him in.

"I don't know," she said. "I loved him before I found out he was cheating on me, even if, like you and Elisabeta, we never really talked about it. But now I can't tell if I love him or not."

"I think if you didn't love him, you would be able to tell that," Alessandro said.

"Why?"

"You are hurt, Lily. I know this, but I also know that a man cheating on his wife does not always have something to do with how much he loves her. We're men," Alessandro said as she tried to protest. "Don't give us too much credit. We mean our promises when we make them, but we are simpletons when it comes to temptation, you must know this. Us cheating on you is not the same as you cheating on us."

"Well, I just cheated on him so I guess we are in the same boat."

"And how do you feel?"

"I feel like I have done something that can never be undone. How do *you* feel?"

"I feel we made the most of a good opportunity."

"Well, you certainly sound like you know what you are talking about."

"I'm Italian. Of course I know what I am talking about."

"You had an affair when you were married to Elisabeta?"

"More than one."

"And she knew?"

"She found out about the last one, and until she did I had no idea how much I was hurting her."

"But she forgave you."

"There was one month at the Carlyle Hotel in New York and a very expensive fur coat and a watch, but yes, she forgave me."

"But it's different for me. My husband has had children, the children I could never have myself, with another woman. Could he be any more deceitful?"

"Excuse me if what I say is not what you want to hear, Lily, but the deceit is the same, whether there is a child involved or not. Would you feel better if you knew of the affair but not the child?"

Oh, but Lily loved the child.

"It's complicated," she said. "Too complicated. I might still love him but I don't know if I can forgive him."

"Yes, I know this. It is the same with my daughter. I love her, of course, she is my flesh and blood, but I don't always feel this love. There is so much else that I feel so strongly in the way."

English as a second language and still he had encapsulated the knotted core of Lily's predicament. She could not know if she still loved Daniel because there were so many other obstacles in the way. And she wasn't sure if she was capable of showing him enough mercy to remove the obstacles.

"I think forgiveness is beyond me," she said.

"I am the same," Alessandro agreed. "You see, we do make a good pair."

They sat in companionable silence for a minute or two, then, with a sigh, Lily got to her feet.

"I need to go," she said. The sun was setting, the greens of the hills rolling away from Alessandro's villa now morphing into smoky pinks and purples.

"You could stay," Alessandro said. "You could stay and I could take care of you."

It was tempting, in a floating-through-the-blue-Tuscan-sky sort of way.

She stepped forward to kiss him a chaste good-bye and he held her for a moment, long enough for her to catch a comforting whiff of passion fruit and sweat and coffee. She caught a glimpse then of what it would be like to stay in his arms, to melt into the bits of him she could see were strong and safe and loving.

But although he had told her he was happy, there was a weight still resting on his shoulders that all the sweet talk and lying naked in her arms would never shift.

This was a man who could build a useless boat in memory of a wife he could not let go yet pushed away a daughter who was right there and surely needed him.

Alessandro was a mistake. A very nice mistake. But still a mistake.

"I feel good," Signora Benedicti announced, sweeping back into the room. "But now I will go home and I will take this lady friend with me."

This lady friend agreed and meekly followed the housekeeper out of the villa and into her rusty Renault.

Chapter 41

"All praise to Santa Ana di Chisa," the widow Benedicti breathed, dialing the widow Ciacci's number into her cell phone after she'd dropped Lily off at the parking lot by the tourist office.

"She's on her way back up the Corso now," she reported.

"Was disaster averted?" the widow Ciacci wanted to know.

"It's hard to say," the widow Benedicti reported. "Partially, perhaps."

"Is partially enough?" the widow Ciacci asked doubtfully. "I can't remember how it works."

"Don't ask me, it's nearly thirty years. And even then we only did it at night in the dark on a Thursday."

"Oh, I miss it though, Benedicti, don't you?"

"Thursdays have never quite been the same," her friend admitted. "Although I often make a *crostata di more* on a Thursday now, so that gives me something to look forward to."

"So what shall I tell Violetta?"

"Tell her that the new *calzino* and old *calzino* were found in a state of partial undress in the living room, not the bedroom, and that upon being surprised by myself, became fully dressed, talked for quite a while—about what I'm not sure—and then parted."

"Was the parting romantic?" the widow Ciacci wanted to know.

"She was in his arms but there didn't seem to be anything too spicy going on. It was more . . . companionable, I suppose you could say."

"No harm in being companionable," the widow Ciacci said. "We'll see you back at HQ? There's a lot to be organized."

Chapter 42

As she climbed the hill from the parking lot to the *pasticceria*, Lily further considered what Alessandro had said about not feeling the love because so many other things were in the way. The truth, if she was honest with herself, was that these obstacles to how she felt about Daniel were not recent additions. They'd been around a while and they weren't pebbles, either, they were boulders. They'd grown moss and sheltered smaller rocks now. She didn't know if they could ever be moved.

And even if they could, this new Daniel, the one who said he loved her but had a family here, the one who had carved out a different life for himself across the world from her, might no longer want her. Whether she loved him or not could well be immaterial.

The gap between them was so wide that she didn't know how a little bit of forgiveness could close it. It could just as likely plummet to the bottom of the crevasse and make no difference at all.

And anyway, did she really need to know if Daniel didn't want her anymore? Would it not be better to assume that he did and leave him before he got the chance to leave her first? Any more than he already had?

She couldn't imagine the humiliation of forgiving Daniel only to have him thank her politely and marry Eugenia.

In fact, she couldn't imagine the humiliation of forgiving him, period. The actual act of forgiveness she could almost come to grips with, but it was a private agreement with herself, not a face-to-face arrangement with him. The very thought of talking to him about it, dissecting his betrayal and her suffering, made her want to throw up.

Until that point she had never understood why some people got divorced so quickly. She could think of at least three couples who'd seemed perfectly happy one day and perfectly separated the next.

Now she knew why: Who wanted in on the postmortem? If it was dead, it was dead. Why drag the entrails out into the open and poke at them with a stick? That would surely only cause more pain, especially to the injured party.

No, she had come to Tuscany, she'd basked in its beauty, she'd found out exactly what was going on with her husband, she'd revived her relationship with her sister, she'd learned to make *cantucci*, and she had spent an afternoon making love to a handsome Italian man—something she planned to never tell anyone else about as long as she lived. She would write the whole trip off in her mind as a sort of secret adventure. And she would stay true to her promise to make sure that Daniel did the right thing by Francesca; she meant that, even if it hurt her bank account. But she would do it from her apartment on West Seventy-second Street.

It was time, truly, to go home.

"Continue straight ahead," as Dermott would say. Continue straight ahead. It was a relief, she told herself, to decide that her marriage was over, because once again she was a woman with a plan. This *i* was about to be dotted.

It was dark by the time she opened the door to the *pasticceria* as slowly as possible so the bell gave only the tiniest tinkle. She stopped for a moment just to take in the strange little place one more time. How did it manage to always smell of roses even when there weren't any? The faint glow of the street lantern outside filtered through the window, illuminating the green glass bowl in which Lily and Francesca had arranged their *cantucci* earlier in the day. Then it had looked like a bouquet of biscotti hearts. Now there was nothing in it but a few lonely crumbs.

How peculiar, Lily thought. Maybe Violetta had come home and thrown the cookies out.

Creeping as quietly as she could, she pushed open the swinging door into the kitchen and slipped through it, only to find Violetta sitting patiently at the table waiting for her. Luciana was propped up in the bed looking as fit as a fiddle, hands clasped neatly on top of her quilts and blankets.

"Oh, goodness," Lily said politely. She had been planning on slipping away quietly, perhaps leaving a note, but maybe it was better to be upfront. "Actually, no, this is great," she said. "I'm glad you're here. The thing is that I am leaving, Violetta. Today. I'm just going to pack my bags and head back to Rome. Stay near the airport, get the first flight home to New York."

Violetta looked shiftily from side to side.

"Mmm, no," she said. She had quite a loud voice for a very small, old person. "No, I don't think so. No, no, no."

Lily was taken aback, but not for long. "Well, yes," she replied, firmly. "*Sí. Sí, sí, sí.*"

"But you agree to stay for one month," Violetta said. "This is a verbal contract."

"Verbal contract? What the—? And about this whole speaking English thing. When exactly were you going to tell me about that?"

"When exactly were you going to ask?"

"*Buonosera*," Luciana called out from the bed with a chirpy wave.

"Oh, Luciana, welcome home. How are you feeling?"

"*Sí. Grazie,*" she said.

"She doesn't speak *inglese,*" Violetta said. "Just me. Lily, is time for us to have a talk."

"All those things I told you," Lily said, remembering the rants she had gone on while the sisters bungled their baking. "All those things! You understood and you never said a word."

"I did not understand," Violetta said. "Why you put your cashmere in the oven? Does not make sense."

"I thought I was talking to a stone! Why would you do that?"

"We want to know more about you," Violetta said with an unconcerned shrug.

"But why? Why did you want to know more about me? And why do it in such an underhand way? Why not just ask?"

Luciana interjected in Italian, which seemed to make Violetta mad, and they argued like baby birds over a single worm until Luciana blew a raspberry and they both fell silent.

"Sorry, what is your question?" Violetta asked.

"You know what the question was! Why did you trick me?"

"Because we want to know how long you would be here so we can get you to pay the rent on our store," Violetta answered.

Lily threw up her hands.

"If you think I'm going to believe that, you are a fool," she said. "And you don't strike me as being foolish. Quite the opposite. What's this all about, Violetta?"

Luciana burbled a short, sharp something to her sister.

"She says to tell you is because we are two stupid old women with nothing better to do than poke our noses in where they are not wanted and meddle," Violetta said.

"That I do believe," said Lily.

"But is true about the rent," insisted Violetta. "Without you we could not stay open another minute."

"Stay open? Your shop? It isn't open now."

"We have trouble," Violetta admitted. "Since the arthritis, the *cantucci* is not turning out so good and those Borsolini *bastardi* down the hill make a fortune selling ugly cookies to fat tourists who won't do the climb up here to our store."

"OK, you know what? Thank you for being honest but that's not my problem, and you know what else, it doesn't matter. I don't care. I'm leaving anyway. You can keep the money I gave you to pay this month's rent for your shop but I'm going home. Now."

The sisters looked at each other.

"We are definitely getting too old for this *merda*," Violetta told her sister in Italian.

"The problem is the money you give us is for last month's rent," she told Lily. "We have no money for this month's rent."

"I gave you five hundred euros!'

"We are behind."

"Well, I'm very sorry about that, but the reality is that you need to get someone else to make your *cantucci* so you have a viable prospect to actually sell, or better still, you need to beat the Borsolini *bastardi* at their own game. I don't know—make what everyone is buying from them, only better, and then maybe you can afford to meet your financial responsibilities. Or talk to the owner of the building and try to come to some arrangement over the rent. Who owns the building anyway?" Lily asked. "To whom do you owe this money?"

A heated debate broke out between the sisters.

"We own it," Violetta eventually confessed. "We owe the money to us."

All Lily could do was laugh.

"You want to trick me into renting a store that has nothing in it so you can 'stay' open when you seem not to have been open for quite a long time selling nonexistent *cantucci* to customers who don't exist?"

Violetta explained this all the Luciana, then they both turned to her and nodded.

"Yes."

"Is this some kind of joke? No? OK, that's it. I'm going upstairs to pack."

"Mention the little girl," Luciana ordered her sister.

"What about the little girl?" Violetta demanded accordingly. "Francesca?"

Lily stopped in her tracks.

"What about Francesca?" she asked. "What has Francesca got to do with it?"

"Francesca has everything to do with it," Violetta answered.

A difficult silence descended on the room. The two sisters' four dark eyes bored into her.

"You know about Daniel?"

"We know about a little girl in need of *amore*. And we know about a darning group that really likes heart-shaped *cantucci*."

"Your darning group ate all our *cantucci*?"

"*Sí*. And they're a hard crowd to please. But all they need to do is spread the word and our heart-shaped *cantucci*—we call it *amorucci* now—could be a very viable prospect. If only we had someone to help us make it. And then there's Francesca. Tut, tut. Poor little broken-winged Francesca."

"This is extortion!"

Violetta cackled like an old hen, then translated for Luciana, who cackled even harder.

"She says welcome to Italy!" Violetta reported, pushing her chair back with an almighty scraping as she struggled to her feet. "But this isn't even real extortion's poor cousin twice removed. Anyway, you might want to think about this overnight."

Lily was astounded.

"There is nothing to think about. I have a life back in New

York, you know: a home, a job, responsibilities of my own. I can't just drop everything and run a *cantucci* store in Tuscany. That's ludicrous."

But she wasn't thinking of her home, her job, her responsibilities, or even of her broken heart or the man who broke it. She was thinking of the smile on Francesca's face as she saw the shape the cookie cutter had made in the *cantucci*.

Lily looked up and caught Violetta's eye. There was a lot of wrinkled skin on that ancient face, but a wink is still a wink.

Chapter 43

It was nearly two o'clock in the morning.

Lily was in bed asleep, having agreed to sleep on it, but still intent on leaving first thing in the morning. This gave the widows another four hours at least to come up with the rest of their plan.

Violetta had taped a tourist office map of Montevedova on the wall and was marking various points with pin tacks.

One marked the room near Piazza San Francesca where Daniel was staying, the other the *pasticceria*, another the roundabout near the tourist office, a fourth the truck drivers' depot, a fifth the back road that wound around to San Biagio church, and another the church itself.

"Widows Del Grasso, Ciacci, Ercolani, and Pacini, are you clear?"

"*Sí*," they answered in unison.

"Del Grasso, you don't look so sure."

"I know what I have to do, I'm just worried about the smell," she said.

"If you take enough food and a bottle of grappa there should be no need to get that close," Violetta said. "Mazzetti has worked out the timing. If we all do our bit, it should run like clockwork."

"You know, sometimes I wish we were really just a darning club," grumbled the widow Benedicti.

"Have you lost your cotton-picking mind?" asked Fiorella. "Where's the romance in darning?"

Violetta and Luciana looked at her, then each other, and smiled. Their matching aching bones heaved matching sighs of relief. They were tired and they were old, but they could rest happy in the knowledge that when they went to meet Silvio and Salvatore in the great beyond, the League would be in safe hands.

Fiorella looked down at her feet and let out a hoot of laughter.

"Look at that!" she cackled. "One blue shoe and one brown one! Now that's got to make a day more interesting."

She certainly had a gift for looking on the bright side.

Chapter 44

Lily had expected a sleepless night after the roller-coaster events of the day, the ups and downs of which ricocheted around her head as she climbed the stairs to her room for the very last time.

But the moment she lay down she fell into a deep, peaceful sleep, waking so early that the friendly ray of light that liked to tickle her chin in the morning was still only climbing its way down the wall.

With the pale golden light dappling on the pretty ceiling and sparkling off the chandelier above her, it was like being inside a glittery snow globe.

She lay there, stretching out in the sleepy warmth, trying not to think of Daniel shouting at her in the alley, of Alessandro whispering to her while he ran his fingers up her thigh, of Francesca smiling at her over a heart-shaped cookie.

Her world had been thoroughly shaken up, there was no pretending otherwise, but when the glitter settled, she would be at home in her old life in New York. She could keep what had happened in Tuscany separate from everything else, to be shaken again—or not—as she saw fit.

She wasn't sad. In fact, she felt a tiny buzz of anticipation in her belly as she got up and started folding and packing her clothes, trying not to look out the window or smell the jasmine that grew up a weathered trellis beside the window or marvel at the general splendor of the green and gorgeous countryside.

These things could go in the glittery snow globe and stay there too.

Her suitcase packed, she carried it quietly down the narrow stairs and entered the kitchen. She knew better than to think she could escape the sisters, but she was not prepared to see them waiting—Violetta standing and Luciana sitting—behind the table upon which they had set out all the ingredients for a massive *amorucci* marathon.

The bins of flour and sugar were at the ready. Dozens of eggs, freshly laid and still sporting coiffures of straw, were stacked beside them. More baking pans had appeared from somewhere and there were bowls of extra ingredients sitting at the end of the table like treasure chests piled with lemons, walnuts, pine nuts, oranges, cinnamon quills, vanilla pods, cherries, dried fruit, and dark chocolate.

Her pastel bowl collection had increased half-a-dozen-fold since the day before, as had the mixing spoons and the cookie cutters. This was a production line, ready and waiting, and she couldn't for the life of her imagine why they had gone to all the bother, let alone the expense, when they knew she was leaving.

Clearly, they underestimated her resolve. Although as she looked at them, unmoving in their black shiftless smocks, it struck Lily that there was a ferocity emanating from the Ferretti sisters that she hadn't noticed before. If they'd ever seemed cute, that was well gone. They looked a little bit like gnarled old rats. There was nothing feeble or quaint about them. They meant business. Indeed, they would not be out of place haggling for shillings in a Zanzibar spice market.

But Lily had looked stronger foe in the eye than these two. She would not be intimidated. She let go of her suitcase and girded her loins for the ensuing battle.

"Good morning, ladies," she said. "You have obviously gone

to a lot of trouble, but I thought I made it perfectly clear to you that I am not staying, so I won't be able to help you."

The sisters said nothing.

"It's been a pleasure meeting you, and I'm sorry I can't be more helpful with your *amorucci* endeavors, but please, here, let me give you this to help you pay rent. To yourselves." She reached into her purse and pulled out her last 100 euro note.

The sisters said nothing, so Lily slid the note into the bowl of oranges and lemons, disrupting the fruit, some of which bounced off the table and onto the floor.

The sisters did not move a muscle.

"Oh, for Pete's sake!" Lily said, chasing the rolling citrus around the room, then trying unsuccessfully to restack the bowl, eventually putting two of the lemons in her purse to get the job finished.

"Right," she said, finally. "It's been a fascinating experience and I'd like to thank you for your hospitality and the use of your kitchen," she said. "But you've obviously got a lot of work to do today so I'll be on my way, as planned. As for Francesca, well, if you see her, please say—please tell her . . ." Her throat closed, making it hard to continue. Such a display of emotion had certainly never escaped her in the Heigelmann's boardroom. That would be suicide.

"Yes, anyway, I would be very grateful if you could just say good-bye."

Nothing. The glaring got a bit more intense, perhaps, but Lily was not going to fold now.

"So thank you once again and good luck."

Still, the sisters showed no response, so Lily turned and pulled her suitcase across the uneven stone floor toward the door. She cursed herself for not getting the wretched thing fixed or replaced because its wobbly wheel had only gotten wobblier.

It got stuck going through the narrow doorway into the shop, then again on the corner of the counter as she rounded the bend, finally collecting the little chair by the front window.

Once she had extricated the bag from the furniture, she found she could not open the shop door. It was firmly stuck and she nearly wrenched her arm out pulling it open, which happened so suddenly the chain holding the bell broke and it crashed to the floor, only narrowly missing her head.

She thought about going back to tell the sisters, but decided her 100 euro tip would have to cover the damage.

She picked up the pieces and left them in a pile on the table in the front window.

The cobbled lane of the Corso was empty, silent but for Lily and her wobbly-wheeled bag. She kept her eyes down, avoiding the colorful window boxes and pretty shop displays, the slices of the valley that hid in the spaces between the buildings.

Down in the deserted parking lot, she climbed into her Fiat 500 and pressed Dermott's on button, but her plan to get to the airport in Rome as quickly as possible started unraveling almost straight away when two of the exits at the difficult roundabout near the parking lot's entrance were blocked off by roadwork signs.

"Turn left," Dermott instructed, and when she disobeyed, through no fault of her own, he ordered her to turn left again, by which point she had been around the roundabout twice and didn't know which left he meant.

"There is no left," she argued, pointlessly. "There's back into the parking lot, up toward the town if you have the right sticker, the main road to Siena, or this other dusty little road."

She took the other dusty little road, which meandered around the back of Montevedova, curling between enormous pine trees between which she could not escape her last views of the beautiful Val D'Orcia.

Was it the color? The acres and acres of green rolling pastures? The bunches of fat grapes that hung lazily on their miles of vines? The copious stands of gracious olive trees? It was all so alive. Everywhere she looked, creation was doing its thing, feeding plants, watering fields, growing leaves, blooming. The buzz in her belly hummed happily along until she rounded a corner and almost rear-ended a large truck that had stopped in the middle of the road. It soon became clear why. She only had to crane her neck out of the window to see that there was another equally large truck stopped on the other side of the road, coming from the opposite direction. The road was not big enough for both of them.

She could hear the drivers shouting at each other from behind the wheels of their respective rigs. Before too long, one got out, then the other, and so she got out too but then swiftly got back in again when one driver, who looked too old to be in charge of such a big vehicle in the first place, reached into the cab of his truck and spryly grabbed a socket wrench.

At that point, Lily noticed a leafy unpaved lane to her right, and she decided that rather than wait around and see what disaster was about to unfold with the truck drivers, she would take it.

The lane was narrow, and quite steep, but after half a mile it opened up and Lily found herself in what she thought was the valley she'd been gazing at from her room. She was sure she recognized Bagno Vignoni in the distance, and even farther away on the horizon, the other little turreted village she had seen from the spa town.

While she was concentrating on that, however, she ran literally into a herd of goats. One moment the road was open and empty, the next she rounded a bend and there they all were, absolutely everywhere, swamping the car, maahing and baahing and stretching up to the next corner and around it.

She sat there unsure what to do. She certainly wasn't game to drive through them. She didn't know much about goats, but thought these ones looked bigger than normal. And some were just babies. She'd squash them, surely.

She turned the car off. The goatherd, if that's what they still called them, could not be far away. It didn't make sense to leave all these beasts untended for long. She would wait it out.

She watched a baby goat get separated from its mother and panic in the mosh pit of other goats. It was trying to keep its head up out of the throng, but it was too small. Its mother was calling it, her head raised, one eyeball rolling wildly as it got pushed farther and farther away.

Finally, she could take it no longer. She pushed open her door, but in so doing panicked all the goats nearest to her, and next thing she knew, the baby had been sucked into the sea of beasts that weren't its mother and dragged away.

A billy goat jumped out of the crowd then and put its two front legs on the hood of the Fiat. It looked straight at her, accusingly.

Lily felt the beginnings of fear. The sour aroma of a thousand goats was starting to stick to her clothes. She turned to look behind her but two goats thrust her out of the way, pushing her farther from her car and into the middle of the road.

They were moving down the hill toward the next corner and taking her with them. She grimaced as she stepped on squishy pile after squishy pile and bade a silent good-bye to her suede Tod's loafers.

The goats were not inclined to scatter, so moving through them was hard work, and it was getting hotter, but at last she rounded the next corner to see that one of the three-wheeled farm trucks so beloved by Italian farmers was parked on the sloping shoulder of the road. More goats milled around it but Lily waded through them to get closer, looking in vain for the driver.

"Hello?" she called out. "*Buongiorno?*"

Nothing but goat voices answered. It was then that she saw the half-hidden signpost to San Biagio tucked between a stand of big leafy trees on the other side of the road. Anywhere else in the world, she might have thought she was dreaming, but in Italy she'd come to accept that a church was just as likely to appear in a hidden lane surrounded by goats as it was in a *piazza grande*.

She trampled her way over to the sign and pushed open a rusted gate. A dozen goats leaped in front of her and scattered up a long overgrown path that delivered her to another gate, which she assumed must be the neglected rear access to the church.

More goats joined her as she wended her way through the undergrowth, then the path cleared and she saw a plain wooden door in the middle of a great expanse of golden stone. This was the church, so surely there would be a priest who could help her, or at least a phone. Or perhaps the goatherd had popped in to say a prayer or drink the holy water.

She pushed open the door.

It was like stepping into a dream.

San Biagio from the outside, even from what little she had seen, was impressive but plain, verging on austere.

Inside it was anything but. Frescoes of cherubs and saints in a palette of pale yellow, blue, and pink adorned the curved ceilings and massive walls, studded with gilded cornices.

Light poured in from the clear windows in the church's massive central dome, illuminating a spot in front of the altar that was itself lit in a smoother hue by a stained-glass window depicting the Virgin Mary.

Lily lifted her hand to shade her eyes and wiped her feet—wretched goats—before starting to move in toward the beautiful altar with its massive statues carved into the wall and a flower arrangement that stood taller than she did.

A figure stood up from a front pew as she approached.

"Lily?"

Her heart skipped another old-fashioned beat. The light streaming from above and behind robbed him of his features, but she could have picked him anywhere. The shape of him, she supposed. His shoulders, hips, head leaning slightly to one side.

It was Daniel. He looked like an angel.

Chapter 45

"That gave us what? An extra ten minutes?" Violetta calculated as she heard the doorbell fall onto the floor of the *pasticceria*.

"Yes, and an extra hundred euro," pointed out Luciana.

"Here, pass me your scarf so I can wave it to the widow Ciacci, will you?" Violetta instructed, opening the window. "She's got the widow Mazzetti over there with the stop watch, but really the widow Del Grasso's our only worry—it turns out she has a phobia about goats."

"So how will she lure old Capriani away from his herd?"

"She has grappa and, more importantly, some of the widow Benedicti's *crostata di more*. If that won't do it he's feeble enough for her to push him over with a decent shove. What about you, are you coming?"

Luciana shook her head and pointed to her bandaged ankle. "Not this time, Violetta. You will have to make do without me."

Chapter 46

"Lily," Daniel said again, the golden light in the middle of the church flaring out behind him.

Lily couldn't think straight. She wasn't prepared. She turned and headed toward the main entrance of the church, struggling with the heavy doors, pushing instead of pulling until she finally wrenched one half open and a goat shot in, a baby one. The same one that had been separated from its mother? It came straight at her, panicked like a puppy or a colt, pushing her away from the door, which slammed shut again.

The kid ran toward Daniel, who was walking up the aisle.

"Maaaah," it said, then stopped, panting, and looked from one to the other.

All Lily needed now was Saint Francis of Assisi to appear and she would know that this was all part of some great celestial joke, not real life.

"You didn't see Francis of Assisi out there, did you?" Daniel asked.

She stared at him, incredulous.

And then she laughed.

It used to happen all the time, that one of them would be thinking something and the other would say it, although she couldn't remember the last time, it was so long ago. How curious that it should happen now.

Her laughter echoed around the empty church, sounding much bigger than it really was.

"What are you doing here?" she asked.

"I was on my way to see a new client in Pienza and got stuck in all those goats. You?"

"The goats. Yes."

He looked at the little kid, which was milling around the pew next to him, then back to her. "I'm so sorry about yesterday, Lily."

Had it only been yesterday? It seemed like a lifetime ago.

"I'm so sorry for everything," Daniel continued. "I came looking for you but I couldn't find you. I went to the *pasticceria* but . . ."

Lily, spookily calm, sat down on the end of the nearest pew. It was so cool in the church, so quiet.

Daniel sat down on the pew across the aisle from her.

For a while there was nothing but the sound of the kid goat scruffling around the altar.

"Happy birthday for yesterday," Lily said.

"Thanks," Daniel replied. "Forty-six."

"What happened, Daniel?" Lily asked. "I need to know."

"Lily, I don't think—"

"Please, I really need to know. I need you to be honest with me. If you can't do that, there's no point in even talking to me."

She was right, of course she was right, but the trouble with the truth was that no matter how he put it, it would hurt.

He could couch it gently, saying the details didn't count, it meant nothing, that he didn't want to cause her any more pain, but really, he doubted that was possible.

He wanted to come clean and there was no easy, no kind, no pretty way to do it.

"I was here on business as usual," he said flatly, "and I had a meeting that didn't go particularly well, so I went to a bar afterward and I met Eugenia."

"When?"

His head was bowed, his fingers clasped in front of him, and she saw his knuckles whiten.

"I think you know when," he said softly. "It's the 'when' that makes it a thousand times worse."

A tear fell silently down her cheek. The "when" did make it a thousand times worse.

"*How could you?* If you loved me like you say you do, how could you?"

If only there were an answer that could wipe away the hideousness of it all, but there wasn't, so Daniel stuck to the truth.

"I don't know," he said. "I don't know. But it was a mistake. A huge mistake and I knew it straightaway, but it was already too late."

So many lives ruined by his *mistake*, thought Lily. By his male stupidity, his selfishness, his thoughtlessness. His own life, hers, Eugenia's, Francesca's, and the little boy she'd never met.

"But you saw her again," she said.

"Yes, the next time I came to Italy. But we never . . . I never . . . She told me she was pregnant and that was that."

Lily closed her eyes and saw the round, full belly that she had ached to have, felt that tiny hidden heartbeat.

"I'm so sorry," Daniel whispered. He meant it, with all his heart he meant it. But he knew that saying it would never be enough. What was an apology, really, when weighed up against his transgression? Nothing but a bunch of useless words.

"Are you in love with her?"

"No."

"Were you ever?"

"No." He shook his head. "I love you, Lily, and that's the truth, but I was—lonely. And stupid. And then there was . . . a child," he tried to soften the blow of that word but couldn't. "I felt I had no choice."

"You felt you had no choice." She sounded cold, dull.

"Lily, honestly, no one could go through what you and I went through and in any conscience make any other decision."

"Don't talk to me about conscience, Daniel! How can you say that?"

"It was an impossible situation."

"Well, you're the one who made it impossible."

"I did. I agree with you. I just didn't see what else I could do."

"So you chose to keep this secret from me for all these years. Can you imagine how stupid I feel? How betrayed?"

Daniel thought of Ingrid. "Lay your heart out like a cloak over a puddle," she had told him. "If you love her, if you want her back, give her whatever she needs."

He had nothing left to lose. Lily was here, listening to him, and there was no point lying or embellishing or hiding anything from her anymore.

"At first, I thought I would tell you," he said. "But you were so fragile after Baby Grace that I was afraid it would be too much for you to bear. And then . . ."

"And then what?'

"And then time passed, Lily, and fragile turned to something else and by then Francesca was two and I knew I had left it too long already, and anyway . . ."

"And anyway what?"

"And anyway, you had stopped noticing me by then."

"So it's my fault?"

"Please! I have no one to blame but myself, I know that. It eats away at me every moment of every day. Can't you see that?"

The truth was, she didn't know what she could see. It was Daniel, her Daniel, but disguised by this shocking deceit that would be between them forever.

"What does that even mean, I stopped noticing you?"

She started to weep before he could answer her—for her lost

children, for his mistake, for the dreadful mess that had driven them apart and would keep them that way and because it was true, she had stopped noticing him. She knew he was lonely because she was lonely too, but it was easier to be busy or distracted or to pour another glass of wine than it was to be hurt.

"You went your own way, Lily."

"You could have come with me," she wept. "You could have done something."

"That's not true. I can only keep up with you if you let me," he said. "It's always been that way. You're the star, I'm just the one catching a ride."

Lily, too, had nothing left to lose.

"It was Baby Grace," she sobbed, unable to contain the pain that was sucking at her lungs. "It was handing her back. I thought I knew what heartbreak was but that car seat, Daniel, that goddamn empty car seat. I should never have thrown it in the Dumpster. I should have sent it back to Grace's mom. She probably never even had a car seat. She probably never even had a car."

"I want to come over there," Daniel said, pleading, tears shining on his cheeks. "I want to hold you."

"No," she wept. "It's too late for that."

"Lily, please. Just let me come over there."

"No," she cried again, even though in a lifetime of loneliness she could not imagine feeling more so. "You must love Eugenia," she said instead. "Or you must have kept seeing her because there's the little boy. There's Ernesto. There are the photos of you all together playing happy family."

Daniel nodded, wiped at his face with the back of his hand.

"Ernesto," he said, "despite Eugenia's protestations to the contrary, is not my son."

"How can that be true? He looks just like you!"

"Well, he looks even more like a Scandinavian backpacker

who came through to pick more than just grapes. We never had a relationship, Lily. It was a fling that had been over for years by then."

"You're just saying that! A woman wouldn't—"

"Lily, Eugenia is troubled. She has a history of being troubled. She requires a lot of looking after. Carlotta is in contact with the backpacker, but he's not in a position to provide in any way, so I do what I can, for Francesca and for the boy. We might play happy family, but that is certainly not what we are."

"You give them money?"

"I give them money. Although . . ."

She sniffed.

"Although what?"

Daniel blew out a lungful of air. "There's something else you need to know," he said. "It's true about my business being in trouble. One of the big corporates has been over here snatching my best suppliers, and I can't blame them, they're offering more than I ever could and trips to Disneyland, can you believe it. I am down to one brunello producer and only two vino nobile and I don't know how much longer I will be able to hang on, even to them."

Lily could not believe her ears. "You want money," she stated plainly.

He laughed, but it was a stunted, disappointed sound.

"No, Lily, I don't want money. I want to be honest."

"Well, I guess you'll be able to sue me for alimony."

"Lily, please. I'm not going to sue you."

"Then what are you going to do?"

"I have no idea. But you know what? Despite me, despite what I've done, how wrong I've been, despite everything, I'm glad you know about Francesca."

Also despite everything, Lily was glad too.

"But is she safe?" she asked. "With her mom?"

"At the moment, I'm not sure."

"Well, what are you going to do, Daniel? And what were you thinking abandoning her like that? You're her father! You can't just run out on her when the going gets tough. That's so cowardly."

"I know it's cowardly," Daniel said, "but I needed some time to think, to work out what to do about this mess, because Francesca needs more than me one week a month and Carlotta when her mother is not well, but I was also thinking about you, Lily. I was thinking that the family I wanted to have was always with you, and how I would never have that."

The kid, still up at the altar, lifted its head suddenly, as though it heard someone calling it, then scampered up the aisle between them toward the door, where it skittered to a halt.

"Should we let it out?" Lily asked, getting to her feet. "I think it's looking for its mother."

"Don't go," Daniel said, standing and reaching for her, resting his hand on her arm.

She looked down at it: his hand with the long fingers that Francesca had inherited, the square nails, the golden skin.

"What do you want me to do?" she asked.

"Don't go," he said again.

She pulled her arm away from him but stayed where she was.

"Don't stay this cold, lonely person," she heard Rose telling her, and Dermott echoing it, and some creamy dessert chiming in too. Part of her wanted to reach out for her husband, to tell him that she could live with what he had done and its consequences, that as long as he still loved her and she loved him everything would be all right. Together they would figure it out.

But those boulders were still in the way and she didn't think she could move them even if she wanted to.

"I know you think you can never forgive me, Lily," Daniel said, his voice thick with tears, "and whatever you want me to do, I'll do it. I'll leave here and come home, forever, or I'll give you a divorce and you'll never have to see me again. Whatever you want, I'll do it."

She wondered then if there was anything he could do that would make it all right.

The kid maaahed sadly at the door. It needed its mother. Everybody needed a mother.

"I love you, Lily Turner," Daniel said, desperately. "I always have and I always will. No matter what. I love you."

She started to walk to the back of the church. He loved her. He always had and he always would.

"Wait," he said. "Lily, please. Wait."

She stopped and reached for the door, but instead her hand found the cool stone of the church wall and rested there.

She believed him. That was the thing. She believed that he had always loved her and always would, no matter what. And that wasn't enough to shift the boulders, but there was still something she could do, a promise she could keep.

She was no longer the same cold, lonely person who had come to Italy. She knew that. She had changed. She slid her hand across the wall and pulled open the door just enough to let the goat out. Then she closed it again and turned to her husband.

"All right," she said, "I'll wait, but not for you. I'll wait until you sort out proper care for Francesca but after that . . . I'm sorry, Daniel. That's as far as I can go."

Chapter 47

Once the church was empty again, the curtains on either side of the priest's confessional drew back and Violetta and Fiorella emerged into the sunlit aisle.

"Luciana will be disappointed about her moment," Violetta said unhappily.

"Yes, but the good news is she still has it to look forward to," Fiorella said. "It could have been a lot worse, after all. Imagine if Lily had driven over the goats, not that I particularly care for goats, although the cheese has possibilities, but she could be headed to Rome by now and on to America never to be seen again. She talked to him, didn't she? And he's very good-looking, isn't he? And she's staying, isn't she? Your plan was successful."

"Well, it wasn't unsuccessful," conceded Violetta.

Fiorella pushed her spectacles up her little pug nose. "Do you like me now, just a little bit?" she asked.

"I don't dislike you," Violetta said as they wandered out to the front of the church. The truth was Fiorella was growing on them all like a toadstool in the winter. Luciana had been right, the League needed a breath of fresh air and Fiorella was definitely that.

Also, she was good on the texting.

"You'd better get in touch with Del Grasso to tell Mario to find Carlotta and bring Francesca to the *pasticceria*."

"Good plan!" cried Fiorella, clapping her hands together. "Sounds to me like more *amorucci*!"

Chapter 48

When Lily walked back into the kitchen a couple of hours later, the Ferretti sisters seemed completely unsurprised.

"This is good you are here," Violetta said as if she'd never left in the first place. "We have trouble with the heart shapes." She held up some literally half-hearted *cantucci*, then shuffled over to Lily, thrusting a cookie cutter into her hand.

As she gazed at it dimly, the bell above the shop door rang and Francesca ran into the room.

"Oh, Lillian!" she cried. "Oh, *amorucci!*"

"We do big favor and look after Francesca this week," Violetta explained, pouring flour and sugar onto the table. "And we take your advice to beat Borsolini *bastardi* at their own game. We do everything they do, only in hearts. So this is good you are here."

Francesca threw her arms around Lily, burying her face in the folds of her soft cashmere cardigan.

"This *is* good you are here," she agreed.

There were not enough words in any language for Lily to express the complicated mixture of pain and joy that churned inside her right then. She took a couple of long, deep breaths, inhaling the strawberry smell of Francesca's shampoo, wondering what else, other than having clean hair, was different about her today.

"Hey, where are your wings, Tinker Bell?" she asked, when she realized they were what was missing.

"Papa is getting them fixed," she said. "And anyway, I am growed out of them." She unfurled her arms from around Lily's waist and licked her lips at the bowls of dried fruit, nuts, and chocolate in front of her. "Would we make the *amorucci* now?"

The old women looked expectantly at Lily who felt the cookie cutter gently pressing a soft heart shape into the palm of her hand.

"Well, yes," answered Lily. "I suppose we would," and she plunged her hands into the beginnings of the *pasticceria*'s first commercial batch of *amorucci*.

Really, what else was she going to do? She was there, Francesca was there, the melted butter and the cranberries and candied lemon were there. It just made sense to pitch right in and get on with it. What's more, as one hour rolled into the next and she mixed and baked and cooled and sliced and baked and cooled and tasted, she kept drifting away from her unhappiness and confusion to find a smile floating on her face. She didn't know quite what it was doing there, but it returned again and again and again.

Later in the evening she headed to the Internet café on the *piazza grande* and sent an e-mail to Heigelmann's saying she was unavoidably tied up with a family situation in Italy and would not immediately be back. She should have called; e-mailing was not a serious way of broaching her absence. But she just couldn't imagine explaining to her CEO that she was in Italy baking cookies with her husband's love child and an ancient extortionate landlady without laughing. It was ridiculous, after all, but an inexplicably good sort of ridiculous.

Because she'd never spent any time in the kitchen, it was a surprise for Lily to discover what comfort could be found there. But the simple process of mixing dull everyday ingredients to create something entirely new and delightful never failed to inspire her. It was so uncomplicated. And Francesca never tired of helping. Together they produced batch after batch of delicious *amorucci*. They were in a world of their own.

After a couple of days, they had made enough *amorucci* to fill all the bowls in the *pasticceria* and so Lily convinced Violetta, with a little help from Luciana, to actually allow customers into the store.

For the first proper open day not many tourists made it past the Borsolinis' shop. In fact, as far as Lily could make out, the Ferrettis' store seemed to be populated solely by little old ladies much like the Ferrettis themselves. They didn't buy anything but seemed very pleased with the free samples that Lily and Francesca set out. And while they may not have put money in the coffers, tourists soon started noticing the crowd in the *pasticceria* and began to dribble in to buy the *amorucci* themselves.

"We have viable prospect," Violetta said to Lily, watching Francesca count out change to give to a large foreign woman who had bought six bags, one in each flavor. It had been Francesca's idea to put the cookies in clear cellophane bags tied with pink ribbons with little red hearts on them. They were quite irresistible.

By the following week, Lily's smile was in danger of becoming a permanent fixture. The hours spent in the kitchen with the old women and Francesca were among the happiest she could remember. It wasn't real life, baking cookies in a sweet-smelling Tuscan kitchen with a child who wasn't hers. But the moments when they stood side by side rolling the *cantucci* into logs, or when Lily wiped chocolate off the end of Francesca's nose, or when they tried to teach Violetta to juggle certainly felt real.

In the afternoons Daniel would come to collect his daughter. At first, Lily's smile faded when he walked in the door and she found it difficult to look at him, let alone speak to him, but after a while it just became part of what her new unexpected routine kicked up.

She even found herself checking her watch if he was running late.

"Could I buy you a drink?" he asked her one afternoon. "Once I've dropped Francesca at Carlotta's?"

Lily could feel the heat of Violetta's beady eyes on her neck and saw that Francesca was watching her carefully. She didn't want a drink, the thought of it made her feel ill, but she did want to find out what was happening with Eugenia, so reluctantly she agreed.

The plan was to meet at a little bar up on the tiny Piazza San Francesca, which looked back out over the top of San Biagio's copper dome from a diffrent angle.

She spotted him from the street above as she approached and surprised herself by thinking how handsome he was, because she did not expect to still see him that way. Two pretty girls moved past his outside table as she watched him, one making a meal of it in her opinion; she obviously saw Daniel that way too. But he didn't even seem to notice the pretty girl.

He was clearly a man looking out for someone else. She felt a lurch, the slightest movement of a single pebble.

"So, what's happening with Francesca's mother?" she asked briskly, nonetheless, as she sat down.

"She's in a residential facility in Umbria," Daniel said. "She's been there before and she's in good hands, but we're not sure how long she'll be there this time. She needs to get the right medication and keep taking it."

"And where does that leave Francesca?"

"Carlotta is doing her best juggling Ernesto and her job, and I'm doing as much as I can while I try to work, but to be honest, Lily, you and the Ferrettis and the baking . . . well . . . you're a godsend." He smiled. "My Lily and baking all in the same sentence. I never thought I'd see the day."

"I guess we've both had days we never thought we'd see," Lily said in a brittle tone that reminded her of her mother. "I'm sorry," she added ambiguously, shaking her head at the waitress after Daniel ordered a glass of red.

"Lily, I know you haven't had much time to think," he started once they were alone again, "but if you could—"

"Don't, Daniel," she stopped him. "Just, please, don't. I'm here for Francesca because for whatever reason I am in a position to help her and that's what I want to do, but I can't do it forever. I have to get back to work; I am running out of paid leave. So don't get your hopes up."

"My hopes are up, I can't help that. And they will stay up where you are concerned, Lily. Forever."

"Well, that's your problem," she snapped.

"I'm sorry, I don't mean to upset you," he said. "That's the last thing I want to do. I'm just glad you came."

"Yes, well, let's try to keep this about Francesca, shall we? What's the long-term plan?"

"I'm trying to sort that out at the moment. We think maybe a nanny would work out until Eugenia is back on her feet, but there's no telling how long that will take, and I need to get back to New York at some stage to try and sell some wine so I can afford it. Otherwise, there is an aunt near Orvieto, but Francesca would have to change schools and she hasn't had the easiest time settling into the Montevedova one so . . ."

They both stared out across the breathtakingly beautiful rolling green hills of the Val D'Orcia. The evening sun fell gently across the landscape. It was impossibly peaceful.

"Francesca took off her wings," Daniel said into the silence. "I asked her if I could get them fixed, just like I have done a hundred times over the past year, and she just took them off and handed them to me."

Lily smiled. "Yes, she told me. She said she'd 'growed' out of them."

"She told you that?"

Lily nodded and bit her lip, praying that he wouldn't tell her what a great mother she would make. She couldn't bear it. But he didn't.

"Do you think about Grace?" she asked out of nowhere. "When you're thinking about Francesca or talking about her or looking at her, do you also think about Grace?"

"Of course I do," he said.

"I can't help myself from wondering what she's doing. How she's getting on at school, how her mom—how Brittany is."

Daniel was silent for a moment, then turned, his green eyes anxious, to look at her.

"I don't know if we have a future together, Lily, if you'll give me another chance, but whatever happens, I don't want there to be any more secrets between us."

"There's more? Please, Daniel, I don't know if—"

"Brittany went to college," Daniel said. "She is a school teacher just like she wanted to be. She got married a couple of years ago to a guy with two younger daughters who Grace seems to get along great with. She is a smart kid, she gets good grades, she likes gym class, she does ballet, she's allergic to tree nuts, she plays the piano, she wants a pony but she's only allowed a cat."

Lily began to cry.

"I should have told you," Daniel continued. "I've had a private detective send me a report every six months since we got back from Tennessee. I shouldn't have done it. But I wanted to know, to make sure she was happy so that I could tell you and make you happy, but the time was never right. I didn't tell you. And I didn't make you happy, but I wanted to."

"What else?" Lily asked. "What else about Grace?"

"She's small for her age, she has dark hair, she rides a pink bicycle."

"Well, I hope she wears a helmet."

"She does wear a helmet. It's pink too, with purple ribbons coming out of it. I have a photo . . ."

"Oh, Daniel . . ."

He pulled his chair closer to hers but knew better than to reach for her, instead handing her a paper napkin so she could dry her eyes. The two girls at the next table looked at her and started whispering but she didn't care.

"I can't believe you did that," she said when she had finally composed herself. "I can't believe you put a tail on Baby Grace."

"I know and I'm sorry."

"No, you shouldn't be sorry." She fought back more tears. "You did make me happy, Daniel," she said. "Once upon a time, you did make me happy."

"I think I could again," he said desperately. "If you'd just give me a chance."

"It's too much to ask. I don't know how to do it."

"I could help you," he said.

"I don't think forgiveness works that way."

"Well, it should."

"But it doesn't. What's done is done." Lily stood up, wiping her face one last time before giving him back the scrunched-up paper napkin.

"Thank you so much for telling me about Grace," she said. "I can't tell you how much that puts my heart at rest."

"I'm sorry, Lily," he said. "I will never stop being sorry."

"Don't, Daniel. I'm tired of hearing it. It doesn't change anything."

"Maybe not, but isn't it better to have everything out in the open?" he asked.

"Maybe for you. You're the one with all the secrets."

"Yes, well, while we're at it, I have one more," he said, but with something of an old familiar twinkle in his eye. "I don't really like polo shirts."

She laughed and had to stop herself from telling him that it was Pearl who bought them for him, anyway. She didn't want to hurt him, she thought, as she walked across the *piazza grande*. She still felt something for him. She wasn't sure if it was love but she was sure it wasn't hate. So what was it?

She was distracted then by the sound of an approaching baby crying and saw that it was the same baby she had seen on her first day in Montevedova, only this time the red umbrella was keeping the late sun, not the rain, off the pram.

The same grandfather gave Lily a cheeky wink as he passed her, while she peered in at the fat little cherub who was squawking in her nest, legs waving furiously in the air, fists balled and flailing.

The old man hadn't noticed that the baby's headband had fallen down over one eye so Lily put her hand out and gently grabbed his elbow to stop him, then reached in and straightened the headband herself, her fingers brushing the baby's hot, damp head, caressing just for the briefest moment her soft thatch of almost invisible hair. The baby screwed up one eye and roared even harder.

"*Grazie*," smiled the old man anyway. "*Grazie*." And he pushed the pram across the piazza. Lily stood and watched till they had disappeared over the crest of the hill, but it wasn't until she was halfway back to the *pasticceria* that she realized her innards hadn't shriveled at the sound of the cries.

Chapter 49

The widows were in their underground HQ a week later, eating *amorucci*, when the widow Ercolani dropped a bombshell.

"Who was that old man I saw you with behind the bus station yesterday?" she asked Fiorella, a mean little glint in her eye. "That was quite a conversation you were having by the looks of things."

Fiorella looked warily at the inquisitive faces around the room. "It wasn't that sort of 'behind the bus station,'" she said. "Trust me, he did not lay a finger on me."

"Yes, but who was he?" insisted the widow Ercolani. "Or would you like me to tell everyone?"

"Have you been spying on me?" Fiorella accused her.

"Yes, I have," the widow Ercolani answered proudly, "and it's just as well, because otherwise how would everyone else in the League know what a phony you are. A phony, a fake, and a fraud."

"A phony?" asked the widow Benedicti. She had grown quite fond of Fiorella. They all had—apart from the widow Ercolani it seemed.

"A fake?" repeated the widow Mazzetti.

"A fraud?" piped up the widow Ciacci.

Violetta and Luciana just looked at each other and shrugged. They had recently decided that when you were this close to a hundred, nothing was really that surprising.

"Yes, all of those things," the widow Ercolani confirmed. "And do you want to know why? She's not a widow. That was her husband behind the bus station. He's alive and extremely well by the look of him."

Half a dozen mouths in various stages of toothlessness fell wide open.

Fiorella looked at Violetta, who just raised what was left of her eyebrows.

"OK, OK, OK, I confess," Fiorella said. "I'm not as widowed as I originally made out. But he did run off with my sister and he does live in Naples."

"And Eduardo?"

"And Eduardo! Of course, Eduardo. Always Eduardo!" She pushed her spectacles up her nose, balled her hands into tight little fists, raised her rounded shoulders, and looked for all the world ready to take on the Italian heavyweight boxing champion, but then Fiorella Fiorucci stunned them all by bursting into noisy uncontrollable tears.

"I was lonely," she cried. "I've been lonely ever since Eduardo left for the war, but the older I get, the lonelier I am. No one notices me. I wore red stilettos and no one so much as looked at my feet. I was invisible until you let me join the League. You are ornery," she said as she pointed to the widow Ercolani, "but the rest of you are like sisters. I've never been so happy." And she cried fit to drown the lot of them in her tears.

"There, there," said the widow Ciacci, moving over to give her a comforting pat.

"What was your husband doing here?" asked Luciana.

"He and my selfish slattern of a sister have run out of money. He came back because he wants to sell my apartment out from under me."

"She can't stay in the League," the widow Ercolani said.

"There are rules, remember?" She prodded the widow Mazzetti, who looked slightly sheepish.

"Now, let's not be too hasty here," Violetta said. "There are rules and then there are rules."

"There are two lots?" asked the widow Mazzetti, who only had one clipboard.

"If recent events have taught me anything," Violetta said, "it's that times have changed and we must change with them. Fiorella, you have been a welcome addition to our League, and the fact you are not a widow is beside the point. You are right. You are a sister. We are all sisters."

"But that's not what—" the widow Ercolani started but was interrupted by the widow Pacini, who hated the thought of anyone being lonely.

"I agree with Violetta," she said.

"Me too," said the widow Benedicti.

"Same here," the widow Ciacci concurred.

"And here," added the widow Mazzetti. "Although perhaps we should think about redrafting the constitution."

"Widow Ercolani, do you care to say something else?" asked Violetta. But the widow Ercolani knew when she was beat. She just shook her head and looked at her feet.

"Right, then. It's decided. Once again, welcome, Fiorella, to the Secret League of Widowed (or Otherwise) Darners. Now, on the subject of darning, progress as you have probably seen is slow but steady with Lily and Daniel. We had hoped there might have been more of a breakthrough by now, but they are seeing each other every day and obviously it's working out very well on the *amorucci* front." There was a chorus of "*sí, sí, sí.*" They really did like the *amorucci*.

"Anyway, it's clear to us that Daniel is not the problem. He will do anything to win her back, according to a granddaughter of the widow Ciacci, who overheard every word of their conversation at the Bar Francesca the other evening and happened to pass it on. It is Lily who is wary."

"That's not all she is," said Fiorella. "Three pregnancy tests in one day usually only means one thing."

Violetta nearly choked on her *vin santo* as Luciana gave a startled cough. Turned out some things still were surprising.

"Lily is pregnant?" Violetta asked.

"I reckon," answered Fiorella.

"She's the size of a breadstick," pointed out the widow Ercolani. "She can't be that pregnant."

"No, she can't," agreed Violetta.

"In the name of Santa Ana di Chisa," cried the widow Benedicti. "It must be Alessandro's! Partial undress must be all you need these days."

"Yes, it must," agreed Violetta.

"But this is a catastrophe! She belongs with Daniel but she carries another man's child?"

Violetta felt a delicious warmth creep over her like a feather duvet. It was her instinct, safe and sound, guiding her toward what was right.

"Yes, she does and yes, she is," she chortled. "Ladies, gather round."

Chapter 50

She should have put two and two together the moment her insides failed to shrink from the cry of that fat baby girl in the piazza.

She was tired, she was pale, her smooth skin was unusually spotty, she had a headache, she had sore breasts. She'd had most of these symptoms before, after all. But she'd expunged the afternoon on Alessandro's couch from her mind, so it did not occur to Lily until she realized her period was late that she could be pregnant.

But she was.

She just knew it. The timing, the nausea, the enormous incongruity of it all. It had to be! Still she ran down to the pharmacy at the bottom of town, foregoing the prying eyes at the busy pharmacy that was closer to the *pasticceria*, and bought a pregnancy test. It was positive. So she ran back and bought two more. All three said the same thing, but they didn't even have to—she felt it. She felt it in her skin, in her hair, in her eyes. She felt it everywhere.

And this time, something inside her whispered that the little angel already nesting there, despite the complications it was going to deliver, had fought this hard to get this far and would keeping fighting all the way to the end. Or the beginning. This little angel, she truly believed, was hers for keeps.

Sitting in her tiny bathroom, the third positive stick in her hand, the terrible wonder of it all flooded through her, starting at her toes, stopping for a moment to spin about the tiny new life forming in her center, then shooting up past her chaotic heart to her whirring mind.

She was having Alessandro's baby.

It was a disaster. A wonderful, amazing, awful, joyful, frightening, extraordinary disaster.

There was so much about it that was wrong! Alessandro didn't want a baby with her. He hardly knew her. She hadn't even seen him since this most miraculous of conceptions. And she didn't want a baby with Alessandro, either.

There was her age, her career, her marriage, the fact she was in Italy and had promised to help with Francesca, the Ferretti sisters, the *amorucci* . . .

There was so much that was wrong. But the kaleidoscope of complications was overshadowed by what was right. Lily wanted this baby. More than anything else in the world, she wanted this baby. She had always wanted this baby.

She walked to her picture window and sat on the sill, watching the ridiculous countryside crawl out of its sleepy state the same way she did every morning. She laughed to herself, delighted, then bit her lip to keep from crying. More than anything else in the world, she wanted this baby.

"Lillian!" she heard Francesca call from the kitchen. "Where are you, Lillian?"

"I'm up here, sweetie," she called back. "Come for a visit."

The clatter of her footsteps up the little stairway swelled Lily's already overflowing heart and when Francesca burst into the room and came running toward her, she couldn't keep the tears from flowing.

"What's the matter?" Francesca asked, as she fell into Lily's arms. "Are you sad?"

"No, honey, I'm not. I'm happy. I know it seems silly but sometimes grown-ups cry when they're happy."

"Why are you happy?"

Her life was so far from the perfection of her dreams that it was laughable. The picture of that huddle of children gathered around her and Daniel as they grew old together lost in the mists of their broken marriage.

And yet she had found the closest thing on earth to a daughter and was now, finally, God and all the saints willing, going to be a mother.

"I don't know," she said to Francesca, giving her a squeeze. "I just am."

"Come on," Francesca said, holding out her hand. "The Ferrettis need you to go on an errand."

Relieved to have some time to herself to digest the topsyturvy turn her future had just taken, Lily agreed to deliver a carton of *amorucci* to a trattoria in Montechiello, another tiny hilltop town about a forty-minute drive away.

"Your first commercial order," she remarked as she picked up the box. "Congratulations."

"You cannot miss trattoria," Violetta said, virtually shoving her out the door. "Is only *ristorante* in town."

Lily could barely remember driving there, her mind was whirring so fast. Should she go home to New York now? It seemed the most appropriate course of action—she needed to see specialists, go through the usual testing rigmarole after all. Or did she? She thought of the smile she kept finding on her face. Tuscany seemed to have put it there so firmly after such a long absence. She had a lot to thank this beautiful corner of the world for.

She parked at the portal to Montechiello and started to climb up to the trattoria with her box of *amorucci*. Red geraniums spilled over the edge of the ancient stone fence that ringed the town, a bright green and yellow lizard basking in the heat flicked out its tongue at her. She poked her own tongue back at it. It was a perfect temperature, the sun dancing across her back, a slight breeze tickling her face.

She pushed open the door to the restaurant. It was dark, with no one behind the counter, but a set of double doors opened out on to a terrace that overlooked the pretty valley she had just driven through.

"Hello!" she called as she stepped out on to it, catching a whiff of the jasmine that crawled up the trellis behind her.

A single table with a white tablecloth that flapped slightly in the breeze was set up at the edge of the terrace. A bottle of wine and two glasses sat on top of the table. Behind it was Daniel.

"Oh, it's you!" she said.

He laughed, and in that moment he looked just like the Daniel she had fallen in love with all those years before. A slightly smudged version, admittedly, a little lined, a little crestfallen, but still, the very same Daniel.

"Yes, it's me," he said. "Would it be too corny to say we must stop meeting like this?"

She smiled back at him and sat down at the table. "I never minded a bit of corny," she confessed.

"I'm supposed to be meeting a new winemaker here, his wife called me first thing this morning, but our hostess now tells me he was held up. She just left me with this bottle before rushing off on some emergency of her own. I know it's early but would you care for a little wine?"

He went to pour her some, but Lily held her hand over her glass. "Not for me, thank you, no."

"I'm sure I could find a white, if you preferred, or a prosecco. It's not champagne, but—"

"No, Daniel, really. I am not drinking."

"Not drinking?"

He looked at her, concerned, and just like that she knew that she did love him, that she felt love more strongly than anything else, and whatever the history, it was up to her to roll those boulders away from the difficult access to her heart. She could do it if she wanted to.

And right then, sitting in the lazy sunshine, a new life radiating in her belly, she wanted to.

Her timing was off, to say the least, but now that she was looking at the future instead of the past, she felt certain again. It was as simple as that; she felt certain about him.

Of course, he might not feel so certain about her, in the circumstances, but there was only one way to find out.

"Will you really love me always, Daniel, no matter what?"

He looked taken aback but answered nonetheless. "Yes, I will."

"Even if I've done something that will change everything between us forever?"

"I don't think that's possible."

"Trust me, Daniel, it's possible. In fact, it's a dead certainty."

"You're scaring me, Lily. Are you OK?"

"I'm fine, I'm better than fine, but I still need you to promise that you'll love me, no matter what."

"I can't imagine what the 'no matter what' would be, but yes, Lily, I mean it when I say it: I will always love you."

"Because I think I know now how you felt after you met Eugenia and found out about Francesca, about having all the right things but with the wrong person. I think I know that."

"I'm so sorry, Lily. I know you don't want to hear it anymore, but that doesn't mean I will ever stop being sorry."

"No, Daniel, things are different now. It's me who is sorry," she said. "I'm pregnant." And even the look on his face could not take away the thrill of those words.

"I met someone here. I don't love him, in fact I hardly know him. And I know you will think I did it to hurt you, but I didn't. I wasn't thinking about you, I was thinking about—well, I don't know what I was thinking about. And I don't know what is going to happen now because I have my job in New York, but I have never been happier than I am baking *amorucci* with your daughter. I don't know where I should go or what I should do, but I can't honestly say I wish none of it had happened because I'm pregnant, Daniel. I'm pregnant, and I really feel that this time it's going to work out. I really do. Somehow without anything to back me up and all the usual evidence to the contrary, I think this time it's going to work out."

Daniel put his glass slowly back on the table. A seed pod crackled nearby in the heat. A motorcycle roared past on the road below them.

"Please say something," Lily said.

"I'm in shock, Lily. What do you want me to say?"

"I want you to say that even though we've made a mess of everything, you still love me and you want to help me and together somehow we'll figure it all out."

"You want me to be happy you're having another man's child?"

"Under any other circumstances I would not even contemplate asking you to be happy I was having another man's child," she said. "But under these circumstances, that's exactly what I'm asking."

"Jesus, Lily, it just seems . . ."

"Impossible? Yes, it does seem that way. But is it? I'm happy you have Francesca. I really am. I never thought I would be, and if I hadn't come here I never would have found that out. But I did come here, I did find it out, and more than that, I'm happy *I* have her. I want to help you, Daniel. And I know it's not perfect but it's better than it was, than we were. We'll have a family. Not the one we dreamed of, and certainly not a traditional one, but we'll have a family. Together."

"I feel ambushed," he said.

"I know the feeling," she told him, but gently. "The difference is I'm sitting here in front of you telling you. You're not finding out about it in a golf shoe. You said you could help me forgive you; well, now I accept your offer. And I can help you forgive me."

"But forgiveness doesn't work that way. Remember?"

"It should. I remember that."

Daniel looked at her across the table, the rolling green hills of Tuscany framing her beautiful face, the veneer that had disguised her for so many years ripped away, leaving her just the way he always pictured her in his mind.

She was blossoming in front of his very eyes, this woman with whom he had shared and lost so much. Could it work? This bizarre patchwork of unrelated children and battle-scarred parents? His wife was bearing another man's child, which wounded him in a way he wasn't sure he could heal. He wasn't even sure he wanted to. Yet he had wanted her to do just the same. And she was looking at him now with such confidence, such faith, looking at him the way she used to look at him long ago when their future was full of undashed hope and limitless possibilities.

The truth was, if he discounted all the things he had done wrong and all the things she had, he still felt the same way about her. But now there was this baby and it would be between them forever, reminding them of all their foolishness and the heartbreak it had caused.

"I know what you're thinking," Lily told him. "You're thinking that this is too much, too painful, that there's no getting over it. But Daniel, I'm probably the only person in the world who knows that *you can*. Maybe not this minute, maybe not this week. But you can. You still love me, you want to help me, and together we can figure it all out."

"I don't know," he said. "Lily, I really just don't know."

She reached across the table and took his hands in hers.

"Well, that's all right," she said. "Because I do."

Chapter 51

Upstairs in the trattoria, Violetta, Luciana, and Fiorella fell away from the window where they had been spying on what was happening on the terrace below.

"Now that," whispered Luciana, "was the moment we've all been waiting for."

"Are you sure?" said Violetta. "He had a funny expression on his face if you ask me."

"Have you forgotten what a man in love looks like?" hissed Fiorella.

"In the name of Santa Ana di Chisa, it was the moment, Violetta," Luciana said. "It was definitely the moment."

"You need to get your eyes fixed," Fiorella agreed. "Trust us, your plan was successful."

Violetta looked at Fiorella, then at her sister. She did trust them.

"Well, it wasn't unsuccessful," she conceded.

Chapter 52

The first Sunday of the following July, Lily woke up and pulled back the curtain in her apartment. It was another beautiful day in Montevedova—all the better for being the inaugural feast day of Santa Ana di Chisa.

The huge *festa* had been months in the planning and there was much to do, as it was an *amorucci*-focused affair and there was a lot of *amorucci* still to be made.

First, though, Lily did what she'd done every single morning for the past four months. She tiptoed over to the crib in the corner of the room and peeked in to see if her son was awake. This ritual, which seemed as ingrained in her now as blinking or breathing, never failed to fill her with the simple bliss of being content, of being lucky, of being exactly where she wanted to be. It was a perfect way to start the day.

Matteo—named for the Italian neighbor of Daniel's childhood—was awake, lying happily on his back, his big brown eyes scrunching up with delight at the sight of his mother, his fat arms reaching for her, fingers wriggling.

She picked him up, kissed the chubby bracelets of his wrists, his dimpled knees, his soft brown cheeks then held him in the air and blew a raspberry into the warm sponge of his fat little belly. He squealed with delight, his bare legs jiggling for joy. It was a sound Lily could not get enough of.

"Will you turn that thing down," Daniel grumbled from the

bed, sitting up to see his wife and child silhouetted against the window, early morning Tuscany shaking itself gracefully awake behind them.

The baby turned to him and held his fat arms out in his direction, wriggling his fingers and squealing some more. Lily then delivered him to Daniel's arms for his morning cuddle.

"I'll feed him," she said. "Then I'm due at the *pasticceria* so could you watch him till the next feeding time and then bring him over?"

"What do you say, Matteo?" Daniel asked the baby. "Shall we do man stuff while the old lady's in the kitchen?" Matteo waved everything he had, which they both took to mean yes.

Lily watched her husband and son nestle down together among the pillows. He was such a natural, loving, hands-on father it took her breath away every day. He took her breath away.

Not that it had been easy—she suspected that forgiveness never was—but they had managed over the past year to put so much behind them that it was once more what lay in front of them that mattered.

She had gone back to New York only once, in her first trimester, to see Rose, have a checkup with her gynecologist, resign from Heigelmann's, and collect a few things from the apartment.

But after that, she had let go of her old life as easily as a helium balloon and not even stayed to watch it float away.

Tuscany was her lucky charm, Montevedova now her home. Her job was being a mother, making *amorucci*, and helping Daniel establish his new business exporting table wines back to the States.

She could not imagine being happier, being more loved or in love. It brought gooseflesh to her skin, tears to her eyes, and a contentment to her heart that she had thought was lost forever.

"I don't need to say it, do I?" she said as she kissed her husband and son, her eyes glistening.

"No, you don't." Daniel smiled. "Now go to work. Matty and I have got a lot of talking about NASCAR and strip joints to get through."

As Lily walked from their new apartment to the *pasticceria*, the Santa Ana di Chisa banners flying from windows above her snapped gently in the warm summer breeze.

The *festa* had been her idea, way back when Matteo was just an egg in her nest.

"So who exactly is Santa Ana di Chisa?" she had asked Violetta one day when she was rolling out a batch of candied orange and pine nut *amorucci*. "I keep hearing her name."

"Yes, I am asking the same thing," said Fiorella, another elderly but sprightly villager who had moved into Lily's old upstairs room by then, and who spoke excellent English.

"This could be tricky," the widow Ciacci said in Italian to Luciana. She had become a regular fixture at the open window, the *amorucci* being far more agreeable to her taste now that it was less likely to be on fire.

"You don't know?" Lily asked Fiorella. "I got the feeling she was someone special around here."

"I try Googling her," said Fiorella, "but nothing is there. I Google myself better."

"She is patron saint of widowed darners," Violetta insisted.

"She is?" asked Fiorella.

"Let's see her dig her way out of this one," Luciana said to the widow Ciacci.

"I wouldn't have thought there were enough widowed darners to get their own patron saint," said Lily.

"We have a league of them here in Montevedova," Violetta said carefully. "And there are perhaps other leagues in other towns. We meet and we fix things and we talk."

"That's what you do downstairs?"

"What stairs?" Violetta asked, fixing her with an intimidating glare.

"So where is Santa Ana di Chisa coming from?" asked Fiorella by way of a distraction. "And when is the feast day?"

"Oh, yes, there must be a party," Lily said. "Or a holiday."

"She does not have feast day," Violetta said. "She is new."

"How do you even get a new patron saint?" Lily asked.

"There isn't one when we first start to look," answered Violetta. "There is Santa Anne for sewing but no one for darning. Santa Catherina di Genoa look good for some time, but we lose her when we find out Genoa claim to invent pesto and everybody know pesto starts here in 1927, but nobody like it so they don't make a fuss."

"Is pesto the one with all the *basilico*?" asked the widow Ciacci. "Waste of *parmiggiano* if you ask me."

"What did she say?" asked Lily.

"Tell her about Santa Rita di Cascia," suggested Luciana.

"There is one widow in our league," Violetta obliged, "now passed away, who think Santa Rita di Cascia is good, but then we find out only reason is because Santa Rita di Cascia has stigmata, a wound on her head that smells very bad, so she become a recluse until near her death, when it smells of cinnamon rolls."

Fiorella looked at her. "And?"

"And this one widow, now passed away, she like cinnamon rolls."

Even Fiorella looked slightly dumbfounded at this.

"So how did you stumble on Santa Ana di Chisa?" Lily wanted to know.

"Was not so much of a stumble," Violetta said.

"What does that mean?"

"It means if we have *festa* or holiday it must be when Father Dominico is visiting Vatican because there could be some problem."

"Some problem?" hooted Fiorella. "Ooooh, I get it. I get it and I love it!" She jumped around the kitchen like the little frog she was.

"Get what?" Lily said, reaching out to stop her bouncing.

"Santa Ana for Anne of sewing," Fiorella said in Italian, between laughs. "And Chisa for '*chi sa*.'"

"*Chi sa*? What are you talking about?"

"Who knows!" roared Fiorella, refusing to speak English. "*Chi sa* for who knows. Violetta, you are the cat's pajamas. You made up the League's patron saint!"

"Well, no one else found one for us," Violetta answered in Italian.

"What are you saying?" Lily wanted to know. She was learning the language but this was beyond her. "I can't understand you."

"Santa Ana di Chisa, she's blonde, like you," Violetta told her. "But not so tall."

And so it was decided that the feast day of Santa Ana di Chisa would be celebrated on the first Sunday in July and that as it was the Ferrettis' idea, *amorucci* would be the patron *dolci*.

Half an hour after kissing her baby good-bye on the day of the inaugural *festa*, Lily was kissing her sister hello outside the *pasticceria*.

"I just can't get used to everything being so goddamned beautiful," Rose said. "Even Al is looking pretty good these days. Who knew? I thought we were beyond that."

"Where is he?" asked Lily.

"He's working on the gondola with Alessandro," Rose answered. "I have a horrible feeling we may end up with one of those things in the yard back in Connecticut."

"Well, at least you're nearer to water," Lily said, giving her sister a hug. "Thank you so much for being here, Rose. All of you."

"Are you kidding me? A summer vacation in Tuscany? I admit, at first I didn't want to bring the family with me, but with every passing day, I swear, those kids are more adorable and Al a little less past his sell-by date. There must be something in the air."

They both lifted their noses and sniffed.

"Rosewater and almond," Lily said. "Are the kids already in the kitchen?"

"You betcha. Those little old ladies came out and snatched them right out from under me."

The door tinkled as Lily opened it to go in. "Are you coming?" she asked her sister.

"Oh, no, I bow to your undisputed superiority in the kitchen," Rose said, with a smile. "I'm going to take a walk in the Italian sunshine with only a large pastry for company if you don't mind."

"See you in the piazza?"

"See you in the piazza."

Lily's happy heart swelled even more when she walked into the kitchen and saw the production line of children gathered around the old refectory table.

Jack and Harry were arguing with each other, as usual, but also competing for the attention of Francesca, who was instead in the thrall of Emily and Charlotte, who in turn were besotted by the extremely beautiful Ernesto.

Violetta, Luciana, and Fiorella sat in the corner of the room, gossiping in Italian, something that, with Lily at the helm of the *pasticceria*, they now had a lot more time for.

The Ferretti sisters were in extremely good humor. They'd started a fund, so Violetta told her, with the increasingly healthy profits from the *pasticceria* and so were both taking expensive medication for their arthritis, which made them far more limber. Violetta in particular had a new spring in her step thanks to the added advantage of a stent in her heart, which had, unbeknownst to her, been giving her chest trouble for quite some years. They both had new dentures.

There were many meetings down the secret stairs Lily wasn't supposed to know about to plan where else this health fund should be spent, and she had noticed that a lot of the old women she often found huddling around the fluted bowls in the *pasticceria* now bore new white teeth and more than a couple had hearing aids.

The sisters, Fiorella, and a handful of other old darners were now in such good health, so Lily had been told, that they were planning a trip to Cremona to broaden their horizons. It was the birthplace of Stradivari, and now that they could hear better, they particularly liked violin music.

In fact, they had it playing in the kitchen, although it was hard to hear it over the sound of the children making *amorucci*.

Jack, at eleven, had been skeptical about the whole business of baking to begin with but actually liked the scientific part of getting the right combination of ingredients and producing the right result, and he was good at organizing the other children to do things for him.

Harry had a thing for knives and so liked chopping, although he had to be watched, and the twins would do pretty much what Jack told them to, unless they were busy fussing over Ernesto, who had no interest in what was going on at all but just loved being fussed over.

Francesca made it clear that she was in charge of the cookie cutter, but as the production line rolled out, she allowed her "cousins" all to have a turn.

For the next couple of hours, Lily wrangled the gang of children as they mixed, baked, cooled, sliced, baked, cut, and tasted so that when Daniel arrived with Matteo, the last of the *amorucci* was ready to be packed up and carried to the piazza for the *festa*.

She and her husband then tottered up the hill, laden with boxes and surrounded by the excitable children, arriving in the square to find it transformed into a humming marketplace built around a heart-shaped table already bearing dozens of fluted bowls, each one piled high with *amorucci*. The table had been Carlotta's idea, and she was there decorating it. She had quite an artistic eye, as it turned out, and had left the Borsolini brothers for good to nanny Francesca and Ernesto and help out in the *pasticceria*.

Alberto had one of four wine stalls on the square. There were two pecorino stands, four salamis, two cashmeres, three souvenirs, three linens, one air freshener, Mario's gelati, five fresh pasta, six fruit and vegetable, a tourist office stand, and a temporary Poliziano. The Borsolini brothers had strangely not received any of the information about the *festa* nor been invited to the planning meetings, and also missing was the parish priest, Father Dominico, who had been called away to Rome for a meeting with the Pope, which for curious reasons never eventuated.

For a couple more hours, Lily worked the stall as locals and tourists helped themselves to the free *amorucci* piled up in the bowls, then bought packet after packet after packet to take home. Violetta and Luciana would be able to afford bionic limbs on the proceeds of the inaugural Santa Ana di Chisa *festa*.

Finally, the crowds started drifting off, and looking up across the piazza, Lily forgot her weary legs as she saw her sister and Al standing at Mario's gelati stand. He too had done a roaring trade: his *amorucci*-flavored gelato proving more popular even than the triple chocolate. It had been Francesca's idea to put the outside bits of the *cantucci* hearts into an ice cream, and commercially speaking, it was an extremely viable prospect.

Rose and Al were leaning into each other, laughing at something Mario was saying and looking far from the pale, rattled creatures who had gotten off the plane clearly not talking to each other a month before.

Harry, Jack, and Francesca were chasing each other around the well, while the twins were playing with Ernesto as Daniel, sitting in the shade with Matteo, chatted to Alessandro. It turned out the two men knew each other before Lily had arrived on the scene, as Alessandro was one of the small wine producers that Daniel was targeting to represent.

They liked each other, which helped when Lily told Alessandro that she was pregnant but staying with her husband. He had been stunned at first but never angry nor possessive of her baby. He agreed to stand back and let Daniel be the child's father and to have whatever role Lily saw fit in the future.

"I have not made the best of fathers," he told her, "but I know you will make a wonderful mother." He was now seeing a beautiful young doctor from Montalcino. And she wasn't the only one Lily hoped he would see.

"Let's clear the *amorucci* off the table and get ready for lunch," she suggested to Carlotta as she watched the various members of her hotchpotch family congregate in different parts of the piazza. Soon they were all sitting around that giant heart shape eating, drinking, chatting, and laughing as they piled their plates with spaghetti thick with anchovies, caramelized onion, and breadcrumbs; orichiette in a rich bolognese ragu; fettuccine with lemon, hot peppers, and pecorino; fried zucchini flowers stuffed with three different cheeses; eggplant dripping in oil and garlic; and crusty ciabatta bread.

Lily sat between Rose and Daniel, with baby Matteo being

passed from lap to lap like the happy fat plaything he was, even sitting at one point in the arms of Eugenia, pale and nervous, but there among them, with her own sister for ballast and her children in good hands. Alessandro sat across the heart from Lily, his girlfriend Angelica on one side of him, confident and strong, lacking the deep-rooted complications of which he was so full. On his other side were two empty seats populated at different times by various children and causing Lily a little anxiety until across the piazza she saw another young woman with a boy of about three shyly approach the rowdy group.

"Come on, come on, sit down, I've been waiting for you," she called, waving them in next to Alessandro.

"Everybody, this is Sofia and her son Massimo."

Alessandro stood as his daughter slipped in next to him and pulled her little boy onto her lap. Lily knew he wanted to leave, but she also knew he wouldn't. He was a decent man. Slowly he sat down and introduced his daughter to his girlfriend. The next time she looked, Massimo was in his lap.

"I see you, Lily Turner," said Daniel, handing her Matteo. "I see you."

"I know you do," she said with a smile, and she kissed the top of her baby's head, thinking for the thousandth time that there was no better smell in all the world.

Then, out the corner of her eye, she saw Mario packing up the last of his stall.

"Get Al to swap chairs with one of the kids, will you?" she asked Rose, and carrying her plump brown boy on her hip, she walked over to Mario and brought him back to the table, sitting him beside Carlotta, so close that their elbows were touching. They were two shy, stubborn people, but Lily was certain they were made for each other and would, one day, realize it.

In the shade of the duomo, a handful of elderly friends watched on, all eyes glistening behind variously thick spectacles.

"Santa Ana di Chisa willing Daniel will live a long and healthy life," Violetta said, "but one day that Lily is going to make a hell of a widowed darner."

"Not that you need to be widowed," Luciana reminded her.

"Not that you need to be able to darn," added Fiorella. "Because it doesn't really matter how you get rid of the hole, does it? Just that you do."

"A mended sock certainly lasts a lot longer," agreed Violetta, handing around a bag of chili pepper and chocolate *amorucci*. "In fact sometimes the darned bit is stronger than anything else."

"It could end up being your favorite part, I imagine," said Fiorella. "Even if to begin with, you didn't think it matched."

She looked at Violetta, who smiled.

"All praise to Santa Ana di Chisa," she said, and her friends all agreed.

"All praise to Santa Ana di Chisa!"

Acknowledgments

The older I get, the more people I have to thank, but the less I can remember who or why. What's that about? So thanks, everyone, everywhere, for all your help. I need it and can only apologize if I fail, here, to thank you personally for giving it.

One person I could never forget to thank is my dear friend Bridget, who shared with me the story of baby Stanley, the newborn she held in her arms for just six days before his biological mother changed her mind and wanted him back. Such difficult days . . . subsequently illuminated by another baby, the stellar Stella, whose arrival made, and continues to make, Bridget and so many other people so very happy.

My cousin Frances Kennedy in Rome deserves at the very least a great big kiss for just being such a cool chick and all-round support system and for introducing me to Montepulciano, the real-life Tuscan hilltop town on which Montevedova is based. Go there—it's pretty much as described, minus the *pasticceria*, although there's a fantastic one called Mariuccia in nearby Montalcino. Stock up on *dolci*, then go to Abbey Sant'Antimo and listen to the monks' Gregorian chanting. Now that's what I call a day in the country.

Tuscany is as drop-dead gorgeous as everyone says it is and all praise to Santa Ana di Chisa for helping me convince my Australian BFF Ronnie into coming with me on my second research trip to save me from being lonely. Even more saintly praise should be heaped upon her husband, Raoul, who I had completely forgotten speaks Italian (and cooks and cleans and drives). How ever would we have found the Prada outlet shop without him? Two GPS systems, two guide books, and a map certainly weren't getting us there.

I carelessly left my own husband, Mark Robins, at home during this research trip. He was busy building a large boat called the Dawn Treader for the third installment in the Narnia film franchise, and it just didn't seem right to drag him away from his twelve-hour working days to trip around the Tuscan countryside in a navy blue Fiat 500.

Unlike Santa Ana di Chisa, Mark Robins is a real saint.

As usual I would like to thank my wonderful agent, Stephanie Cabot, without whom I might still be stuck in an office writing captions about cellulite on the thighs of Hollywood movie stars. And I'd like to thank Denise Roy, my amazing editor at Plume, for making me work harder than I'm naturally suited to. I hope you appreciate the results as much as I appreciate the opportunity to work with such a class act.

More than anything, though, I would like to thank the readers who continue to e-mail me to tell me that they like my books. Most of the time I am at home, on my own, stuck in front of the computer, halfway through the new one, with only the dog and perhaps a little something sweet for company. Often my head is in my hands, and I am wondering what the hell I am doing. Sometimes I am drawing up a list of other things I could do instead, although that can be quite depressing as there don't seem to be that many jobs for five-star resort inspectors or chocolate tasters.

Then, just when I am seriously starting to consider what role I could fulfill at the circus—that doesn't involve heights or working nights—I will hear the friendly little "bing" of an e-mail arriving. More often than not it's someone who has taken the time and effort to say they've just finished reading something I've written and they'd like to say thank you.

I can't tell you how much this fills my heart with joy. "Hey, circus, find yourself another fat and/or bearded lady," I will cry. "Stick your five-star resorts where the sun don't shine," I'll continue. "Get those dark chocolate truffles away from me at once. I don't need to taste them!"*

So to those of you who have written to me already, *grazie*; so often you make my day. And to those who have yet to get in touch but think they might like to, visit my Web site at www .sarah-katelynch.com, and you can e-mail me from there. I look forward to hearing from you.

This story, by the way, this book, is about mending broken hearts. If you haven't ever had one, count yourself lucky. But if you have, well, never forget that we're all in this together. I know some breaks are worse than others, but I also know that we will get our happy endings if, as Tinker Bell says, we believe in them. And if we look in the right places.

---

*Actually, I would never say this.

Also by Sarah-Kate Lynch

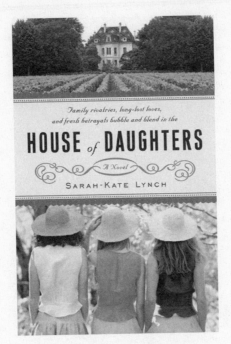

ISBN 978-0-452-28938-3

Available wherever books are sold.

www.sarah-katelynch.com

Plume
A member of Penguin Group (USA) Inc.
www.penguin.com